STONE WICKED

JAY WILBURN

ISBN:

Book Layout: Lori Michelle
www.TheAuthorsAlley.com

1

"**WHO THE HELL** are you and what did you do to get in here?"

"I got old," Stone Wicked said.

Perkins chuckled at that one. "Do you recall your exact charge, Inmate Wicked?"

Agent John Perkins, that's what the ID he showed the one orderly on duty said his name was, waited on the frail old man on the couch to answer. James Fanny, the orderly, standing off to one side, knew Stone Wicked wasn't going to answer, and he didn't.

Perkins lifted his eyes and scanned the facility from the dayroom. James couldn't see the fellow's mouth or nose because of the medical procedural mask the agent wore. James wore one, too. It was policy now, with the Covid-19 pandemic in full swing. The old man did not have one on.

Months before, James swore that Corona virus was over-hyped like West Nile or Bird Flu before it. He ate crow on that one, as friends who worked in hospitals told horror stories of hallways full of the dying, with no beds to put them in. It had a very end-of-the-world feel as the economy shutdown hard. He hoped it wouldn't last long, though.

This place sounded spooky quiet when the TV was turned down. An episode of the Tiger King was paused. James had been sitting on the couch with Stone, watching it. He meant to just listen to a little as he worked, but ended up sitting through three episodes before Perkins had arrived. The visit was scheduled, but James had forgotten. That stuff was the guards' business anyway. James was a big man with broad shoulders, broad everything. His ass print still depressed the couch cushion next to scrawny old Stone Wicked.

Perkins, who sat on the wood coffee table across from Stone, violating the six foot rule himself, lighted his eyes on James where the orderly stood off to the side with his arms crossed under his clipped staff ID. "How many other inmates are here?"

James tilted his head at the couch. "Stone is the last one left. The second to last one died nine years ago. That was before I got here."

"Inmate Wicked, you mean?"

James swallowed. "Sure. Yes, sir."

"Is there no guard on duty?"

James glanced at the harsh light spilling off the tiles from the glass doors out front. "Dawes is on duty. He stepped out to grab lunch."

"Leaving the place unmanned with a prisoner on hand?"

James sighed. He hated the stink of his own breath in these masks, no matter how carefully he brushed his teeth each morning. "You're getting into guard business, sir. I clean the floors and clean the patient. Not looking to get in trouble or to cause it."

Perkins' mask puffed out with a sigh of his own. "Running fast and loose with the rules here at the Scully Elder Care Facility. I suppose you fellas have it kind of easy, with one old man to guard."

"If you say so, sir."

Perkins nodded and added, "Kind of high-priced digs for one prisoner."

"If you say so."

"I do say so, Mr. Fanny. I do. Do you know why I'm here?"

"Interview with the prisoner, but that's guard business again, Agent Perkins."

"And the guard is out to lunch," Perkins said. "I'm here because the Alabama prison system hired me as a consultant to recommend prisoners to release early on account of the pandemic, and facilities to close to make up budget shortfalls on account of the pandemic."

James took a deep breath. They told him these masks didn't restrict oxygen flow, but he felt like he couldn't get enough of it just then. "This one would make sense. The prison's been waiting on old Stone here to up and die so they could close it down anyway. He keeps not obliging though."

"Do you know his prison history?" Perkins asked. "His charge? Any details like that?"

James suspected a lot of things. Stone Wicked had his phrases, things he repeated often in answer to questions, whether those pat answers fit or not. Then, he said other things, sometimes in a short mumble, and other times like he was blurting out a confession.

James let most of it roll right out of his head after a shift, but some things were just too dark and weird to ever forget.

"He's not talkative, and I'm not sure he remembers all that well anymore, sir."

"Any paperwork here on him that might tell me those details?"

James shrugged. "That's guard business, sir."

Perkins stared at the orderly without saying anymore.

One time Stone Wicked, Inmate Wicked, between bites of squash casserole, had said, *She was turned inside out when she finally died. There were so many colors. More on the inside than just red.*

Squash casserole wasn't typical on the prison menu, and if it was, it'd probably be inedible. James had taken to cooking lunches and dinners for himself and making enough to heat up for Stone, too. It was easier and the old man would actually eat most days if he was presented with something worth eating. It was easier than fighting the vendors to deliver on time and correctly. If you only had one patient, you could be flexible, even in a global pandemic that might yet take down the world, if people outside Scully, Alabama were to be believed.

After the "inside out" comment, James was careful to not turn his back on Stone for a while. They warned you not to get too friendly or casual around the inmates, even the harmless looking ones. Especially those. Usually, Stone didn't move at all, but other times when James was busy with something, he'd glance up to see that Stone had crossed the dayroom to one of the windows without the orderly noticing or hearing a thing. If Stone had decided to sneak up on James in a moment like that, it could get ugly, he supposed. That vigilance only lasted a little while, though. Routine was a sedative.

That didn't change the fact that Stone Wicked might well be an elder serial killer, for all James Fanny knew.

James unfolded his arms and said, "Alright, I do know we have paperwork, but it's incomplete."

He waited for the agent-consultant to explode at that. No guard on duty, incomplete paperwork on their one inmate, it really was looking like a Micky Mouse operation here. If he stayed long enough, wait until Perkins saw James pull out homemade turkey, dressing, and gravy for lunch.

Perkins surprised James by saying, “Doesn’t surprise me. No one has complete paperwork on him. No charge listed. They have his date of transfer here from Birmingham and to Birmingham from another in-state prison, but not the date he was transferred into state. Any of that stuff in your file?”

“No, just medical stuff mostly. Even that is scant. Stone is healthy, other than being elderly. Not even a birth date. Like you said, no charge listed. No date of sentencing. Thought it was weird, but you know . . . ”

“Guard business,” Perkins grumbled.

James nodded. “Guards assigned here won’t know either. Everyone is recent transfers, mostly older fellas that might not be up to the pace of a bigger facility. Our admin is back in Birmingham and hasn’t visited any day I was here. I’m here most days.”

“Spoke to him,” Perkins said, “and his assistant director, a woman named Mandy. He politely told me it was my job to tie up this loose end. She nodded along politely, too.”

“Consultant business,” James said.

Perkins actually laughed. He narrowed his eyes at Stone, who stared off to the side. “Inmate Wicked, you’re quite the living mystery. Do you know your date of sentencing?”

“It got bloody,” Stone mumbled.

Perkins leaned forward. “I missed that. What’d you say, inmate?”

Stone didn’t repeat it. James only knew what he’d said because it was one of those phrases the old man mumbled often, sometimes in his sleep.

Perkins sighed and looked to the orderly. “You catch what he said?”

James shook his head. He wasn’t sure exactly why he didn’t translate the mumble for Perkins, but he just didn’t. Didn’t seem right to.

One time, Stone Wicked had said, *One of her eyes was busted up and one whole ear was missing. After the first one was down, the second one started laughing in this shaking hooting sound. That was when the first bitch's chewed up ear fell right the fuck out of her mouth. You ever seen any shit like that before in your life, Fanny?*

James Fanny had not, in fact, seen any shit like that before in his life.

Agent Perkins, Consultant Perkins, had turned his attention back onto the subject at hand. "Inmate Wicked, repeat what you said for me, please."

No response. James could tell Perkins that in his current state he wasn't going to get much out of Stone. No blurted confessions, for sure. But the orderly had gotten a laugh out of the guy and shifted some of the heat of the slack procedures of the facility off of his back, so he was inclined to leave that impression without saying any more.

"You know your birthdate, prisoner?"

Still nothing.

In the silence, James could hear someone screaming in the distance. What the hell? Then, he realized it wasn't human. A bird, a cat, or something else was making that noise. Whatever it was, he hoped it stopped or Perkins started talking again soon.

Stone Wicked was getting a little twitchy.

"I know you were transferred here from South Carolina," Perkins said, finally. "Don't know the date. I know you were transferred to this elder care facility back in 1992. Been renovated twice since you been here. I know you came here from Donaldson Correctional and were in Ventress before that. Any other Alabama prisons you parked in I haven't mentioned?"

"Was in the spring, I seem to recall."

"Okay. Okay, that's something. Spring of what year?"

James didn't have the heart to tell Perkins that if he asked Stone when Christmas was, he'd likely get the same answer. Was just another one of his phrases.

"What year were you sentenced?"

Nothing. Stone's eyes looked longingly at the Tiger King frozen on the television screen, James thought. That weird animal screaming was still out there somewhere. At least it wasn't getting closer.

"What about from South Carolina? Where was your prison

home there? I was a state bureau agent in South Carolina before I retired. Not when you would have been there. Do you remember the facility name, inmate?"

Stone's eyes closed and he bowed his head. Didn't look asleep just yet, but definitely out of it.

"I'm going to take a trip back to Carolina and see what I can find on you from that end. I'll be back, though, with whatever I find on you. I promise."

Perkins finally stood and James saw him out, locking the glass doors behind the agent with the guard's keys.

As the lock was still turning, Stone Wicked mumbled from the couch, "If'n you hold a dead man by his beard, the teeth still click together as you walk. Ever seen anything like that?"

This fucker was almost definitely an old school serial killer, right in their midst, James decided. And this was less than a minimum security facility in its current state.

He might have missed those words this time, if Stone hadn't said something similar once before. It gave Fanny a chill. And, no, he had not seen anything like that before.

James sighed deep and returned to the couch. Stone Wicked's eyes were open. He stared out the window instead of at the frozen Netflix miniseries.

"You want me to start your program again, Stone?"

Nothing. No response and no proclamations about clicking teeth.

"We can do lunch early, if you cotton."

After another nonresponse, James nodded and reached for the remote near his surviving butt imprint on the couch. At least that screaming animal noise outside had finally stopped. Someone had come out and ran off their screeching cat.

"You want to hear a story, James Fanny?" Stone Wicked asked, without looking at him.

"Sure," James said as he stood over the old man.

"It's a long one." Stone looked up. His eyes shined brighter than usual. "Do you have the time?"

James sat down on the coffee table where Perkins had been. The wood creaked.

"It gets bloody."

James swallowed and nodded.

"You an Indian, James? You look a little Indian. Maybe Mestizo. Am I supposed to say Native American now?"

"Don't worry about it, Stone." James shrugged. "My mama was white and Latina. That means Spanish. Puerto Rican, in her case. My daddy was descended from Freedman, a former slave, adopted into the Cherokee tribe. Intermarried with Indians for a few generations. A lot of this history was oral, passed down from my great grandmother, who really did look like an Indian. We called her Big Mama. You know how oral family histories get. Probably as much legend as true facts, if you're lucky. So, I'm a bit of everything, I guess."

"Nothing wrong with that," Stone said. "This will be a story your Big Mama wouldn't even have heard. I'm a lot older than you'd guess, even your wildest guess. And I'll be surprised if you believe all of it, but I swear to Christ every word will be the truth, as well as I remember . . . "

During that first session of Stone Wicked's story, James' ass started to hurt. He moved to the couch next to Stone. He got up only once to let the guard, who smelled like liquor, back in at 2:00 PM, but that was enough to break the magic for a while. Stone petered out after that, so James made him a late lunch/early dinner.

Until then, Stone Wicked made up for all the years of mumbled answers and shouted complaints in that single afternoon.

The tale did get bloody.

2

I'M OLDER THAN you think, but I don't remember the exact date. Was in the spring, I seem to recall. Some doors are closed to me. Others open for a glimpse. And some days, like today, the lock is jimmied, and I get to slip through for a good long while. Maybe that bastard, with all his questions, shook things loose in my skull for me. My mother called me hardheaded. Most my family agreed, but they're all dead now, so what the hell do they know about any damn thing anyways, I say.

My brother was last to go, and he had the lowest opinion on me of all of them, but I hated him, too. Traitors and deserters are always hated. We may get to that later, I guess, because it happened later.

I got myself into some trouble in Georgia. Nothing that would involve the law, but the sort of thing that might have a pretty girl's father and brothers out for blood. I wasn't quite twenty, if I remember right, and she were but sixteen. Before you get shitty with me, that sort of thing wasn't out of bounds like it is today.

I mean, unless you break a girl's heart, and she starts saying you tricked her. Lucky she didn't right out claim rape, I guess, but, either way, I found myself on a series of trains and coaches heading out west.

Wherever you go, there you fucking are. That how the saying goes in those drying-out meetings the alcoholics go to?

Right, anyhow, I was prone to the same fuck-ups in new towns. Weren't always girls, but always something. Running from my troubles turned my story, the one I'm about to tell you, into a western of sorts. People still like westerns, do you think? Hard to keep track of what's in style any given moment.

STONE WICKED

I could tell you a lot of story before I get to the real story. If we both live long enough, maybe I'll fill in the pieces I can remember. Skipping the boring parts here, as best an old man can, it was because whisky, gambling, and pussy were cheap back then. Do fellas still call it pussy? Alright, good stuff then.

It got cheaper the further west you fled. Problem was, the cost accumulates and then vices grow expensive and deadly. I joined up with a gang of piss-ants to help pay for my expensive habits. We got into a little thieving.

Again, still nothing big. No horses, no coaches, no banks. Some bad asses could hit that stuff and threw enough lead to get away with it, but there were easier targets. And that was our jam. That still how you say it? That's my jam?

Really? I feel like that phrase just got started. I swear I saw it on the Netflix just the other day. Okay then, that was our modus operandi: soft targets, like the terrorists do these days.

The last job we pulled should have been the easiest, but you know how that shit goes. It's always the last one that fucks you up.

Me, Frank Goodall, his brother River, and some dumb ass named, ugh . . . shit, I don't remember anymore. We'll just call him Jimmy Dumbass. We hid out in the woods close to a ranch house for three days. The amount of days a resurrection usually took in the Good Book, right? Then, we closed in on the place late that last morning, when we was sure the place was abandoned. Oh boy, were we sure. Three days sure. All the men out. All the ladies gone to a revival supper closer into town, which weren't close. No one home for lunch that day, and we were going to be long gone before they got back for dinner or washing.

That was the motherfucking plan, anyway.

Jimmy elbowed a window, spreading broken glass into the parlor. It was single pane and thin, but it sliced through his duster in multiple slashes. The boy hissed like he'd been stung.

"Son of a whore," he said, as he reached through to work the latch. Mr. Dumbass managed to slice the webbing between his ring and fuck-you fingers on a shard of glass still pinched in the frame of the window. Turned out it wasn't even the kind of window you could open.

Frank said, "Pull up on your reins, Jimmy. We don't have to climb in through the chimney like summer rats."

Frank took hold of the brass knob and just turned it. It swung open on unoiled hinges, like a groaning witch.

Not sure what Jimmy was thinking. No one out there had locks on their doors in those days. You could bar the door in storms, but someone had to be inside for that. Maybe that's where the boy's mind was. If that were the case, you'd likely get buckshot to the face before you elbowed out all the glass to crawl through a window. You get what I'm saying?

River said, "Your hand's weeping like a bitch on her monthlies."

I might have some of the slang wrong at this point, after all these years, but that's the gist of what he said.

Blood trailed in a healthy flow up the back of his hand and into his sleeve from his upraised palm. It was the same sleeve he'd sliced up at the elbow. He adjusted the sleeve and held the wounded digits down by his side. He dripped all over the porch boards and down the pant leg on that side.

"Should wrap that up, Saphead," Frank said, as he walked inside.

River followed, then Jimmy leaving a trail over the threshold, and lastly me, not trying to track through it with my boots. I liked my boots. There would be times the boots were the last thing I was able to hold onto, just my boots and my guts.

"Once we're flush again," Jimmy said, with the blood running out of his closed fist like he was juicing a tomato, "I'll get some sage hen to nurse it and my long stick."

"We're going to have to ride a ways before we can do that," I said. "Would be nice if you weren't painting a red trail from the window to our camp for the ranchers."

"Leave it be." Jimmy shoved me, adding a spot of color to my collar. I shoved him back into a grandfather clock as old as time, and probably brought over on sailing ships from Old Europe with the first printing presses in the New World. The old thing bonged, clanged, and something long, thin, and metal clattered loose inside.

The steady ticking of time from the weighty pendulum fell silent and left the room heavy. Was one of those sounds you don't realize is there until it's missing. However long that box of gears and Swiss magic kept time moving, it had final come to a halt and progressed around the wheel of its face no more. I had stopped time, you see.

River started to speak up on the subject of Jimmy's hand, but Jimmy said, "If you Angelicas can't still your mouths, maybe you can put them to use servicing me since the whores are still a ways up the trail."

River and me were about to set upon him, to get his face flowing like his fist, but Frank shouted, "Stop fucking around and start searching for the loot."

As I recall, civilized people didn't say fuck quite as much back then. Not until the World Wars and beyond, but we weren't civilized. Frank might have said cocksucker more than motherfucker, but that's neither here nor there.

We cursed each other under our breath after Frank called us down, but we spread out to do the job finally.

Jimmy did finally take up a cotton napkin to wrap up his fist. Found it folded on a marble-topped service table next to the big family eating table. The dark wood was polished brighter than any mirror I had ever shaved in. Was from trees that didn't grow within a hundred miles or more of that ranchland.

Everything from the napkins to the table legs screamed of unnatural wealth out in that part of the world. Lended credence to the rumors of what we heard might be hidden there.

River pulled a drawer full of silver cutlery polished as bright and bold as a brag. "Frank?"

"Stuff's heavy," Frank said, "but we may take some yet. Leave it for now and let's search what we came for first."

Frank started testing the floorboards with his boot heel. When he found one he thought didn't sound right, he'd rest on his haunches to probe it with his fist. Then, he'd move about testing the floor elsewhere.

Jimmy stopped at the foot of some stairs, past a deserted kitchen with the windows open to vent some heat and allow for fresh air. If Jimmy had come by the back porch, he could have spared his hand. I wanted to say it out loud to him because it was a good dig, but Frank and Jimmy were already pissed for different reasons. Being honest, I was still a bit of a pussy back then, too.

Jimmy leaned forward and looked into the upper floor from below. "Hello, up there."

The other three of us froze and stared at him as he remained staring up at whoever he might be talking to. When nothing happened, our hands dropped to our lead pushers and we waited some more.

As I watched, dark spotting spread into the slashed material around Jimmy's elbow. Could have been the flow that ran up his arm earlier, but I didn't think so. The fancy white napkin balled around his hand and between his fingers showed a spreading stain in murder red that couldn't be denied on that field of pristine white. Then and now, made me think of the shroud around the mutilated Christ who wouldn't stay dead.

Jimmy set one foot on the bottom step and took hold of the ornate carved railing with his good hand, leaving Mr. Dumbass none to draw with. The three of us leaned forward as Jimmy set his full weight on the step.

I expected a creak, like from the door hinges, but there wasn't a bit of give on that step as polished as the table. Made we wonder why the hinges were so neglected.

Frank whispered the man's name and, since the stairs were church mouse quiet, he heard him well and turned his head. Jimmy looked us over, all three of us tense as coiled springs and ready to strike. "What?"

"Who the hell were you talking to up there?" Frank whispered a little louder.

Jimmy shook his head. "No one."

River glanced at his brother and then me, with his hand still set to pull iron, and asked, "Why'd you say, hello, then?"

Jimmy shrugged. "Just checking."

"Checking for . . . " Frank dropped his hand from his weapon and we followed suit. "Are you . . . If there were someone here, don't you think all the glass breaking and clock bumping wouldn't have already . . . "

When Frank wouldn't go on, Jimmy held up both hands in a questioning way. "What, Frank?"

"Nothing. Nothing at all." Frank turned his back. "Just keep looking. We don't want to drag out our visit."

Jimmy clomped the rest of the way up the stairs. We searched the place downstairs, going through every cabinet, cubby, and closet as Frank went on tapping the floor with his boot.

A crash upstairs froze us. More thumping and crashing noises brought us to the stairs.

We looked to Frank and he called up, "Jimmy, shout if you need help."

The commotion stopped and from upstairs Jimmy said, "What?"

Frank sighed and said, "Sounds like you're fighting someone."

After a pause, Jimmy shouted back, "Just searching in a hurry."

The crashing recommenced and we walked back to pick up where we left off.

River spoke low, even though there was no way Jimmy was going to hear any of it. "We may need to get rid of that whoremonger sooner than later."

"Not today," Frank said. "Getting shed of him and giving him reason to tell tales might be a mistake. As early as tomorrow, we might hash it, but not today."

I drifted off into a small parlor with a great big piano. I couldn't figure out how this room fit the rest of the house. Seemed like it made one wall longer than the other, which wouldn't match up outside.

I was fixated on the piano, though. It was a shiny black grand piano and not the rough wood uprights I'd seen up to that point in my life.

I touched one of the keys like I expected the thing to bite me. Pressed it slow and felt the spongy resistance a third of the way down. The white surface had to be polished bone. I suspected as much then, and knew it in my heart before I left the house running for my life maybe twenty minutes later.

Once the key was fully depressed, it gave a quiet, low resonate sound that was hardly greater than a whisper, but still too full and rich for that tiny ass room.

I marveled. I marveled at the sound, at the existence of a thing like this, not just in the dusty Wild West but in the world at all, at how they must have built the instrument in the room or the room around it because there was no way it would pass whole in or out of the parlor door. I marveled at it all.

The crashing finally trailed off upstairs and Frank found a hollow sound he liked. It was still there when he tested it with his fist. "Help me get up these boards."

By the time his younger brother and I got there, he'd already found a seam and was bringing up the section of false floor. The uneven section coming up looked big enough to be a raft.

Then, Jimmy started yelling from upstairs. The three of us paused. None of us ran to check and no one grabbed for a weapon this time. We'd reached the "crying wolf" stage of things, I suppose.

After a moment, Jimmy's hellraising settled into what we could tell wasn't pain and wasn't exactly distress, either. "Get up here. You have to see this. Come on!"

Frank looked longingly at the section of raised floor he hadn't yet pulled free to reveal its secrets. "I know this is it."

Jimmy insisted, "You have to see this. What's taking you so long? Get the hell up here!"

Frank stood and we took the stairs.

Jimmy had stopped yelling, finally, right as we were trying to track him at the top. The top floor was well lit from a number of windows in each room, all opened. The higher floor was hotter than below, as was always the case, but there was a cross breeze.

The rooms were trashed from all of Jimmy's deviltry, but they were fine and ornate trashed rooms. Not the sort of thing one would expect from ranchers. I suppose the bunkhouses on the other side of the property were probably closer to custom for the region, but who knows? They might have had brass fixtures, crown molding, and foreign clocks, as well.

We tracked Jimmy to a doorway that had been pried open in what looked like the back of another fancy bedroom. The bedroom hadn't been rifled much, yet, as the locked door in the back corner had drawn his attention early. The frame was splintered and hardware that included a keyhole lay on the floor. The discarded knob and lock fixture wasn't brass. It was a duller, harder metal.

The smell of the extra room hit me full in the face and then Jimmy stepped aside, revealing the figures chained at their necks to iron poles bolted in place on stone blocks.

The things shackled in there couldn't be human. I didn't know what the fuck they were.

3

IT WAS AT this moment I started to believe hell might be a tight dark cave. It'd be confirmed for me not long after the discovery of this tiny, hidden prison behind the master bedroom of the finest, most extravagant house in the West. That and maybe the fact that coming in this house was the biggest mistake of my years, up to then, in a life full of Christ-fucking mistakes.

Their goddamned eyes, I have to start there. Black pits, they were, but not voids, not emptiness, the sockets stuffed full and solid. Claw marks in the filthy faces led me to believe their eyes had been shredded into mash. The sores over their naked bodies led me to that jelly mash of eye meat getting infected and not treated. No doctor knew of this room, or the souls chained inside, by God or by Scratch. The filth over their scarred skin hinted that something dirty had been packed into the diseased and blind sockets by madness, for the pain, or as additional torture. The end of it, with us small-time bandits staring through that broken doorway upon those broken creatures, was a solid black mass crusted in place of their eyes and hardened like veins of coal needing a pickax to ever be broken free again.

They couldn't see us, but must be they could hear us through the discolored pus oozing from their ears, or through the cracking dried blood around their flaring nostrils, they could smell us, because they went from cowering and shaking to reaching for us and moaning. I'd bet my life they never reached for the deviants who locked those iron collars around their necks and left them there, locked until the flesh under and around the iron edges had been rubbed raw and sticky thin. A dark part of me was thankful because the chains stopped the abominations in their barefooted tracks before they could reach us.

I don't know what they made of all Jimmy's screaming before we got up there.

The four of us backed up a step each, just the same. Still, we didn't look away or flee that open living tomb stench that was filling the house, filling the goddamned world.

"Dash," River whispered, harsh, like a child trying to avoid saying damn.

"Christ on the fucking cross," Jimmy breathed out a little lower.

They were naked and their skin was grey. Cracks webbed every part of them, making them look like they were made of a strange desert hardpan. No telling if those indentions and running cracks were through the unbathed filth that coated them, or their ruined skin beneath.

I wanted to say they were all men once, but I can't for sure. Their genitals were sliced and abused multiple times. Shredded, in some cases. Swoll, knotty, and twisted in others. More than a couple crotches were mangled and caked solid black like the shit in their eyes. God knows whether any manhood ever dangled there, and Christ's daddy had surely turned his eyes away from that room long before we ever opened it.

The floor in that hidden torture chamber was cave grey in the middle, a shade or so lighter than the prisoners' flesh. The corners and edges below where the chains were bolted into the walls were black, a shade or so lighter than their packed eyes and crotches. The smooth, impacted shit along the base edge of the room was curved into a sort of snowdrift of filth.

The moaning continued. A few of them opened their mouths and white strings, that looked more like fungal growth than saliva, strung between the weeping surfaces inside. Those that still had tongues licked them out, as white as the piano keys, but they had nothing to say, were they still capable of speech.

"I can't be here no more, Frankie," River growled in a voice that was half begging child and half madman gravel. "No more. Take me away from here."

Frank locked down on his brother's arm and River acted like his boots were nailed to the bedroom floor and his knees locked.

Frank had to wrestle his little brother backward, and maybe that was exactly what River was begging for him to do.

I moved my ass in a backward shuffle all on my own.

Jimmy Dumbass stepped forward, toward those reaching hands with fingers that hardly ever numbered five on any of them. He reached, too, with the hand wrapped in the fancy cloth napkin, thick enough to be used to sew a waistcoat. His blood had soaked scarlet through most of it.

Then, a single drop of blood fell from his elbow through the straight clean tears of his sleeve from the window glass. The wine-colored drip burst small and sprayed minuscule droplets around its point of impact where the fine wood floor of the master gave way to the grey-white scratchy spread of fecal filth in the hell room.

I never before, nor never since, saw a single drop of blood turn two different colors on the same floor, but I swear to bleeding Christ that drip was black in there with them and rich burgundy on the polished boards out with us. Never seen that illusion since, and I've witnessed a lot of spilled blood.

Those tortured creatures lashed out and snapped yellow, green, and black teeth hard enough to split some of the ones they had left, casting bone crumbs onto the shitty floor. They growled and roared with the shrill passion of abused animals.

One managed to hook a split fingernail under an edge of the bloody napkin and tore it away from the wound. Jimmy let out a high little squeak, but still didn't back off.

Those chained men jostled each other for position as they twisted and pulled around that napkin. They struggled to suck the blood from the course cloth. Others fell to lick up the blood squeezed out of it from the violent competition above.

If Jimmy's wound had been closed once, or was starting to, it reopened with the cloth pulled away. The blood dribbled thick onto the filthy floor, turning black on impact.

A few grey men broke from the napkin to reach for the growing puddle. Their collars pinched and wrinkled the flesh of their throats, squeezing clear fluid from the unhealed abrasions. They fell to their faces at the end of their chains and wiped their fingertips through the blood before bringing it to their dry, cracked lips. They slurped the stuff up and moaned in quivering ecstasy.

One of them chewed through one of his own remaining fingers and kept sucking up the blood as long as it would come.

The rest of us, save for Jimmy, backed out of the bedroom door.

Jimmy drew his gun and smeared the grip with greasy blood. As he raised the weapon, more of it dripped out from under the barrel. The thirsty monsters reached for it. He fired all six shots in deliberate, one-after-the-other, fashion. And the asshole managed to miss the cluster of bodies five times.

The one bullet that actually hit, on the fourth pull, tore away a bit of one man's shoulder. That wounded creature turned in two full circles, hunting for the smell of fresh blood, and wrapped himself up in his own chain. A few of his fellows took him down and attacked the wound. Even on the ground, being fed upon, the wounded man was still trying to suck up his own blood, too.

Jimmy holstered his bloody empty piece and turned to us on the retreat. "Give me one of yours."

"Like hell," Frank said.

River finally moved on his own and the brothers took the stairs.

I lingered a bit longer.

"Stone, help me end this."

"Shouldn't have started it," I said, as I turned to take the stairs two at a time going down.

I took hold of the front door when I got down there, but Frank yelled at my back, "Help us get this trap open. Hurry, I want to be out of here."

Less than ten minutes away from the end of our gang, I knew then it was a mistake not to bail out that door right then, but I turned to help the Goodall brothers, anyhow, with that crazy howling from upstairs filling the fine house.

4

FRANK HAD CALLED that false section in the floor a trap. I think he meant trapdoor. Trap was probably the right word for it, then and now.

We pulled it away to reveal a dirt floored space under the main house that dropped waist deep. As Frank eased into the space, I looked over my shoulder longingly at the closed front door. I think I tried to listen for hoofbeats coming for the noise of that string of gunshots from upstairs. I listened for them through that break in one of the front windows, but my ears were ringing too loud to hear anything distant. I sure heard that fucking animal bloodlust howling that Jimmy had unleashed, and apparently still watched, upstairs.

"Eureka," Frank said, muffled from below. He was dragging something. "It's heavy. Help me, would you?"

River dropped down with him. The brothers dragged a dusty, cobwebby trunk into view. It looked for all the world like a proper pirate's treasure chest, even though we were some five hundred miles from the Gulf and easily twelve hundred from the closest ocean. Still, had to be an easier haul than that piano, even if it was pirate treasure.

They hoisted and I muscled it up over the edge of the floor with them. Thought we were going to have to waste time working on the lock, but the latch just folded down and Frank swung the heavy lid open on the powerful smell of mahogany. It was a welcome replacement for the death-in-a-latrine reek that had taken over even the bottom floor.

My mouth went dry when I stared down on the pile of collected treasure.

None of the pieces were the same color or size. Some was carved, but not most. It was all polished to an impossible sheen. Brilliant, even in the low light coming through the room. If it weren't for the skulls, I'd have not believed it was all finely polished bone. There were a couple cow and horse skulls in the shiny pile, but most of the skulls peeking out with empty sockets were clearly human.

Frank ran his fingers through the stuff, stirring and clicking the pieces about. Yellow, ivory, parchment brown, and speckled black, all the bones, pieces both complete and broken, were carefully worked smooth and marble-fine by patient hands.

I'm not sure what he was thinking. Looking for gold underneath? Thinking maybe there was value here he didn't understand? I never got the chance to ask.

I still don't understand it to this day. Even after everything that happened later, and all the secrets underneath the world we think we know that were revealed to me, I don't get what it was all about. Why they did it. What it meant to them. I was not their kind.

Jimmy finally started down the stairs at a casual pace, with all that goddamned hooting and howling continuing upstairs.

River asked quietly, "Should we take it with us?"

Hell, I knew the answer then and now, but Frank was staring wide-eyed at the stairs where Jimmy had stopped. River gave a choked noise from the back of his throat when he looked.

I turned, last and slowest.

There was Jimmy Dumbass, standing stiff and bug-eyed with the four barrels of what must have been a custom quad-barreled rifle pressed tight against his lower back. The kid, in a three-piece black suit with a skinny black tie knotted under his chin, holding the gun on Jimmy couldn't have been a day over six or seven. Even with what happened next, I swear it's true.

I pulled my own gun without thinking about it. The kid had the drop on Jimmy Dumbass, but I pulled my iron to defend myself, I guess. Frank and River drew theirs, too, and they thumbed back their hammers. I just squatted as low behind that trunk of polished bones as I could.

"Kid . . . " Frank said. That was it. He had no follow up. He either lost the rest of his argument in the strangeness of that moment, or never had it to begin with.

The kid, and that's all he fucking should have been was a little kid, said, "Put your guns away. Put the prizes back where you found them. Do it now."

No shouting. No real authority behind the words. His voice even had that mushmouthed kid accent with too many "W" sounds in words. Creepy as shit.

And prizes. He called those polished bones fucking prizes. We should've gotten out that door sooner. We should have never come. Maybe we should've never been born.

"Kid . . . " Frank got that far and stalled in the same spot again.

"Where did you come from?" I whispered.

The kid either didn't hear me or ignored me. "Do what I say or you'll all die, starting with him."

River said, "We don't care about him."

"To hell with you." Jimmy's voice shook.

"Kid, we'll just go," I said.

Frank was our leader, as best as I can remember, but his mouth had vapor locked on him or something. I never drove a car in my life, but they had us working on engines when I was locked up down south of Birmingham. Of course, I rode in a few cars whenever I was being carted from one cage to another somewhere's else. The last one, I guess, were the van that brought me from my temporary cage in Talladega to here. Makes no difference. Point is, Frank's brain-to-mouth connection had vapor locked.

With a "w" in place of the "r", that creepy bastard said, "Put the prizes back."

Fucking *pwizes*. Jesus Christ. And it was only going to get worse from there.

"We're not dropping our guard, kid," I said. "You've won. We'll walk out and never come back, but we're walking out."

"Don't move," he said, and shoved the gun into Jimmy's back a little more.

Jimmy gave a squeak.

Frank tried one more time. "Ugh, look, kid . . . "

"Goddamn it," Jimmy shouted. "Just shoot this little son of Deuce and let's raise dust."

The boy shoved again. "Drop your guns and put the prizes—"

Jimmy wheeled about and elbowed the quad barrels aside. One

roared off with a sound like a fucking canon. So fucking huge that, through my ringing ears, I swear I heard the windows vibrate and the wires inside the piano across the house zing with the force of it.

The bullet tore a hole clean through Jimmy's flank. I'm not sure if the kid punctured or nicked anything vital, but Jimmy bled like a bitch from both spigots. Hell, all he'd done since we got there was fucking bleed. The round kept going and turned one gold-gilded corner of a landscape painting's frame on the wall behind us into dust.

Jimmy screamed out of tune with the piano and the ring of my failing hearing. He wrapped his hand around the four barrels and turned them so they were aimed right at us.

Frank rolled into the hole in the floor and aimed up over the edge of the boards and around the side of the "pwize" trunk. River scrambled to his feet and ran toward the arch leading to the dining room. I balled up behind the trunk and hoped for the best.

I could see Jimmy and the kid struggling over the rifle in a mirror that covered most of a wall between landscapes. Wet red spread down his haunch, sticky dark through the material of his pants, into his boot on that side. I know from experience that when you got a good bleed going, it always seems to be a lot more than it really is. But fucking Jimmy was gushing the stuff.

He drew his gun, pressed the bore against the kid's pale forehead, and thumbed back the hammer. The kid just stared up at Jimmy around both sides of that barrel. It looked like he was about to murder a baby, he was so much bigger than that boy.

The gun clicked empty. I'd forgot he used all his bullets upstairs, missing the bloodthirsty grey men. He apparently forgot, too. Not sure if the kid knew or if he just had balls the size of cannon loads.

The boy twisted his aim back up under Jimmy's grip. I rolled and prepared to run toward where River crouched at the arch, but then held up because I couldn't remember if I'd seen a door out that way or not.

The rifle boomed from a second barrel. This bullet furrowed the underside of Jimmy's forearm and blew his already cut elbow to bits. Blood, bone, and gristle vomited out from the gaping mouth of the fabric of that sleeve. A lumpy, puckered sponge of yellow fat squeezed thick from the upper arm into view through the empty cavern of Jimmy's missing elbow. I'd never seen anything like that before, and had no words to describe it then.

That arm fell away from the barrels in a ragged mess, dead-alive down by Jimmy's side. His own empty shooter clattered to the floor and he grabbed the barrels again, with his remaining arm across his body. Again, that rifle, with two possible live barrels remaining, swept over our position like Jimmy was trying his damndest to include us in the bloody, flesh-ripping fun.

All my senses were scrambled by then. My ears rang until there was a hot ball of molten iron pain in the center of my skull that made it hard to think or act. My eyes felt like they were bulging in their sockets. Colors looked too bright and unworldly. The red of the blood and gory bits especially. The sun yellow of the leaking fat, too. I saw steam rising off the rifle from under Jimmy's fingers and I swear I heard a sizzling noise, although that can't be true because my aching ears were like they was stuffed with cotton for days after. I expected to smell burning flesh, but I smelled a rich minerally water, like some still pool deep under the dark ground suddenly released. Like a deep, cold well when the cap is first popped off on a hot, humid day.

I remember an aunt I had who had slowly lost her mind. Started cussing like nothing I'd heard before or maybe since. At the end, she screamed that her hair was burning. She could smell her hair was afire and she needed one of us cocksuckers to put it out. She fell dead to the floor in the midst of that last fit.

I know about strokes and brain tumors now. Then, it could have been a demon of the Devil himself killing her from the inside of her soul out, for all I knew. Smelling that pungent water stink and my eyes bulging with adrenaline overload until the walls looked like they were melting, I thought my brain was going to pop and I was about to drop dead there like Aunt Cocksucker.

Jimmy lifted his boot like he planned to stomp the kid into the floor. Should have been easy to do, but the little boy levered the rifle out of Jimmy's grip and swung it all the way around until he clubbed Jimmy right across the jaw and chin with the wooden butt of the weapon, polished bone bright. Jimmy's lower jaw skewed out of alignment and he struck the floor hard, leading with his goddamned head.

The boy rolled the rifle the rest of the way around with the butt planted in the saddle of his shoulder, ready to fire those last two barrels like some traveling Wild West Show sharpshooter.

"Kid . . . " Frank said, as he peeked up over the edge of the floor. "Put the prizes back. And take your licks for your sins."

I didn't like that bit at all. River Goodall must not have cared for it neither because he fired on the boy from the cover of the arch. Of course, he missed. Didn't see where that bullet went. There was a lot more missing back then than any movies would have you believe. A lot fewer gunfights than people would probably think, on the average, but my life ran just a touch over average beginning that day.

The kid swung around and blasted the wall next to River's head. Plaster and wood slat exploded out and twirled away in every direction. An eruption of dust followed that. River slapped his hands and his gun into his eyes and folded away to the floor. I thought it might be the dust in his eyes. Frank maybe thought his brother was hit.

"River!" Frank yelled. Then, he raised up from his hole and took aim, showing his gritted teeth.

The boy took a step toward River and the ruined arch, but then wheeled back around on us. Frank and the boy fired at once. I smelled that thick wet odor and the whole world seemed to waver like I was underwater. I thought at the time my eardrums had blown and that was what fucked my vision for a moment. Later, I wasn't so sure of anything.

Frank missed the boy, who seemed to be wavering from side to side, and the slug splintered the stair railing behind the boy. Frank took one to the chest, high and off center. He staggered backward and hit his ass against the backside of that hole in the floor.

The boy broke open his weapon over his forearm like a proper rancher or gunman would. Then, he fished around his pockets for more bullets.

Frank folded open the fabric of his shirt, that was already sticking to his chest around the wound. The bullet broke his collar bone. I could tell because a ratty piece of it had poked out through the dark bleeding hole, showing shit-colored marrow in the core of the bone. Frank's bones were dirty and rough compared to the prizes in the trunk I was still using for cover.

Frank was sucking air. My ears were ringing too awful loud to tell if some of that sucking sound was coming from the wound. The bullet was a touch high to hit a lung, but a broken collar bone was prone to popping a lung, I knew.

He raised up his shooter in the arm that was shaking below that broken collar. He'd probably have done better to switch to his dummy hand, but he was running on piss and rage at that point.

I rolled over to get low and spotted the boy just beginning to thumb in the fresh bullets he'd finally found. His fingers were all clumsy, the way any kid would be. I hurt for him a little, but that goodwill wouldn't last.

River got up blinking. Was just the dust after all. He took a steadier aim on the kid. This was going to be ugly, no matter how it played out.

Both brothers fired off their rounds about the same time. I had a gun in my claw, too, but I'd forgotten all about it. I'd become an addled spectator to this whole disaster. If we were having this much trouble with one little kid, how would we fair against the adults in the family once they came home?

If I had to hazard a guess, I'd say River was the one that was on target because Frank's arm was a sapling in the wind. Every shot threw him one way and then the other, but he kept pulling the trigger anyway.

I got that wavering underwater view of the world again. I didn't smell no water this time because the house was full of the hot stink of smoke and spent gunpowder. But that boy wavered like he was made of water. He still fumbled those four new loads into his open rifle, but his body sort of rippled with shadows and popped over a couple feet to the left. Then, he rippled and was a few feet to the right again. The last time, he shifted forward a good bit, closer to me. By then, River was reloading and Frank was dry firing as his arm drifted to the floor.

The boy's teleportation, if that's what it was, wasn't like sliding from place to place like he was on skates. That creepy little shit folded out of space where he was and rippled back into reality in a new spot. With all this time between then and now to think on it, I believe in my heart that he was shifting out of the path of River's bullets.

The kid locked his four-barreled rifle closed and raised his eyes onto us.

Jimmy started shaking and convulsing on the floor. In his fit, he reached out for the kid's leg. As he tried to grab on, the boy folded and swirled with shadows. I swear there was a pop this time as he vacated one space and reformed standing all the way over where River knelt.

I may have lost time and missed the boy's true passage, but that don't erase the fact that some fucked up shit was going down in that house.

River locked his roller home, whether he was finished recharging his weapon or not, and endeavored to take aim. The boy knocked the gun out of River's hand with the fat end of the rifle.

Frank started yelling, but I couldn't make out any words in it. Was like he was speaking in tongues. He climbed up out of that hole in the floor with his good arm. The bad wing was folded up against his side.

I got dripped on with gouts of blood too dark to be healthy. The stuff matted my hair where it plopped on me, cowering where I did. Small bubbles popped in Frank's wound around that broken, protruding bone, like hot grease around cooking bacon. Then a couple spurts of wine-colored life ejected before the whole thing went back to a sizzling suck on Frank's inhales.

It was at that moment I was dead sure we'd all be goners before the day's end. Either fed to the shit-eyed blind fuckers chained upstairs, or skinned with our bones polished up in the overstuffed prize trunk. Maybe both at once.

Then, I heard something crawling underneath the floor. Maybe felt it more, really. My ears were shit by then, ringing and aching to the point I was surprised they weren't bleeding. But I felt whatever it was crawling under the floor. Not in the packed dirt under the house, I mean. Whatever it was down there was flipped upside down like a spider and pulled its way along the underside of the floorboards. Over whatever joists were under the house, it was coming for the hole. I could see the floorboards pressing upward in its path toward me and the trunk, like it was operating under reversed gravity down there. That, more than anything, convinced me I needed to move.

I'd never been in a gunfight before that day, believe it or not. Kinda crazy to remember being that guy not accustomed to throwing lead and having it thrown back. Would come a point where gunfights were quaint compared to the horrors I was going to see.

So, I was afraid to the point of being frozen in place at the thought of being shot. If the Goodall Brothers had made it out of that house, they might have seen fit to dump me off with Jimmy. As it was, I would have probably stayed put longer and gotten sucked into whatever horror befell the rest of our gang.

But seeing those fucking fingers wrapped up around the edge of the floor from below, crawling along the underside of the boards, fingers like witch's digits crossed with thick, furry, discolored spider's legs. I would have much preferred it been a giant spider. The hands were shadowy and cracked sulfur yellow through blue dead flesh. Other fingers, for there were a hell of a lot more than two hands coming out from under there, were blacked like smeared ash. There were more hands for sure. More than eight, were it a spider-thing with human hands.

The brothers screamed together but out of tune with each other as I scrambled around the bone trunk and to my feet, in a sprint to the door. I did not look back to the thing crawling out the hole, but I glanced over to see the boy folding in and around Frank and River. The boy still had his long gun, but he was using a knife to cut the brothers as he whipped past and between them, over and over.

He cut them deep, flayed their flesh in long meaty strips, all lumpy pink. It took a second for the juicy red blood to seep through that raw exposed muscle, like the cuts had been so quick and clean that the body needed a beat to remember it should be bleeding.

Clothing had ripped open. The lips of the more shallow wounds rolled back, like leather splitting and losing its tension. There was exposed bone in a wound on River's side. In Frank's gut, layers of separated muscle, more of that puckered yellow fat, and something light purple never meant to see the sunlight bulged out of the weeping opening. That was the one that woke him back up screaming.

Jimmy, that fucking bastard, snagged my boot as I turned tail for the last few feet to the exit. Like the serpent trickster from Genesis striking at my heel. He stuttered my step, nearly wrapped one of my feet around the heel of the other. I felt myself going over on my face and, to this day, I got no fucking clue how I stayed on my feet, struggling for balance all the way to that door.

Maybe I've been struggling for balance the rest of my life ever since, huh?

If I had fallen, I'd have met the same fate as the rest of the gang. I'm sure of that, even though I can only guess at what they went through.

I clawed open the door, stumbled over the porch, finally did overcompensate, tumbled down the porch steps, and, crawling through the dust of the ground like the snake in the Garden myself, cursed by God to travel on my belly eating the dust along the way.

It was the hissing behind me that made me roll over and look back into the darkness of the house from the sunlight.

Hands pressed against the inside glass of all the first floor windows across the front. Dark fluids smeared the glass and ran down the insides of the house with liquid infection. Not blood. Not human. Maybe not there at all, I wish I could make myself believe. Some of that liquid evil dripped out onto the porch from the broken glass in one of the panes.

The screaming continued inside, but that shadowy little boy stood in the open doorway staring out at me. He dropped the rifle on one side of him and Jimmy's boot where he'd been dragging the man by one leg.

The boy wielded long curved-blade knives in each fist as he charged out at me from across the porch. I shuffled and struggled to get up and run, but my limbs were lead-filled and some connection between my brain and my muscles was misfiring. I just kicked up a little storm of dust around me as the boy leapt off the top step and flew toward me in the air.

He broke apart, smoky and watery, before he reappeared in that doorway, still clutching his carving knives.

The screaming inside had faltered, and the windows were smeared black in the fluid wash. I heard a couple notes from the piano inside and around the corner, I'd swear. One of the brothers was moaning. It might have been Jimmy, there in the doorway, but I don't think so. Another begged for his life in sobby blubbers. I think that were Frank.

God damn, I've heard a lot of fuckers beg for their lives over the years and, most times, they don't get it. By the time you're begging for it, your fate is pretty well sealed, I think.

The boy came at me again, taking the steps. He made three

before he snapped back to the inside edge of the house. Four more attempts to chase me out into the sunlight had the same result in rapid fire. The boy's image blurred with motion and flashed with his vanishings and reappearing.

My eyes rolled in my sockets, sure I was dreaming this, going mad.

I got up to my knees and heaved up a clear string of slobber from my insides. Tasted of thick acid in my throat. Made mud in a small dribble under my face in the dry earth.

As I found my feet and wavered on my watery legs, I dared to check the boy's position. I expected to stare down the rifle. If he couldn't hold himself together in the sun, for whatever dark magic reasons, he could plug a bullet in me. If I went down that way, I found that preferable to any hands inside that house getting a grip on me.

The boy had his rifle but returned it to strapped over his back. He stared at me. Marked me with his eyes. He knew me. Would recognize me anywhere. I thought about the fact that the sun was going down eventually, and this boy was memorizing me for later. Life was changed for me now.

He turned his back finally and started up the inside stairs, dragging Jimmy by one leg and River Goodall by one flayed arm. I saw bone through the ragged tears in the bloody flesh of that arm. I recognized River by his clothes more than his scared face. Flesh peeled further off of him as the tabs of his skin caught of the edges of each riser. River's eyes, out of the mangled remains of his face, lighted on me in terror as his lolling head bumped its way up those steps out of my view where I perched out in the sunlight.

River's lips, such as they were, still moved, but it was only Frank's begging from deeper in the house I could hear.

Might have lingered there on my unsure legs a while longer if the door hadn't slammed on its own.

I stumbled away with a hitched step, in the direction of where we hid the horses. No thought of getting my partners out of there crossed my mind.

I only thought of getting away, riding hell to leather anywhere but here. I thought about the fact that there were other members of this family out in the sun who would be coming home eventually. Not sure what breed of devils they was either, like or unlike the boy, but we'd seen them go, in the morning sun, looking all the world like human beings. Either way, the sun was going to set on me no matter how close or far I was at the point darkness covered me.

I took Frank's horse instead of mine because it was better. Didn't take nearly enough supplies because I was about running, not thinking about living.

I never thought ahead. All my family accused me of it long before I was on the run to prove them out. My brother especially gave me hell about that, mostly before I left. After I came back, he had a list of other gripes for me. I would prove him out again.

I would be chased. Chased by a marshal and his bitch sidekick, it turned out. Wasn't exactly the predator I expected on my trail, but that species of horror I'd encountered in that house, making me the lone survivor and only witness to its evil, wasn't done with me either.

If that fucking pair of law dogs hadn't driven me into that cave, things might have gone different. Who knows though? Maybe it was the evil in the form of a little boy toting a four-barrel rifle, who marked me, that drove me in that fateful direction in the first place.

Seems about right.

5

THAT'S AS FAR as he got in the story that first day. He teased the chapter about the marshal, a sidekick, and some cave. Prison Orderly James Fanny tried a couple times to get Stone talking again, but it was back to Netflix, changing sheets, fixing meals, and assisted bathroom breaks, complete with helping an old man wipe his ass while he grumbled and complained the whole time.

Routine has a strange way of lulling people right out of curiosity. Prisons, even ones with one elderly inmate and no real guard to speak of, thrive on routine. The one break in that routine was when James had to treat a rash on Stone's ass. The gauze found their way to the biohazard bucket hanging on the wall nearby. Sometimes the orderly didn't bother with that procedure because it was up to him to empty the thing anyway. That day it was the closest disposal though.

As James helped Stone get his pants back up, the old man pointed at the hazard bucket and said, "That's what the symbol on the back of the burned skull looked like that day at the mill."

The orderly kept his eyes on the old man and didn't pursue it. Stone Wicked was prone to say cryptic dark stuff like that, so James tried not to think on it too much.

James almost forgot the whole episode before Agent John Perkins showed back up. Perkins took the remote from Stone Wicked and turned off the TV instead of just pausing it. Wicked crossed his arms, but didn't say anything about it as Perkins set up a camera on a tripod in front of Stone this time.

James stood off to the side and waited. He didn't say anything for fear that Perkins might send him away. James really wanted to hear this.

At least the guard was here and awake this time, for what that was worth.

Fanny and Perkins both wore their blue medical procedural masks. The pandemic was getting worse and the prison system in Alabama was taking it seriously, if not many others in the state. Stone's exposed face was in need of a shave.

Perkins got the video on the camera recording and watched Stone on the digital screen instead of in real life, as the agent stood behind the tripod for the whole interview this time.

"State your name, inmate," Perkins ordered.

Stone stared at the floor. His eyes were watery and hooded. Even with his arms crossed, he looked more lost than defiant. At least to James that's how it appeared.

Perkins said, "Agent John Perkins, contracted with the Alabama State Prison System, interviewing inmate Stone Wicked in the Scully Elder Care Facility of the Alabama State Prison System in Scully, Alabama. Also present, Orderly James Fanny of the Scully Elder Care Facility. Can you confirm everything I said is true, Mr. Fanny?"

James stood up straight, even though he wasn't on camera. "Ugh, yes, sir, all of that is true. Yes."

Perkins added, "Date and time are marked in the video. All times are Central U.S. times. This is my second interview with this subject, but the first recording."

After a pause, Perkins raised his voice a little. "Inmate Wicked, are you with me?"

No answer.

"What kind of day is he having, Orderly?"

James wasn't sure if this was part of the official record or not. He just tried to answer without thinking about the camera. "Hard to say. He's been cloudy lately. Very quiet today. Just sitting and watching TV the way you saw him when you came in."

From the angle where he stood, Orderly Fanny could just see the red front of the biohazard disposal bucket on the wall of one of the exam rooms. Not the one he had treated Stone's rash in. He considered the black symbol of a petri dish with tendrils of disease leaking out of it in perfect three-part symmetry.

Perkins sighed and said, "Inmate Wicked, I'd like you to attune to me as best you are able. Just got back from South Carolina. Visited

Robert G. Hucks Detention Center in Fuller Beach, South Carolina. You would have known it as Grinder State Prison in your time there."

James attended to this.

"Grindfield, you say?" Stone asked.

Perkins stared at Stone Wicked a moment, started to reach for something in his pocket, but then stopped. "I don't know what all you boys used to call the place, but Grinder State was what its name was prior to the 1980s, after you would have been gone."

"The Grinder," Stone mumbled with his arms crossed and his eyes cast down.

Perkins picked up on the words though. "That's right. Some of the guards still call it that, or the Grind House, too. What do you remember about the Grinder?"

"It got bloody."

James barely heard the mumbled words, but knew the phrase from past conversations with Stone Wicked. Agent Perkins picked up on this mumbled bit, too, it seemed.

"That's also correct, Inmate. Do you remember the specific years you were in The Grinder?"

Nothing.

"Do you remember when you were born? When you were sentenced?"

Nothing.

Perkins looked to James and James took that as an invitation. "Did you find his birth or sentencing dates, Agent Perkins?"

Perkins shook his head ever so slightly and returned his attention to the digital image of Stone on the camera's little screen.

"You were transferred to Alabama, temporarily it was thought at the time, at least, in the fall of 1979."

Stone nodded his head but didn't lift his eyes. "That's right."

"You remember that, Inmate?"

"Was in the spring, as I recall."

Perkins sighed and said, "No, it was in the early fall of 1979. Probably still hot with Indian Summer the day you were transferred."

"Was hot as hell, as I recall," Stone sounded more lively, even though his posture hadn't changed. He didn't mumble this time.

"Hottest summer on record, up to that point, for the Carolinas," Perkins agreed. "You were transferred temporarily forever to Alabama because a storm damaged the prison pretty severely that summer of '79. Locals around the area, old enough to remember, swear it was a hurricane, but near as I can find, it was a tropical storm that missed South Carolina completely. What do you remember about that storm?"

"It got bloody."

"Yes, it did. Sections of the prison got flooded. Inmates escaped their cells and a couple bad characters escaped the prison altogether. There was a riot. A number of guards and prisoners were killed. Got bloody, as you said. The names of those killed are on a monument outside the fences of the new prison. Big slab of black marble with a rough edge. The names of the deceased are carved into it real nice. I'm not sure it's all that comforting to the families of the dead, but it's nice and kept clean, as far as I can tell."

"Just the guards or the prisoners, too?" Stone's eyes swept over Agent Perkins and then away.

"What's that now?" Perkins leaned forward, pulling his eyes off the digital screen and looking on Stone directly.

Stone hesitated, but then said, "The names of the deceased . . . the dead prisoners, too, or just the guards what got killed etched into that pretty stone you saw?"

Perkins smiled, but it only seemed to really lift one corner of his mouth. Made the smile into a bit of a sneer or a smirk. "Only the guards who passed, I guess."

After a pause with nothing more from the inmate, Perkins asked, "What was your part in that, Inmate Wicked? You a rioter or a hider or what?"

Stone chewed at the inside of his mouth before he spoke. "Hot as hell down there in solitary. Place leaked all the fucking time. Dug the damn prison down into the ground spitting distance from the ocean. What'd they think was going to happen? Stupid as hell."

"Were you in solitary during the storm of '79?"

"Don't recall. Everyone in The Grinder was in isolation at one point or another. Guards got more nervous when we behaved than when we gave them shit. Couldn't win."

"What do you remember about the riot?"

Nothing. Maybe he remembered something or maybe he didn't, but, either way, he said nothing. Perkins waited a good long time to make it awkward, but Stone looked like he was going to doze off long before he broke.

Perkins tried again. "You remember what the Grinder was like after the storm? Consolidating down to a couple cell blocks?"

Nothing.

"Did you know an inmate named Alias Orwell there? Probably would have been when you were in solitary."

Nothing from Stone, but James made a mental note to Google the name later.

"Wasn't the storm or the riot that got you moved officially," Perkins continued. "Grinder had a bad outbreak of tuberculosis. Started in the spring of '79, and only got worse after the storm. Did you catch it?"

"Was in the spring, as I recall."

"You caught TB in the spring of '79? At Grinder? . . . Inmate?"

James couldn't take the awkward pause. "That's just a thing he says. Doesn't mean he really—"

"I know, Mister Fanny. I have this under control. Thank you."

"Yes, sir. Just we have no record of him having had TB, is what I'm saying."

"Yes, Mister Fanny, we don't have much record of anything on Inmate Wicked." Perkins wiggled his fingers as he traded his attention between the digital screen and the man himself. "Turns out South Carolina wasn't your state of sentencing, and the Grinder wasn't your first prison, either. We don't have a record in the Carolinas of when or why you were sentenced. We don't have the date of when you were transferred in. Just that you were . . . from Georgia. Do you recall your time in Georgia, inmate?"

If he did, Stone didn't say. James remembered Stone mentioning Georgia in his story about fleeing west. Fanny decided not to say anything on it either.

"Am I getting any closer to where your long institutional life begins, Inmate Wicked? You clamming up on me?"

Stone answered by staying clammed up, arms crossed, eyes watering and half open.

"Found an old yellow and brown crusty piece of paper with your name on it in a warehouse-sized file storage room, Inmate Wicked. Wasn't your transfer paper, but some other nothing about you being questioned concerning other inmates giving you some trouble. You were as closed-mouthed then as you are now, according to that paper. The page was from 1954 and mentioned off-hand that you were transferred from Blood Mountain. You remember Blood Mountain at all?"

"Other prisoners always starting shit," Stone grumbled. "Was the Cubans the last time."

"Was the Cubans that did what?"

Nothing.

"Tell me about the Cubans, Inmate Wicked."

Nothing still.

"Were the Cubans at Blood Mountain? Were they the ones giving you trouble in that incident report from 1954?"

Same nonresponse as before.

"When did you have trouble with the Cubans, Inmate Wicked?"

"Was in the spring, as I recall."

Perkins sighed and muttered, "The fucking spring."

James wasn't sure Perkins had said it loud enough for the camera to pick up, though.

During this whole exchange on the Cubans, James fixated on the year. Stone was already in prison in 1954? He was transferred from another prison before that. Quick math made that 66 years, plus his time in Georgia before that, plus however old he was at the time of sentencing before that. It all seemed to track, if Stone was in his 80s or 90s. James also thought of Stone's wild story from some days back, after the agent's first visit, a story that went from western adventure to a stone cold horror story, leaving the orderly thinking the teller was drifting into hallucination part way through. Stone would have to be pretty damn old to have lived a western, horror-western or otherwise. The fact they still had no start date on him left James to wonder.

"At any rate, can't find Blood Mountain," Perkins said, breaking the silence once more. "Not a town or a prison, in any search or on any map. Can't get anyone on the phone that knows either. I debated a good long time on whether to come back here or go looking there first. What is Blood Mountain?"

Stone's lips shifted a bit, but that was it.

"Guess I made the wrong choice. The Grinder . . . Blood Mountain . . . If it's another prison name, you've stayed in some sinister sounding facilities. With a name like Wicked, I guess that fits. Anything you recall about a place called Blood Mountain? Anything at all?"

Nothing, it seemed.

"I got myself another mystery to track down then." Perkins turned off the camera and took apart his setup. "If he says anything else, anything remotely useful, would you call me?"

James thought about the story of the haunted ranch and he nodded without considering mentioning it. Perkins held out a card between his fingers. James looked at it, then up at the agent.

Perkins tilted his head and wiggled the card he still held out. "Did I give you one of these last time?"

"No, sir."

Perkins spoke just above a whisper, "Then, how you planning to call me?"

James took it. "Yes, sir."

"Cell. Email. Either one, or both. Anything that sounds remotely helpful about his past. Anything at all, at any time."

James nodded but offered no information in that moment. He did offer to see Agent Perkins out but was declined.

James waited until he heard the guard reengage the lock behind their visitor. Might not have been a more wasted lock that existed in the entire Alabama prison system, James thought.

"You want your show back on, Stone? Or something to eat?"

"Hot as balls," Stone snapped, as he unfolded his arms.

"Need the air turned down?"

Getting no answer, James started to finger through his keys for the one to the thermostat cover, perhaps the second most wasted lock in the system.

But Stone cut him off. "No, not now. Then."

James stared a moment, hands frozen over his keys. He'd realize hours later he was still holding them just like that. "You mean, back at . . . The Grinder?"

"There and Blood Mountain. Grindfield was a filthy place, though, full of filthy men."

James thought about asking about Blood Mountain in particular, maybe the beginning of the story Perkins cared about. Almost did so, too, but he waited. The moment felt fragile.

Stone broke the silence first this time. "You want to hear about that cave?"

James really did.

6

MARSHAL ELLIOT CRAWFORD and his bitch deputy, that's who. Don't know that deputizing women was allowed back then, but I guess you fuck around far enough west, it doesn't make a great goddamn what civilized people in the east think about anything.

She was Annabelle, last name spelled "S" "Y" "N" "E", but pronounced "Sin" as in fucking your sister or torturing a dog because you're having a bad day. Annabelle Syne. She couldn't have been no more than 5'5" or five-and-a-half tall, at the outside, but would turn out she'd be the one I should've been watching.

She had this whole speech worked out when she saw me on the train, years later. "Heading back out, looking for trouble, Stone? Mind if I tag along? There's a few people who've been looking for you a long while, me included. Et cetera. Et cetera. Bullshit. Bullshit."

I'm getting ahead of myself because this was back to our very first meeting.

Crawford was this tall drink of water. His knees would regret bearing all that height and bulk before our days of cat and mouse were over. But it would be her, in the end.

Everyone assumed they was fucking. Couldn't nobody see any purpose for her other than that, on account of her being just about the right size to slob on his cock standing up if it had a little upward curve in it. Couldn't say, myself, of course. Been called a cocksucker plenty, but never made it true. My guess was that she were more comfortable riding in pink canoes than breaking studs, a lot of the more rough and tumble women out there, back then, were. Some of them looked more like men than women. If they wasn't whores or wives, they were bulls, mostly.

I'm saying she was probably a lesbo. Okay, you were just staring at me like you weren't getting it. Okay. She didn't look like a bull, though. Looked like she'd blow away on the wind if you didn't know how the story would end.

Apparently, that devil family at the bone ranch from hell sicced the law on me. Said we stole. Said I messed with their boy in some manner, as much a lie as the first one, way back, that pushed me west in the first place. On top of, every wronged man in the west pinned all the gambling debt and thievery of the rest of the gang all on me. Being the last one left alive came with its downsides. Was enough to get me my own marshal and bitch bull.

The whole fucking time I struggled to stay ahead of him in the desert, I kept imagining Crawford sitting in those fine parlors listening to the devil family's lies. That black magic boy trying with all his might to keep from phasing across the room. All that grey human meat chained up over his head.

He'd tell me later, he never visited the ranch, which makes sense now. I feel like he would have sensed it. If not him, then Lady Syne, for sure, and he'd listen to her, trusted her instincts and intuitions, he did. He always did. Probably saved his life a couple more times than he deserved. Fuck 'em both, I say. Fuck 'em both for chasing me into that goddamned cave.

I kept trying to circle around them in the day and the night, but together they were too wise to fall for it. Tried to box them in and set a trap, but they were too wily for that shit and had me running for my life and freedom again. Facing trial didn't scare me near as much as facing that family, with them knowing where I was caged up.

Water was running short out there in the hot, dry, sandy nothing, but I kept going.

That's when we got to the black mountain. At the time, it had a name. Was part of a crumbling range, there in the driest parts of the west. Was an Indian name, I'm sure. Every fucking state in the Union has a bunch of shit named after the Indians that used to live there, like every road atlas is written in their blood.

Point being, you ain't finding that place on any map today. You couldn't find it if I had the satellite coordinates for the thing. No reason to think it fell down in the meantime, even though it's been a spell. I'm sure it still stands, maybe made of volcanic rock with no natural explanation for it being there, or maybe its schorl tourmaline or some mineral spinel that would give geologists a hard-on. But it also isn't there. I'd say you'd only find it if they wanted you to, but I don't believe they ever wanted no one to. I think a fellow like me only finds it because I was marked from the business at that ranch, and the law dogs found it because they tracked me so well. Fuck 'em both.

On any account, they decided to waste a couple bullets in the sand to keep me from skirting that mountain. So, I pressed forward, found a cave opening that was deeper than it first looked, and I traded some shots back. I hoped to hide, but Frank's horse bolted from me and gave up my spot.

Now, I'd be lying if I pretended, after all these years, that I could recite our first dialogue there, shouting back and forth at each other, with our voices echoing off the shiny black rocks of that unnatural mountain and all its broken pieces scattered about that rough cave entrance like an alien landscape on some distant *Star Trek* world.

We had plenty of shouting matches over that long misadventure. Other, quieter, conversations, too. Especially me and the marshal. So, all those back-and-forths blend together after all this time. But for the sake of the story and introducing the key players, I'll give my best estimation of what was said.

Marshal Crawford cupped his hands around his mouth, from their high-ground perch, and bullhorned something down at me like, "Come out and face the music, Wicked."

I shouted back, "Fuck your mother's twat with a sharpened railroad spike."

Crawford's lady bull had to throw in her two cents. "Look, mister, we're taking you back, one way or the other."

"If you two assholes want to get back home alive to see any of your loved ones and watch the evening news, you'll leave me be."

Shit, there were no TVs back then. Scratch that last bit, but you get the point.

Okay, so he said, "That's enough of that. You're coming back with us no matter how hard you make it on yourself. We got water and know you don't. We got food and know you don't. We got the only ride with any chance of getting you out alive, and saw your horse take to the hills without you. You aren't on the hook for anything that'll get you hanged, so come on."

Elliot, Marshal Crawford, never said words like "ain't", not that I recall, anyhow.

Annie Syne bleated out. "We also got more bullets and know you're almost out, you piss ant."

"Fuck you, cunt," I said. "Go suck your man's cock. The men are talking here."

"I don't suck his cock. That's just a vicious rumor."

"Whatever you say. Put something in your mouth to keep you from interrupting so much."

I'm drifting off into fantasy here. Something was said back and forth. Probably not all this, but something.

At some point the marshal pulled her back for a word. Something along the lines of the nice way to tell her she needed to cool her tits.

I decided to slip out from that narrow hiding spot and make my way around the mountain. No idea how I thought I was going to get away with it and stay ahead of them, both on horseback and with them having the drop on me, but I guess I could already feel there was something suspect about that crevice and what lie beyond.

I didn't get an ass hair's distance into the open before she popped up and took a shot, kicking up more sand. I fired up on her, to at the least try to make her duck or maybe to put one in her skull to be quit with her. I came close, real fucking close, but she didn't duck.

Her next shot came real the fuck close to me, too. I didn't feel the wind of it. I think that shit is pulp mag storybook stuff, but I did hear it ricochet two or three times off those black rock surfaces behind me. Stuff didn't even chip from the bullets, as I recall. Had to have been as hard as that Hugh Jackman's metal claws in that movie we watched the other day.

Her jumping bean bullet finally broke into some weaker rock out from the mountain a bit and that came apart. Stone chip shrapnel cut me at least a half dozen places, like a bunch of stinging bees. I ducked back into the crevice, leaving the light behind as I searched for another path of escape.

And now I was bleeding. Bleeding in the cursed dark.

So, I went deeper, didn't I? Of course I did, or we wouldn't be talking about this shit, now would we?

I thought I found hell on that last job at the ranch. Maybe that crazy house was a waystation of some kind, but I'd found the real gate to hell under that black mountain, and I was crawling into it.

7

FUCKING HELL, I hate tight spaces. Always have. I could feel the walls crushing into my chest, poking into my back, scraping as I dragged myself into the darkness. I don't know how much you read those clickbait articles on the Internet, but more than one dummy through the years has gotten himself pinned in a tight space in caves. Even when they're found, they're wedged in so tight, there's no getting them out. They suffocate like that, with their chests and backs pressed by rock. Nothing to do but take their pictures for the clickbait.

Well, I was that dummy that day. Marshal Crawford weren't going to take my picture and I don't know how hard he or his bitch were going to work to get me unstuck if I wound up that way. I was still spooked by the devilry at the ranch, and I was going to run to the end of the fucking Earth, if that's what it took. I guess, in this case, I was willing to crawl straight down into Hell.

So, that's what I did, wasn't it?

Finally, that fat man's squeeze let up and I was pawing my way down into the dark. Was a pitted track, threatening to twist my ankles or suddenly open up and I'd fall down into a dry well pit from which no one would ever fish me out again.

The cuts on my hands smeared little lines of blood, like shitty skid marks on the walls of the tunnel, on both sides. Particles from the gritty surface irritated the openings in my skin, but I couldn't keep going without feeling my way through. The shiny, hard, black stone outside gave way to other species of rock the farther I went.

As the passage widened beyond my ability to reach both sides at once, I stuck close to the right-side wall. I used the dim light to judge what was just ahead, but held to the wall just the same, leaving my thin blood trail for whatever predators might be interested in me, from behind or ahead. The rocks themselves seemed thirsty for it, too.

I didn't notice until later, but I could still see, even down in those descending depths, long after the sun had no reach. Spots were glowing around and above me. Other light was bleeding out of the air, green, like toxic energy, and dead dull white, like the burn off a ghost of some sort.

Scraping and scratching echoed around me, so I kept going to stay ahead of the marshal on my tail. Never dawned on me such noises might be echoing ahead from some evil that called this cave home.

I felt the sharp edges on the wall to my right and drew my hand back in a hurry, like something got teeth on me. Were bones, but really old ones. Didn't have a word for it at the time, when all those bones, in all sorts of skeletal shapes, stuck out from the wall like carvings in stone, but those walls, extending several feet up into the rising ceiling of the cave, were chocked full of fossils.

There were people that knew about dinosaurs by then. Wasn't long before everyone was all a titter about them, the way school kids lose their shit for dinosaurs today. Probably, back home, back east, every damn body was a buzz with it. The Brits, then the city folk, and out to the South and the boonies later. Preachers wouldn't get their dicks in a knot about big ass lizards until later. I wasn't paying much attention to the news of the day back then. Wasn't everything just waiting on the other side of a computer keyboard, like today.

These fossils were something wholly different though.

There were large bones, like those of giant reptiles, dragons I thought of them then. But protruding from those rocks in betwixt those monster skeletons were the bones of people, too. The individual bones were separated from the joints and spread out, like the poor bastards had been blasted from their skin and embedded in the stone just as the pieces started to spread apart. Half-buried skulls, like things melting into the wall, sinking into the surface, hung jaw open in mid-screams of terror and pain.

I swear, had I not seen those polished bits of bone in the prize trunk earlier, I'd have had to conclude these were carvings, some bizarro art installation out in the middle of damn nowhere. Would have made not a lick of sense, but more comforting than the idea that any of this could be real. I was beyond comforting.

I heard the voices, harsh and whispery. Thought, logically enough, they were coming from behind me, so I continued forward. More human bone art marred the wall as I went deeper through the low glow of the passages. These calcified and fossilized forms appeared to be trying to claw their way out of their stone prison. The spaces between their restless resting places were decorated with fossilized marine life.

I knew how far we were from any ocean, too far for sea creatures, too far for pirate chests full of polished femurs, but had been told all my life that such sights were from Noah's Great Flood. Maybe, at the time, that explained away for me the leviathan bones I'd passed earlier, and perhaps I convinced myself that the human remains were those of the sinners that had hurt God's eyes and heart with their debauchery and mockery as Noah built his big boat.

Don't clearly recall my thinking at that exact moment. Everything we remember is shaded by what happens later. Especially if that shading comes from something earth-shattering, like what lie at the hot bottom of the cave system under that black mountain.

I moved through some passages but passed other openings. I had the presence of mind to realize I needed to be marking my path if I hoped not to get lost down there forever. Wanted to shake the law on my tail, sure, but I wanted to get back to the daylight again, eventually, too. Would have been stupid to chalk an arrow for the marshal to track me, I thought. So, I tried to use the formations and memorize some landmarks for myself. Left at the eight-armed starfish fossil on the way back. Second passage under the dragon claw after that. Keep straight at the dog-looking thing with two heads and saber fangs. Like that.

As the caverns opened wider, the twisted bones of giants barely held onto the walls where they was pressed all the way from the floor into the uneven luminescent ceilings. Not dinosaurs, mind you, motherfucking humanoid giants. I'm not sure what they looked like, with their skin and hair still on. They were contorted and the eye holes in their skulls didn't line up right. Could have been the movement of the earth after they were dead and buried. Could have been deformities, on account of being so tall. Elliot Crawford had trouble with his knees, like I told you, and he wasn't no super giant. Any way you cut it, I saw the evidence of real giants that once crept the Earth. The Bible had an answer for that, too, so I kept going.

Maybe I thought I'd stumble upon the gopher wood remains of the Ark itself down there. For all I knew, this was Mount Ararat. There was something Biblical or magical going on, it seemed.

Place started to get hot the deeper I went. I didn't have much experience with caves. Not much experience with any damn thing back then, but I thought I knew caves stayed cool. Steady warmer in the winter, and cooler in the summer. The only answer was if I was in a volcano or found myself a passage to Hell. That black glass surface of the mountain out there should have warned me something was amiss.

I was hearing all sorts of scratching and clatter and voices and footsteps by that point. Wouldn't have been surprised to round any corner and find the marshal or his woman drawing down on me.

What I did find was beyond surprising. More than shocking. It ruined reality for me.

8

A DIFFERENT SORT of light, a different quality of illumination, filled in the space as I progressed onward. It was a dark light in fire colors. It made the shadows and edges deeper.

You know those *Lord of the Hobbit* books what came out some many years ago? I only saw the movies. Well, parts of them. They run long for me. But you know those parts about mines and smelting machines deep down in the ground? It was like how I'd imagine that if those stories were real.

The fire light. The smoke stink. The ringing sound of what could be falling hammers. The grind of turning things. Heavy things, twisting into the rock for their own reasons.

And the smell. Sulfur, I guess, like any story about Hell and demons. But more than that. Worse than that. This stench, Jesus Christ, it were like setting a body's rotten, impacted shit alight while still inside and then cutting them open to let the aroma escape after all that cooked pressure built up real good. If you can imagine that horror, you might be part way to how it really was for me down there.

I pressed on because I thought the worst that could happen to me was getting caught, getting taken back. That's probably how every soul gets to Hell, I imagine. They always think they're running away from it, while the whole time marching toward it.

I started to slide. A greasy sort of soot covered the rocky floor as it ramped down and around from the tunnel I was fleeing through, down into a sprawling chamber that wound down and down and down through cavernous spaces like cathedrals. The anterooms to Hell, they really were.

I never got a great look at any machines. That grinding noise and volcanic furnace glow floated out of pores in the walls and floors of those endless chambers. Could have been machines deeper down, but also could have been something organic, or animated, at the very least. Something that grinded its armored sides against enormous tunnels still too small for it. God knows what. Devil knows. Some evil and horror not meant for human minds, on any account. Something too big to even be housed in the horror house back at the ranch. Related, though. Were all related.

There were growths, too. Alien gardens hung from ledges and crevices in the ceiling, spilling down vines and glowing blooms of flora not meant for places where sunlight shines, maybe not meant for this Earth, above or below. In other spots along the walls and smaller chambers cut through to other tight places, fungal gardens sprouted and twisted out from where they fed upon dead things, or things that wished they was dead.

Animals in the process of corpsing, humans, too, I believe, moved about in those feeding vegetative abominations. One spot of growth was close enough for me to see struggling paws and hooves. They reached out of the fungi, blind and desperate to feel a world that wasn't all darkness, decay, and digestion.

Then, people, too. They was trapped under there and in all that. By God and Sonny J, they were as grey as the poor souls from that filth chamber behind the master bedroom of that ranch house, the place I left my whole gang to be tortured, too. These grey men lifted up with the fungus growing into their backs like a new hide. Tendrils of the stuff weaved through the skulls and out of the ruptured skin of their faces. The colorless roots of fungus twisted around into a screen in their blind eye sockets. As they turned and shifted in their living prisons, I couldn't tell if there were any conscious thought left in their half-eaten mush minds, but some lizard instinct still had them struggling, writhing in it and against it. Chalky, ashen sores opened up at the folds near their elbows or turned necks. Blood seeped from those wounded joints, only it was blackened from whatever poisons flowed through them at that point. Before any of it could drip over, white threads of growth broke through the grey skin, sopped the stuff up like gravy, and retreated back into the bodies. Nothing wasted.

Would that have been the worst of the horrors, I'd count myself lucky today. Might have just surrendered myself to the marshal and his pet to be taken on to the sane punishments of humankind. I wasn't lucky, though. That weren't the worst of it. The real horrors were carnivorous, as they always are. And they had no intention of letting me go. Wasn't their way.

The real masters of that realm under the black mountain were goliaths. Easily three or four times the height of even the biggest men I'd seen. There was nothing natural about them, even though they sported two arms, two legs, and a head that went with their size.

They wore robes I mistook for cloth, pulled tight around their frames despite the heat. Weren't no cloth, though. Those coverings were leathery stuff, made from the skins of smaller creatures, all sewn together. If it wasn't human skin treated to be rubbery and elastic, then I have no idea. The bony jut of their knees, elbows, shoulders, and spiny vertebrae stuck out sharp and obscene without breaking their coverings, whatever they really were.

There was flesh on them. It was all dark and lumpy, like flesh made from disease. Maybe kin to the fungus they grew on other living things for purposes I'd never understand. Not as long as I lived, and I've lived long, you know. But whatever that rotten, burnt stuff was over their sharp bone structure, it didn't cover their skulls. Their heads were all exposed bones that swept down like long animal snouts, like bleached bones sitting in the desert sun, only down there where no sun had ever reached. There was enough sinew weaved around to allow the long jaws to open and snap closed. White tongues, longer than any I've ever seen, licked out from between the most forward fangs and then back in. They cast their vision around from beady red eyes that set deep inside the bony pits of their sockets.

And they fed.

More grey men, not yet sacrificed to the fungus or vines, trailed up naked from the lower chambers in the deeper cathedrals of that place. Those same scars around their genitals and eyes as we'd seen in the room What's-His-Name uncovered back at the ranch.

Fuck. I was frozen on that slippery ramp of stone leading down into that living hell.

Those men, if they used to be men, brought the carved remains of other grey meat up with them. The great bone gods in their leathery robes snatched the offerings away from the hands of their blind, filthy slaves with animal hunger. Their strange jaws ripped, twisted, and tore loose bites. Entrails, pink muscle, and dribbling red blood spilled from their cheekless skulls.

Clawed fingers, twisted in spirals of exposed bone and tight flesh, poked loose pieces back in like talons. There were too many joints in those long fingers, easily a dozen knuckles along the lengths of each one. They were deceivingly sharp, I'd find out the hard way shortly.

They lurched their heads and necks as they chewed and swallowed, like strange dinosaurs swallowing whole slabs of meat. Severed bone and ragged cartilage crunched as they made some small effort to chew some of the bites before swallowing everything in big chunks.

One of them snapped early and caught a grey man by his shoulder instead of the partial slab of meat he offered. The man screamed from a raw throat, but it seemed to be more reflex than any real passion. Maybe death was a relief for his kind. The others waited patiently under this great creature with the slab of meat. It gnawed into the man's body, burst his organs, and slobbered gore down its own misshapen body. The blood rained thick on the grey men underneath. Their speckled tongues lapped out to taste the spillage themselves, but they mostly just stood still, waiting.

I turned and made an effort to climb the slippery incline back into the cave passages leading up. All thought of the marshal and escaping custody had left my mind. Escaping the horrid fates down there filled my world.

I could get no traction on that sooty rock, but I kept scrambling. The alternative to keeping trying was too awful to imagine or accept. I didn't make a sound, I swear it. I would have screamed if I had any voice left in me. Obviously, I needed to get out of there silently, but I had no control and was truly trying to scream my fucking head off. I couldn't get any of that rancid air to stay in me after what I'd seen, though.

Still, they fixed on me. Every single soul, or soulless monster, within dark sight marked me. Even the blind fuckers bringing meat, probably made of themselves, and the eyeless things used as fertilizer for twisted mushroom gardens, all turned my way and stood still, as if staring.

I scrambled hand over hand, still trying to gain ground as I was doing very little more than holding position at best. I turned my head and saw them all watching, as if I were the most interesting thing to come their way in ages. The sunken red eyes of those exposed-skull gods were the most terrible and always will be. As long as I live, being seen by those things will always be my greatest terror. When I end up in Hell one day, I know exactly what the front porch looks like, and what will be sitting out there waiting for me.

All those horse-headed monsters, maybe a dozen of them in sight at that moment, all folded open their hide robes, revealing their hideous nakedness. They folded open their jaws wide enough to hide their eyes and expand the flapping valves of their gullets, the dark voids within. And they screamed, high and shrill, to end the world and tear my sanity in two.

The grey men responded to those screaming cries by breaking formation and running toward me in a mad rush of ruined flesh and murderous intent.

I'll never know how I did it, beyond the dark magic and motivation of fear, but I got my ass up that greasy slope with wave upon wave of grey meat on my trail.

9

THE BONY MONSTERS charged through the crowd of their grey men with their leathery robes flapping behind them, screeching the entire way. They ran on all fours, like cats, pitching their front limbs back between their legs as they propelled themselves forward in predatory chase. There was no outrunning them, I feared. No way something as fragile as a man could escape these things in their own lair without becoming their next meal, or degraded into one of their grey slaves, worse than being eaten, I'd bargain.

I scrambled up into the mouth of the smaller passage that had led me down into this place. The monsters propelled and clawed their way up the greasy face of the wall under the trail. I heard them crash and clack against each other as they jostled one another to get to me first.

They caught me twice before I was through the narrows and on my way up through the maze of caves again, with those eyeless and cockless grey bastards running after me. I don't know if it was two different ones what cut me, both sharp-boned hands from one of them, or two impossible fingers from one hand, spread wide enough to gash me in two separate places. Don't matter really, I guess. Either way, I got sliced through all my clothing and deep along my back. If that one had kept scratching me as deep as it did for another couple inches at most, it'd have severed my spine and that would have been the end of me. You'd be cleaning up some other old man's shit seven days a week. That cut was deep and threatening, especially accounting for me not nearly away or safe yet. The second cut opened the side of my pants and separated the muscle of my right thigh almost to the bone. That was the one that nearly cost me everything down in that cave.

After that, I was more lurching forward with that leg than proper running. You probably noticed me limping on that side. Right? These days I think I limp on both legs. Sort of waddle my way through life, without end or relief. No matter. That day in that dark twisted pit I was running hell to leather, injured or not.

I'm not positive when those oversized bony bastard lords of the caves squeezed through the passages behind me, in amongst all those grey half-men, but they were coming and still screaming for blood. It was the grey masses that barreled up behind me, hooting and barking like wild animals.

Should have been pitch as midnight down there so far from the surface. I should have been lost from the sun forever, but that green radioactive poison glow still spilled down from the ceiling and out of crevices where bones older than time turned to stone in the walls. I should be thankful that ghostly light showed the way, but I have nightmares for what else it showed me.

Those naked minions of the monsters that fed upon them in the depths battered each other as they bounced off the uneven stone walls of the pass, never slowing in their pursuit. I didn't waste a lot of time looking back, but when I did, a couple of them dropped to lap up the blood I was spilling from my cuts. When they did, the others ran over the top of them and trampled those thirsty fools to death.

It was the screams. The screams of their masters, weaving through the passes with them, drove them onward after me.

One wrong turn could have cost me everything. One dead end or one slip into a side tunnel would have been the death of me. Not sure I remembered the way in my fear or just guessed lucky, but I never dreamed of hesitating. Those monster screams drove me on, too.

Things opened up a bit. I didn't remember this much space on the way in, but I had no time to ponder my mistakes.

I felt better when I saw the marshal and her pointing their guns at me. At least I knew I'd come the right way and was maybe closer to the surface now. I wasn't sure the sun was going to save me at all, but I still wanted to escape this black place.

The law dogs were so shocked to see me and the pack I trailed that they made no effort to snag me as I ran bleeding right between them and up the passage they'd just emerged from. Their mouths hanging open like that might have been comical in other circumstances.

The two of them fired on the mass of grey flesh behind me. They downed a few of them, I know because I heard the victims cry out even over the ringing aftermath of the blasts. I'm sure some of those grey men took to feeding on their wounded fellows as others crawled over the top of them to get to the three of us.

I don't know if Marshal Crawford and Annabelle caught sight of the monsters at that point or if their first glimpse came later. Might have been they decided running was their only real chance as the grey men kept coming like a plague of rats. They caught up with me quicker than I liked, as neither of them was injured at that point.

"Left. Left!" Crawford yelled. And I left lefted.

"Right."

"Center!"

Maybe I owe him my life. Maybe I'd've found my own way, but I shudder to imagine.

Those grey fuckers kept coming, goddamn their shit-packed blind eyes.

Then, I saw real light. It was white and overbright in a way that made me think of death. But I plunged out, headlong, into the burning desert sun. I kicked sand and pebbles out from under my boots as I told myself to keep running, to not trust the sun to save me.

Still half blind, my hat that inexplicably stayed on my head shaded my eyes a little.

I scaled the rock face above that narrow opening of cave I could have easily missed and never stopped wishing I had. Crawford and Annabelle Syne emerged in full run below me after I was more than halfway up the rocks, dribbling bright red drops along the white stones.

They'd been shooting at me from up here not long before. Now, they were following my blood trail to get away with me. We were all fugitives at that point, traitors and deserters.

A few of the grey men staggered out into the dusty light. Even with their eyes destroyed, they raised their arms against the heat cooking them. Almost every last one of them bled from somewhere they'd cut themselves along the way. I don't think any of the ones that made it this far had been shot, but they might have been better off if they had.

I topped the rocks and the horses the marshal and his girl had followed me on reared and shuffled about in fear, maybe at me, probably at what was coming.

Other grey men tried to pull up, still within the relative cool of the cave's jagged mouth. The bodies behind them forced them out.

I should have known better, but I was exhausted, bleeding, and scared. I stopped where I was for a breath as the other two still climbed up behind.

Then, the screeching rage of the monsters followed us. I'm not sure if it was Elliot Crawford or Annabelle, but one of them screamed like a girl as the first skull-faced beast started wriggling its way out of the narrow opening. Our mutual hell had just fucking begun.

10

THOSE MONSTROUS THINGS were worse in the light. Even in the bright sun, their eyes glowed hellish red. They scrambled out with all the grace of baby birds. They stretched and sniffed the air for us, whipping their heads from side to side after the black mountain gave birth to them, one after the other.

One of them spied us and charged after us. The others followed. Their terrible claws, the same ones that marked me, tore through the confused grey men in their path. Dirty flesh unzipped and bones sliced through clean to the marrow. It bothered me and still bothers me to discover how many colors are in a man. People say we're all the same on the inside, but I don't think they fully appreciate how horrifying that statement is. Seeing all those organs exposed to the light they were never meant to see, same as these monsters who had no place in the light but hated us enough to hunt us out into it, it turned my bile inside. There were even more colors, in all shades of poison and filth, when those organs burst as the monsters tore their slaves in half in their rush to seize us. It splattered everywhere in a pasty soup. Of course, blood ruled all. Red splashed their leathery robes and their misshapen flesh. It pooled and pearled on top of the hardpan, turning the layers of dust to crimson mud. The surviving grey men fell to their knees to avoid the claws themselves and then chewed that bloody mud to squeeze out the salty flavor of the dead between their lips.

I turned tail, praying the monsters would occupy themselves with the marshal as I retreated. I played them dirty, too. I swatted one horse's rump to get it to flee riderless as I hopped onto the other and kicked it into motion.

As the horse under me, that I believed to be the marshal's, set to gallop away from those horrors with me willingly enough, I started shedding gear to lighten the load, with no regard for the future or thought to surviving that desert beyond that moment. Yanked the ties to the bed roll and let it fall to the sand behind us. I cast off food stores, cast off water, and I would have cast off the saddle, too, if I wasn't planted in it and could figure out how.

People these days mistakenly think horses are like cars. You just fuel them up and drive them as long and as far as you need. That ain't so. You can get short sprints out of them, but they'll give out in a hurry under the best of conditions. Being chased through the desert by those skeletal demigods is obviously far from ideal.

Instead of setting out to the open desert, I turned us toward rocks and box canyons beyond the black mountain. It was still mighty far, but I needed to put something between me and them.

I looked back and saw the marshal and Annabelle had made it to the horse I'd tried to run off to leave them helpless. They took the opposite direction as me, with them both on the same horse. They didn't stand an ice cube's chance in the Devil's asshole, I thought. Figured they were done for. The herd of monsters split in two to pursue, so they didn't do much good for me after that.

I set my eyes forward and kicked my stolen horse to ride as hard as it could for as long as it could. If I'd had to ditch it to feed those monsters once we reached cover, I would have done it.

Then, I spotted my original horse trotting around the desert from where it ran off from me back during the shootout. I guess I stole that one, too. That sort of thing could get you hanged back then. Not that you give much of a shit about that when the devils are on your heels. If I had a way to drop that horse on purpose as a sacrifice to buy me more time, I would have. As it was, he set into a run along with the one I rode, and they took up a little two horse stampede through the hot wastelands together.

I cut a look over my shoulder and saw I had three of the fuckers on my trail, and gaining ground. They screeched and cried and snapped their bony jaws at me. The bulbs of blackened flesh that covered their lower skeletons separated and closed over and over as they galloped after the horses. Wet bone showed through the gaps on the extensions. Ropy cords of sinew pulled taut like they were the only things holding these things together and allowing them to move so godawful unnatural fast. A sick yellowy fluid leaked out from between those loose knots of flesh, like festering wounds. Wouldn't have doubted all their blood was that seepy color. Maybe they fed on blood day and night in the dark bowels of the world to make up for that thin stuff pumping through them.

A smoky steam rose off their bodies like they were ice cold in the sun or were burning alive under it.

The riderless horse pulled ahead, and my newest ride started to flag on me. Those bone monsters showed no signs of giving up, short of feeding on my colorful insides. I whipped the horse with its own reins, as if all the fucker needed was encouragement and a firm hand. The beast was frothing foam from its dry mouth and heaving for breath between my knees. I was good and royally fucked. Not to mention I was still bleeding like a bitch to encourage those walking skulls to keep coming. I was about to be the distraction for the other horse to get away.

Well, enough suspense, because obviously I got away since I'm telling you this story. If there is a god that still listens to people and cuts us breaks, which I very much doubt at this late stage of life, he up and turned that other horse's ankle. The horse gave a scream of its own as it folded and flipped ass over tea kettle into the sand. The bastard nearly tumbled into the path of my ride and would have brought us down in a heap, too. We just skirted by. That seemed to encourage my stolen mount to keep going where it was ignoring my cries, kicks, and flicks.

I heard bones snap as that poor horse rolled a few more times behind us. Once two of those monsters plowed into the fallen horse teeth first, the real rending began. They heaved its body in the air and tore their shares of the meat away in two directions. The horse literally split in two. Intestines stretched out between the open halves but quickly all fell out to one side. Bright spurts of blood, and what I think might have been a light purple liver, spun up into the air, catching the sunlight over the glistening surfaces.

They slammed their halves back into the ground and thrashed their bony heads from side to side, burrowing down into the flesh. Fur and muscle parted as they bit, tore, and chewed and chewed and chewed.

But one was still on me. One was determined to have me. It would have caught me twice, or maybe three times over, if it had just kept running. But it pulled up and tried to grab multiple times with its many-knuckled fingers, throwing off its stride. Those reaching hands. That screeching cry.

I should have faced forward, but I couldn't look away. I couldn't.

Its hide cape flapped behind it. Had to be human skin. There were no whites to those sunken eyes. They didn't really glow, either, not in the sunlight anyway. They were so bright because they were shot through in needle-thin red veins that sprayed out from the deep dark pinprick of their black centers. This one had a long purple tongue like a giraffe, too. Never seen a giraffe at that point, but the day I did, that tongue reminded me of that creature licking his out, impossibly long, as it scratched the horse's haunches down to the pink on one of its grabs.

Those scratches got the animal moving. It felt like that last monster followed us forever across the world, fleeing south like we did, but couldn't be. We wouldn't have survived. Wouldn't have lasted.

It peeled off and headed back. Maybe it wanted some of the meat they already caught. If it was about the meat and blood, though, they would have stayed down in their caves with their endless supplies. It was about me. I was the violation. I'd stuck my nose into their dens twice. I had no reason to think the bullshit at the ranch and hellscape under the mountain were related, but it wouldn't be much of a story if they were random supernatural events with no through line, now would it?

At the time, still riding for the cover of more natural mountains and canyons after the last monster had given up the chase, I thought we had finally gone too far from its black mountain lair for it to keep pursuing. Later events would undercut that assumption, I'm afraid.

I still dream about those monsters. Who wouldn't? They marked me. They infected me. I'd never stop paying for angering them.

I don't care to talk about this anymore.

11

JAMES FANNY DIDN'T push Stone for any more details that day. He wanted them. He less than half believed anything he had heard once it became a monster story, but it was a good monster story. James could kind of believe in ghosts, Ouija boards, UFOs, cryptids of various types, and the like. Stone Wicked's story required a very different framework of the world than James was ready to accept. It required way too big of a hole in reality than maybe the slight thinning of the veil other supernatural ideas needed. Still, he wanted to hear it.

A couple days later, James found a note he'd jotted down. It was just a name, but not one that meant anything to him.

Alias Orwell

He sat on it all day, tickling at the back of his mind. Alias wasn't even really a name. James only had one prisoner, though, and if someone suggested they knew another name for Stone Wicked, he wouldn't forget it. So, this was something else.

Alias Orwell.

Then, he remembered what it was from while he was staring at his TV at home that night, but not really seeing it.

This was the name Agent John Perkins had asked Stone about after Perkins visited the prison in South Carolina.

James was hungry for story, so he looked it up. It turned out to be another man of mystery, like Stone Wicked himself. Whether Alias Orwell was a real man or not was hotly debated. James didn't feel like there should be so many mysteries in a prison system. Guilty or innocent? Maybe. Prisons were full of innocent men and the wrongly accused, if you believed all the bullshit that spewed from the mouths of the most terrible men alive, men who belonged in cages, or more likely belonged in the ground. Mysteries around how many people they hurt or who else was involved? Sure. But mystery around whether men in custody were real at all? When they were born? How they got there? Those kinds of mysteries shouldn't be. Stone Wicked was novel, a harmless old man, old as the dirt he sprung from, drinking buddies with Old Adam, perhaps. Add another man of mystery with a strange name and doubt about when and if he lived at all? Now you had a troubling pattern on your hands. And Alias Orwell, if even half the shit written about him were true, was a troubling figure, to say the least.

If he was real, Alias Orwell had been a priest in the late sixties and seventies. Maybe earlier, too. The timing wasn't solid. One source said he was a carpenter that worked for the church and not an actual priest. James wasn't Catholic, but he was pretty sure churches didn't keep on their own carpenters, unless you counted Jesus himself.

Children had been Orwell's prime targets. Not exclusively, but mostly. It wasn't clear whether he was diddling them the way too many predator priests had been known to do, partly because there wasn't much left of his victims when they were found. It was the adults he killed, or the pieces of them that turned up, that finally got Father Alias Orwell caught.

How long he was in prison wasn't clear, either. Another kinship to Stone, James noted. The escape date appeared to coincide with a hurricane that struck Grinder State Prison in Fuller Beach, South Carolina in the summer of 1979. Whether it was really a hurricane or not appeared to be in question. One source claimed the prison was attacked by a monster. The fact that Stone Wicked was there at the same time, according to what Agent Perkins found, made James pause over the monster theory a bit longer than he would have normally.

After all that, the timeline grew even more vague. Alias Orwell, if he really existed, might have been killed in the 1980s, died of natural causes some time later, or still roamed the earth. Not likely, but as Stone Wicked appeared to have memories of the Wild West, who knew what powers of longevity Orwell might share as well?

The descriptions of killings attributed to Orwell, after his escape in 1979, splashed bloody across the Internet in gory, splattery detail. Many of the sites were True Crime archives that collected obscure and forgotten tales of serial killers' exploits. Some of the description was clinical, but much of it had a salivating, lusty quality to it. There was a visceral, vicarious narrative that invited readers to lose themselves in this sort of hero worship of evil violent men. There were stories of female killers, too, but most often women were the victims with timeless, pretty faces framed by out-of-date hairstyles. Men were the predators and objects of real interest.

Orwell, if any of it was to be believed, did not discriminate on gender, age, or race when it came to his prey, post incarceration. This random indiscretion, as much as the many discrepancies in the contradicting accounts, made James Fanny doubt the stories.

A family of four was slaughtered in a car on a deserted highway, between isolated farms in upcountry South Carolina. They were then strung up on barbed wire, high between the trees. Even with all this pageantry, they weren't discovered until years later, with their flesh dried and their bones picked over. Like earlier victims, there wasn't enough left to show what else he did to them.

He might have mutilated a game warden in North Carolina. He might have partially eaten some runaway teens found stuffed in a drainage pipe on the Carolina beaches. Or he might have crucified a homeless man just off the highway in Fernandina Beach, just over the Georgia line. From there, he might have started killing along the Gulf Coast, or butchered hookers in Virginia. He might have been responsible for the deaths of a bus full of senior citizens, or it could have been a terrible crash, depending on who was telling the story.

It was probably all bullshit, but Agent John Perkins had asked Stone Wicked about the specter of Alias Orwell for a reason.

James Fanny could picture Alias Orwell walking out of the storm-ravaged ruins of the prison with the surviving guards too tied up in containing a violent prisoner riot to notice. If Grinder State was in the same spot as Robert G. Hucks Detention Center that replaced it, then it was a short walk to a quiet section of beach, past a stretch of marshy grasslands. The details around that storm and riot, though contradicting, were quite specific in their agreement about the weather. It was hot and muggy. It was clear and calm the next morning. A man walking out of prison, insane and free, would stand on that windblown beach and take a moment to feel the breeze in his hair and clothes, probably still in his prison jumpsuit, or whatever prisoners wore there in 1979. He'd take in the feel of the sunshine on his skin. That's where the picture ended, though.

Alias Orwell either had to turn left, to go north to cannibalize runaways, or turn right to hike southward to crucify homeless men. He couldn't do both. Unless he took out a bus single-handed and flayed a game warden before doubling back to kill along the Gulf. Would he stop by the prison to see how repairs were going? He'd have to check on them again before he went after the hookers in Virginia.

No, none of it lined up and none of it made sense. Never mind that there was no pattern in the victims, the killings, or Orwell's supposed history before he was arrested. James thought there were some few examples of killers who changed up their modus operandi, but that was the rare exception. The Alias Orwell legend felt to him like those late night History Channel shows that tried to tie every object in history to aliens or Egyptians finding America first.

But Agent Perkins had asked, and now James wanted to ask why.

This depressed him. He was surprised by his own reaction. Why did he care about this seemingly unrelated related individual? Seeing the bullshit around the killer priest stalking the beach, woods, and mountains somehow tainted Stone Wicked's wild tale for him.

He never really believed any of Stone's ravings were true, but there was a certain gothic synchronicity to the story, told in broken pieces, from the unreliable mind of the old man. He thought maybe gothic stories weren't supposed to be bloody or full of grotesque monsters, but he wasn't sure. Maybe he had half suspended his disbelief, the way he knew professional wrestling wasn't real even when he was a kid, but it was more fun if you pretended it was real for the sake of the show. It was easy to do in Stone's case, to hypnotize himself a bit, because the man was stored here alone, like some mysterious magic object, isolated from the more ordinary prisoners. He had to come from somewhere, but no one knew. The mystery deepened because there was an outside agent tracking Stone's trail deeper and deeper into the past as the old man doled out the bloody pieces of his tale a little at a time, teasing reveals, teasing hidden truths, teasing some underlying meaning to all the madness he was spewing.

Digging through the nonsense timeline of Alias Orwell ruined that magical half-suspension with enough light to show the disconnections from reality. The desperate attempts by careless conspiracy theorists to glom together unrelated facts and overreaching fictions made James feel stupid for playing along. It forced him to admit that any magic or mysterious shadows left around Stone's story and past was one flashlight away from being shown to be addled bullshit.

James also had to admit to himself that he had been seduced by the game that it was a special tale just for him. Stone didn't share it with Agent John Perkins or anyone else. These were stories just for him.

Not a worthy use of his time.

And trusting prisoners was a mistake. You weren't supposed to get close, even if you only serviced one man of mystery, whether he was elderly or not. Something he had done had gotten Stone in here, and if Perkins was asking about a legendary serial killer, then maybe Stone Wicked was one, too. Maybe some of those killings could be attributed back to him, ones that occurred before 1954, back in Georgia maybe. Stone said some twisted things from time to time, too, bloody things, serial killer things. And by God, his stories of monsters in the desert were serial killer delusions for sure. Stone Wicked probably saw nothing but bone and sinew when he looked at everyone. Every person who wasn't him was a grey man with shit for eyes and no soul.

Depressing.

James went about his work oddly depressed for a few days. Stone stayed quiet and surly through most of it, and that was fine by him. He figured he was done with Stone's story anyway.

He was mostly over it and past it when a call came into the facility for James from Agent Perkins.

"Is he well?"

James didn't have to waste time asking who Perkins meant. He pulled his blue procedural mask down under his chin, even though he wasn't supposed to. The guard around the corner didn't even have his on today. "Physically fine for his age. No real change. He's been in a bit of a dark mood the last few days, but nothing out of the ordinary."

James thought that might be a little projection on his own part, but wasn't worth mentioning here.

"Not talking at all?" Perkins sounded disappointed through the landline. He was probably on his cell, wherever he was.

"Nothing beyond grunting and complaining. Short comments about what he wants for meals or what he doesn't like. Calling me to help wipe his ass when he's decided to play helpless. The usual, I guess."

"I found some discongruent facts in Georgia I'd really like some answers on I think only he can provide."

Discongruent? James wasn't sure that was really a word, but it communicated an idea and images to his mind. That was all any word was meant to do. He pictured Alias Orwell, a man he had never seen, maybe a man who never was, standing on a beach in the wind and heat with a ruined prison still in violent chaos behind him through the marshes. Alias needed to turn north or south, but couldn't do both at once, though the True Crime serial-killer-worshipping bloggers would have you believe otherwise.

Discongruence, manifest in flesh. James leaned out from the phone's alcove and eyed the back of Stone Wicked's liver-spotted head. The mystery incarnate.

James wanted to ask about Alias Orwell on the spot, but decided against it.

"You still there, Fanny?"

"Yes, sir. I guess you got me curious and thinking again. That's all."

Agent Perkins chuckled, causing the line to crackle a bit. James had no idea why making this near stranger laugh made him feel so good, but it did. Maybe John Perkins just gave him back what Alias Orwell stole. Of course, Perkins was the one who introduced Orwell in the first place, that poison pill. Words creating ideas and images.

Perkins said, "I'm going to be there in the next day or two. I have to try to get some answers, however unlikely that might be, no matter what mood our mysterious inmate might be in."

"Yes, sir. He'll be here waiting, of course."

"Don't suppose he's revealed anything about his past you forgot to mention."

James swallowed and then shook his head. Remembering he was on the phone, he said, "No, sir. Nothing like that, but, like you said, you have to come ask anyhow."

These stories are mine and mine alone, James thought in the dark corners of his mind where magic and monsters might yet be half real.

"Keep him alive, fed, and his ass wiped clean and dry until then."

James laughed a little harder than he meant to. "Will do. I'll see you soon."

After hanging up and pulling his mask back up, James stepped out and stopped in place with a shiver. Stone Wicked stared right at him over one bony shoulder, with a surly sneer of disapproval. Probably had more to do with James laughing too loud over Stone's show than the idea that Stone could see into his mind and soul, which was how that stare felt in that moment.

Finally, Stone turned forward and paused what he was watching. Without looking back, he asked, "What's happening in a couple days?"

"What do you mean there, Stone?"

"You said you was seeing someone in a couple days. You got family or friends coming, or was that business?"

James had a sudden urge to bark at Stone that it was none of his business, but that wasn't exactly true, as it was all about Stone, and James wasn't a guard, not to mention this wasn't an environment that required that sort of thing at all.

He walked around to the side of the couch where Stone stared down at the remote cradled in his leathery hands. "Stone, that was Agent Perkins. You remember him from before?"

He didn't expect a response and he wondered briefly if Perkins would disapprove of James forewarning Stone like this. But then Stone nodded.

"Well, Stone, he was in Georgia and apparently found out some stuff about you that he needs explained. He's coming to see what you might tell him."

"He say what he found?"

"Not particularly. He called the facts discongruent."

Stone laughed. It was a harsh, crackly sound. It made James think of a bad phone line, even though they were in the room together.

Stone glanced at one of the windows. "If I could remember how, I'd teleport on out of here before he came to bother me again."

James chuckled. "That'd be quite a trick right there."

Stone chuckled with him and then said, "You know there's a Georgia over there, other side the world, in Russia?"

"I do. You ever been?"

"Never left the States except you count the territories before they became states. Been in one jail or another since then."

Impossible. James didn't have those dates handy, but the contiguous states had been states too long for it to match what Stone Wicked was claiming offhand. Still, it was tempting to half believe for a little while, for the sake of a good story.

"Well, he's going to ask you about the Georgia next door to us, I believe, and whatever it was that happened to you there before you found yourself in South Carolina years ago."

"Should have never come back, that's what?"

"To Georgia, you mean?" James found himself circling around the couch and hovering over the old man, between the table and the seat beside Stone.

Stone still cradled the remote. The TV had switched to the scrolling screensaver for the streaming services. "You want to hear what happened when the marshal and his bitch finally caught up to me again?"

James licked his lips. They were dry. He lighted on the couch next to Stone in answer. "They survived the monsters in the desert?"

"Dark miracle that it was, we all survived and brought the curse of that place, and the devil touch of those things from under the black mountain, with us."

After another pause, James confessed, "I want to hear all of it, Stone."

Stone pursed his lips and gave the slightest nod that could have been an age tremor, but it wasn't. "I remember all that blood. Remember the crunch it made when Crawford clobbered that preacher that undid his pants and tried to take his cock out. Blood leaked thick down between his eyes, dripping heavy off the pointy tip of his nose and then, as the flow picked up, other trails ran down over his lips."

"Jesus, Stone. The marshal hit a preacher?"

Stone seemed to fade out. His eyes glazed over, like he'd lost his anchor on the present. James thought he'd screwed it all up by interrupting.

Stone blinked a few times and shook his head. It made a little loose skin under his chin waggle. "No, that part came later. Got it mixed up. I have to tell you about the stuff that happened farther south first. Is that okay with you, Fanny?"

James nodded. "Sure, Stone. Tell it your way."

"You might think I'm giving too much detail for it to be memory, especially after all this time. And you're right. I forget things a lot, but I'm also haunted by what happened back then. There's a lot I've forgotten, or maybe even reinvented since then, even on my clearest days, which are fewer and far betwixt, but there are bad moments of high emotion between all the blank spots that will pop back up on me out of nowhere. Sometimes they'll replay over and over, for hours or days, before they go back to rest, but always just under the surface, always ready to pop back up on me. Hadn't told anyone most of this stuff for a very long time, you know what I mean?"

James gave one quick nod. "I do."

"Sometimes I look up at a cross and can't remember if that's Jesus H. Christ up there or Old Malcolm Blank." Stone started laughing hard enough to shake his whole body.

James waited it out. He didn't get what was so funny. It wasn't the craziest thing Stone had ever said, but it was weird enough to make James think of serial killers again.

Stone stopped laughing finally and his grotesque smile smoothed back out into a more solemn expression. "After that ranch house and after that black mountain, I was a cursed man the rest of my days."

James didn't move again until well past Stone's bedtime, when the old man finally drifted off mid-sentence. He'd have to remove the remote from Stone's hands and carry the frail man to bed after that leg of the story was complete.

12

THE HORSE DIED under me. I've read a few westerns, from one prison library or another, and I absolutely hate it when some city-livin' writer overuses that turn of phrase where the bandits or heroes rode their horses to death. That's ridiculous. That ain't how it happens. Can you imagine going to the trouble of buying or stealing a horse and then literally riding it to death? Why? So you're stranded? Never mind the morals of it. It's boldfaced madness.

But that one time, after being chased and nearly brought down by those bone-faced devils from under the mountain, I rode that horse away and he fell dead on me while we was still in the desert.

I'd already shed all the gear, supplies, and even the water on account of the weight and because it didn't matter if I had a lake's worth of water if those things got their claws into me again. I cursed myself the fool afterward, crossing that hot land with nothing.

The horse fell dead and I almost got my leg crushed under him good. Nearly reopened my wound in the process. As I was checking on him and getting from him what I could salvage, I saw a deep slash along his thigh.

My cuts were ugly with infection and barely scabbed. I already had the hints of the bad fever that was to come, but the wound on that dead horse was black with active rot and, though there was no heartbeat left in the animal, the flesh around that dark mess was pulsing, throbbing up like an extra heart born just under the putrid surface of that dead, diseased animal thigh.

It scared the shit out of me and I shuffled myself back away from it, even with all the agony in my abused leg muscles. Was a good thing I did, too. The fucking thing exploded like a squeezed boil. Worse, really. Was an actual explosion rather than a pop. Meaty chunks of cystic flesh sprayed out every which way. Black tar veined with bloody pus splattered the sand out several feet from the animal's corpse. The puddles of muck started to sizzle and smoke. The stuff was crawling about, either from the heat or because some living disease in it was seeking out something else to infect. I swear to you the stuff burned so hot it turned swatches of the sand into a poor quality black glass, full of bubbles of poisoned gas.

I got my ass up over my boots again and started hobbling away as best I could. I had nowhere in mind to go, other than away. Away from that shit. Away from the lair of the monsters.

That cursed animal's wound kept moving, even after it ejected everything that was festering inside it. Looked like the body was trying to turn itself inside out from the ass forward, and was succeeding at it. Bones snapped and bled shit-colored marrow as they were forced out of the rolling lips of the wound, but still bound up in the exposed muscles prolapsing out. The head and legs disappeared in that writhing mound of flesh that kept folding and folding over and over itself. All manner of viscera squeezed out of that writhing mess. Solids and liquids of yellow, green, and red, but mostly that black color of disease.

I hobbled onward, just trying to get far enough where I couldn't hear that sloppy noise anymore. Then, I kept going until I couldn't see it no more. As it got dark and all my burned and blistered parts started freezing in the dry night, I kept going until I couldn't think about it no more. And that was quite a while.

The West ain't all dry desert, mind you. Even the desert ain't all desert. I found a river cut that still took me southward. Nearly killed myself climbing down into the rocky depths. It was lush and wet down there. Cooler by degrees. The water had a mineral alkaline taste, but I drank it anyhow. Ended up throwing up to nearly turn my own self inside out. I was thirsty as hell and drank some more anyways as I traveled onward through that cut. All sorts of blackflies that called that wet gash home had their feed of me. Couldn't keep them out of my wounds, either, which refused to heal up clean for me.

It may have been the flies giving me something like malaria. Might have been something ugly in the water that got me so sick. Probably have to give it to the cuts the monsters gave me, although my legs didn't rot, blacken, burst, and fold inside out on me, like what happened to the horse.

Still, by the time I crossed another dry stretch and reached the village, I had lines of bright red infection trailing through my veins. Their doctor was busy with other dying folks that got sick to death before I ever showed up. Might have been lucky timing for me, ironically. If everyone in town had been healthy, they probably would have run me out for being sick and having no money.

As it was, they rolled the bloated corpse of some woman with flies all over her off a cot and onto the floor. A part of her split open and leaked clear fluids as men with bandanas over their mouths dragged a wet and greasy smear out the door as they took her to the burn pile for bodies they'd set up just outside the town.

With the cot still spotted with her green and yellow shit stains, the doc dropped me in her place on the damp canvas, in a little stone building all my own connected to the deserted town store. Wasn't no door on it. Hot as a sealed Dutch oven during the day and colder than a mountain stream at night, without the refreshing qualities.

Some fox or coyote came along in the night through that open door. It sniffed at me and started to chew. I was too fevered to know real from delusion, but I'd swear I felt the bastard's needle teeth sink in and tear. In the dark, I thought I saw a flap of hairy meat folded away from the shredded muscle underneath where the little fucker had opened me up. Tried to cry for help, but I was too weak and dehydrated to make a sound. Had to kick it three or four times in the snout to finally get it to leave me be. Couldn't do much more to help myself after that.

A pack of dogs stood outside, growling for a while. Their eyes seemed to glow. I knew I had nothing left to put up a fight if they decided to set upon me. But they started to whimper and scurried off, tails between their legs.

In half English and half Spanish, the doc told me I was out in that open stone crypt three to four days, but that couldn't be right. No one was feeding me or nursing me, really, during that time. After the desert and that much time on the cot, I'd have been long dead and dragged to the burn pile instead of healed.

Must have dreamed the coyote bite because my leg was fine. The wounds from the mountain devils were gone, too. Just the faintest scars in the flesh left behind, and those would vanish in time, too. The lines of blood poisoning had retreated as well. I might have conjured the coyote bite in a fever dream, but I saw and felt the wounds of the bony scratches and saw the advancing blood poisoning when I was still lucid, so I knew those were real.

After surviving all that, I had to be on my way to being immune to everything.

I was still shaky as hell as I climbed up off the cot. Still had a touch of fever, as well. But I made my way around and found the doc making his rounds. Relatives doled out water to the dying and the doctor's visitations consisted of identifying who had died in the night. Folks left out cooked food for the dying who could not eat it and I stole that to replenish myself when no one was looking.

Someone had filched my gun while I was out, so I didn't feel the least bit sorry for feeding and hydrating myself. From the looks of it, the town was going to be barren of life before too long. I lost count of how many died while I was there, helping haul the bodies out and setting them ablaze.

If I had a lick of sense, I would have left right away to avoid catching whatever manner of plague they were stewing in down there. Black Death. Cholera. It looked a little like severe dengue fever, but folks didn't typically die from that. I got no idea. It was nasty, though. Medieval in its horror and despair. Truth was, I was beat. Still hovering a fever. Out of energy. Not keen on hiking horseless through the dry lands again, unarmed and alone, right away.

Did I tell you what town it were? Garacto, the people called it. I found it on a map some time later. They had the village marked just on the Texas side of the Rio Grande, north of Reinosa. That couldn't be right, though. I never saw sign of any river and there's no way I went that far south. Marshal Crawford said we barely got into the Texas border when he and the bitch were chasing me. Must have been a different Garacto. No idea what the word meant. Some bastardization of Spanish, probably. The place isn't on any map now, unless you find one from the period rolled up in a museum somewhere maybe. It got good and forgotten on account of what happened next.

When Crawford and Syne rode in on fresh horses, I was good and fucked. The people had taken to me since I was the last healthy soul still on two feet and was willing to look helpful. Even the doc was feverish and the rare few that got over whatever nastiness was afoot could barely breathe or stand up for too long. I wasn't far removed from that weariness myself. Even still, they didn't like me well enough to get on the wrong side of the law for me, with all their other troubles.

Fortunately for me, they had guns but not the strength to keep me from taking them from them. So, I helped myself when I saw the pair riding in like ghosts out of the wilderness. I've never been so disappointed to see anyone still alive.

Fuck 'em, I said.

Checked the rifle I took off a moaning man in the middle of the chapel floor and leaned out the door post to fire my first salvo. If I weren't so shaky, or if I were a little more lucky, everything might have played out differently. I got "what ifs" for ages though. Still don't rightly know what activated the madness, then or now. All I can tell you is what happened next, and it was batshit crazy.

My shot went wide. So wide I'm not sure the pair realized they were even being shot at just then. I kicked a few splinters off more than one building to mark my failure. Then, that stray bullet winged a couple sick folk dying on their cots under the shade of a saloon porch. One man and one woman. Cut a furrow through his shoulder. If he'd been in his right mind, it'd have probably smarted, but it barely bled. Got her a little deeper through a fat roll on her hip. It was a through-and-through and hit nothing vital but hard lumpy fat squeezed yellow out of that puckered hole and hung there like a little shelf fungus mushroom growth on her flabby discolored skin.

Crawford and his girl looked about to try to get the lay of what had just happened. Other folk, barely conscious and wavering on their feet, looked up from their miseries, as well, for a lazy gander. Gave me another chance to make right on my attack. I got closer with the next shot, but still only cut the air near them. Also, gave them a bead on where I was.

They dismounted and returned on my attack, pock-marking the front of the church as I scrambled back inside. I kicked a few folks on my way through. Might have set them off as well. The wounded man and woman from the porch had to already be rising up. A few of the dying inside the church put up a little more struggle as I pulled weapons away from them to continue my fight.

Wasn't no official back door on the little sanctuary, but I made my own with the butt of the rifle and my shoulder. There was a ton of old sun-bleached lumber and other debris piled up back there. I had no more than emerged into that scrapyard in the sun when the commotion inside the church-turned-sickroom rose to a dull roar.

I turned about, prepared to fire back through my new exit, thinking the law was right on my ass. I held off because I couldn't see shit standing in the sun behind the place and staring back into the sullen, hot darkness. There was a ton of movement, though, back and forth. Too many shadows in motion. None of those people living out their final moments in slow agony should have been able to stand, much less dash around each other like those figures seemed to be doing.

Then, one of the shadows came for me.

13

IT BOUNDED OFF doorframes and the scant furnishings as it blundered forward. It was all claws and teeth and I didn't think the fucker was human, even after he plunged out into the sun with me. Fast as fuck. Drooling. Leaking from sores. Discolored with disease and filth, but still alive and human.

I backed into sharp splintered points of the broken up wooden trash behind the church. The feral man charging out after me broke off the ends of the boards on the back of the building with the force of his exit. He tore open his cheek and shredded one of his eyelids in the process. The man screamed. Could have been anger, pain, or both. Definitely madness.

Had so little time to think, I swung the rifle instead of firing it. Dropped all the other guns I'd collected down around my feet in the process. I broke the dude's jaw at the hinge on one side and changed the shape of his already ugly face. He staggered. Maybe that's not the right word for it because he was all forward motion and wild attacking energy. I changed his course just a mite.

Instead of tearing into me like I'm sure he intended to do with whatever soup he had left for brains, he caught me with an elbow shiver along the side of my temple. I staggered. Cut open my pants on a rusty curl of metal in all that junk. The both of us tripped and stumbled on the guns I'd dropped. I used the rifle as a crutch as I lost my balance and shuffled face-first into the back of the building to the left of the jagged opening. Lucky I didn't blow my fucking fingers off ham handing a loaded gun like I was.

The madman impaled his belly on a broken board and leaned over it, not really standing, not really on his knees. He slobbered pink and red down the grey length of that trash wood speared inside him. Groaned like any ordinary asshole would in a similar state. The guy's shirt was pasted with sweat and God knew what else to his bowed back. I could see a wet peak where the rough end of the board had exited the guy's back around kidney level, or was stretching out the skin and shirt there if it hadn't actually broke through. I never got a good look to tell which was the case, but the dude appeared to be on his way to dead. That's why I let my guard down with him. That, and the fact there was a bunch of other shit going down.

Shouting rose up from the street around the front of the church and other town buildings where I couldn't see. I was still aware that I was committed, in spirit at least, to a shootout with the visiting law that had been interrupted by all this. The commotion inside the sanctuary had my immediate attention though. No barroom brawl in real life, or that I seen in movies since, compared to the horse shit going down just then.

Folks was slamming into the inside walls hard enough to shake the whole building. Hell, I could feel it in the ground through my boots with my feet going numb. Boards bowed out where the nails couldn't hold snug from the force of those impacts, as the place was beat to shit from the inside out. Dust spit out from the sides, too, like passing bullets, but the only projectiles were bodies.

I lifted the rifle back up into proper firing position. Gave a passing thought to needing to collect the other weapons shortly. But I eased around and back over to the opening in the wall. I took a shuffle step into the shade to get a better bead on what was up. Right next to my head was a sliver of thin skin, stuck to the end of a board glued there with blood muck and dancing a little in the wind. Must have been a piece of the guy's cheek or eyelid. Pretty gross, but it had been a gross visit to Garacto and the scene inside was all consuming.

They weren't just fighting, those sick fucks that had been flat on their backs moments before with no hope of walking out of that chapel again, much less getting athletic. They were ripping into each other with their bare hands. Cursing one another. Damning each other in the most explicit terms as they tore out each other's throats, bellies, and faces with their bare hands and teeth.

I think I know what you're thinking. Weren't no zombies. I've seen those movies. Even the ones with the fast zombies wasn't anything like this. These crazies were alive. They bled out and died like living folks. They spoke like living folks, if not how people normally conduct themselves in church. They were just insane, criminally and violently insane.

A big fat woman, who'd been moaning all day and literally bleeding out of her ass thick and heavy enough to soak through her cot and drip like a leaking faucet on the floor, was now kicking and stomping some half naked dude's head into pulp. His blood and brains splashed up her exposed legs as high as her swollen groin. It mixed with the blood and shit still running down the back of her thighs from her prolapsed anus. Not sure what happened to her skirts, but the bloody, shitty blanket that used to cover her strung across the floor behind her to the overturned cot. A piece of skull bone stuck out from between her toes where it had buried into her foot. I know she felt it because she let out a whimper each time she stomped again, but she wouldn't stop.

A man with a mustache and beard glistening in fresh blood rose up from the whistling hole in a young girl's throat. The bits of skin and gristle fell over his teeth and lips as he stopped chewing upon spying me watching him. The gore peppered the dying girl's face as she clawed at her own ragged throat and then beat her tiny fists against his spread legs.

He stepped square on her face as he moved on me, and the bones crunched under his boot. There was nothing left after he stepped off, but she kept clawing and trying to find him with her fists.

I raised the barrel and took careful aim as he picked up the pace, closing the distance between us. I couldn't help but think of everything that proceeded this moment since my life came unanchored from the natural world. All those moments seemed unrelated, except in their irrational violence. The tortured souls hidden behind the bedroom wall at the ranch, the chest of bones, the boy that couldn't have been human falling upon us, the things under the mountain, the grey men, and now this bloody nightmare all flashed through my head as the bloody man ran at me.

He hit the doorframe with a hammer crack and spun out of view. If I'd tried to fire, I might have hit some other maniac deeper in the building, but I'd have missed the one set upon me. It didn't last long, though, as he climbed back into view and entered the last room between us, a lot slower than before he split his own head open. I took aim again and curled my finger to the trigger.

Two sets of hands locked into his greasy hair and pulled him backward off his feet again before I could take my shot. The women tore into him with their bare hands. I had no idea what Velcro was back then, but that's what his scalp sounded like as they peeled it back from his blood-sticky skull. The other bitch dug into his throat with her fingers and the skin dimpled deep like putty. It changed the tone of his growls and screams, as if she was playing his throat like a musical instrument. Women didn't keep their nails long back then, especially not in middle-of-nowhere villages, but she kept at it until she broke the skin and dark blood bubbled and frothed up from where her digits disappeared into his neck.

Believe it or not, he broke loose and slammed those women's heads together hard enough to cave in their foreheads. Their eyes didn't line up after that. The women went after him with their teeth next. They didn't tear away chunks like wild animals, exactly, but they held on as he fought back to his feet.

He set eyes upon me again and I stared down the barrel of the borrowed rifle at him. He showed his bloody teeth and advanced, dragging those mad women along with him where they still had their jaws locked on him. I almost took my shot, but then his eyes rolled up and the threesome of gore collapsed in a heap.

I waited there a bit longer and one of the women with a concave forehead looked up at me as she was chewing. She got to her hands and knees. Stepped on her own dirty dress and nearly faceplanted again, not that there was much more damage to be done, either way. She got to her feet, but jacked her clothes around to where one bruised tit popped out.

Then, she was staggering toward me. I would have shot her, but she was bobbing and wavering so much, I'd have missed for sure. Mind you, I was aiming for her body, center mass, and she had a lot of mass, but it's not easy to hit a moving target, even then, so I waited for her to get closer.

A taller skinny man, think he might have been the town's priest, hit her from the side. Sounded like punching a side of beef until they struck the edge of the next doorway from where I stood half in the sun and half out. Then, the sound was the snapping kindling noise of breaking ribs. That took a little of the fight out of her, but she and the priest tore into each other there against the wall.

I couldn't see it all, just around the edge of the door there, but the priest took hold of that loose titty and stretched it way out until it resembled nothing on a human body. The skin started to rupture in long fissures before it tore all the way loose and plopped on the floor right in front of me. I could see the spongy fat through the ragged wound and the world got real spotty around me.

Backing out of that space, I bent over and stared at the ground between my boots, just trying to breathe. I felt like I could pick out every individual grain of sand and grit on the hard ground there, at the same time it all seemed to be getting farther and farther away.

That's when the asshole hit me from behind and drove me into the back wall of the church, to the side of my opening there. I tasted blood and struggled to get turned around on the one that got the drop on me. Something sharp bit into my lower back and I was sure I'd been stabbed.

That dude from the junk pile still had the thick broken board sticking through him as he tried to rip me in two there against the wall. His breath was sour. Not the smell of death, but sure enough the smell of his guts coming apart inside him as he went on breathing.

I tried to get the gun up between us, to eject his brains out the top of his head, but couldn't get a lick a space. He was all hands, teeth, and impaled board poking into my stomach.

He tore my sleeve twice with his teeth as I fought to keep those snapping jaws away from me. I finally seized on the board itself and used it to twist and lever him off of me. It was slick with his blood, but I still managed to take a few fat splinters deep into the heel of my hand.

Finally got the rifle up to head level, but had the butt of the gun up and was holding it choked up on the stock, almost to the barrel. I got out from between the wall and his weight, but he was back on me before I could get the thing flipped around to take a shot, so I took a swing instead.

I connected solid with the side of his head, broke the skin. Would have loved to have hit him just a couple inches higher and do him in, but I caught more jaw than skull. Broke the hinge the rest of the way with a gristly tear and snap. His face lost its shape, but he kept hold of his grip.

He wasn't trying to bite me at that point. His elongated mouth and crooked lower jaw wouldn't allow it no more, even if that were his notion. But he headbutted the living shit out of my forehead, more than once. Nearly scrambled my brains and clobbered the sense out of me. I might have just stood there until he succeeded in beating me to death with his bloody, broken face, but it was the clawing and growling in the church behind me that woke me up again.

I double-handed jacked the gun butt straight up. Under where his chin had been before I angled it off of true center. His lower jaw shattered, then, as I cocked his head back toward the blazing sky. Gave him that floppy, collapsed old man face look we all come to in enough years with age or bone cancer.

I got free of him at that point and would have been wise to run, but I was younger and full of adrenaline-poisoned fear. And if I had a lick of wisdom, I wouldn't have spent most of my life locked up, so there you go. There you fucking go.

My back was to the wall and though he was rocked and drenched in his own blood coming from more than one leak, he wasn't out. Probably could have worked the gun around to have the business end on him again, but not quick and not graceful-like neither. So, I decided on another clubbing instead.

Didn't know what baseball was at the time, but we all have instincts to be violent when the moment calls for it. Even when the moment doesn't. If you learn nothing else from this story, maybe that's the takeaway. But I swung for the fences, as the kids say, and twisted his head around. I probably cracked some vertebrae at least. I didn't sever his spine because he didn't collapse on the spot.

I did get my first solid look at his guts. The spit of wood still in him had migrated to the meat in his back where it still barely held on by the splinters. It left the puckered raw opening in his belly exposed. It wasn't exactly gaping like I'd have expected. No open hole straight through like in cartoons before they all turned woke or PC or whatever you call it. There was something purple in there. Something else pulsing, like it was in time with his heartbeat maybe. Had a little of a diseased pussy look to it. Angry and hot.

The guy's knees made to buckle on him and he staggered a bit to keep upright as he slowly fought his head down level on whatever damage I'd done to his neck. If I'd given him another breath or two for his body to catch up to how bad he was hurt, he'd probably have fallen on his own right there. But I was staring at that obscene, puffy opening into his seeping weeping stomach and it made me feel violated, endangered.

I backhand swung the rifle to get him off his feet and laying down like he should have been. Didn't even get a fraction of the power behind it that I'd managed in my earlier attacks. Still, the damage must have been dished out all around at that point. He toppled, stiff, to his side. The rifle split along the wood like a corked bat and all the pieces came apart in my hands. I held onto the barrel maybe a moment longer, trying to think what I could do with it, but then dropped it next to the body. He might have still been alive, in the technical sense, but had made it far enough to death's door so as to not matter anyway.

A couple of the surviving crazies in the church tumbled into the back room behind me, still wrapped up in the business of fucking each other up. I didn't give them the time to find their way out the opening I'd made, but started to run instead.

I no sooner rounded the corner than seven of those mad fuckers were squared up, circling and snapping at each other. They were bloodied up pretty good already. One had part of her scalp ripped away and hanging by a hairy thread. Another had his chest clawed until it looked like raw hamburger left out a touch too long.

Another dude had an eye dangling from an inch or three of optical nerve. The other eyeball had gotten popped and the thick jelly had run partway down his cheek until it stuck in mid-ooze like hardened pus. At the time, it reminded me of a busted boil of an abscess in the clove of a heifer's bum hoof. These days you can watch people popping those things in compilation videos like it's porn or something.

I shouldn't have focused so much on that guy. He was swinging wild, spitting and barking like he was raped by the Holy Ghost and convulsing in tongues. The others were roughed up, sure, but they could still see. I don't think they had the sense left to evaluate their conditions or their odds. I think they were hurt enough to take breath before they laid back into each other. Then, they saw me with my blood and guts mostly still inside myself and they couldn't abide it.

The six of them came after me and I tripped over something behind me. Fell to my butt. Kept going ass over tea kettle, rolling up into a heap. God help me.

14

It was enough for them to catch up, so I made to evade. Had nowhere to go except into the midst of the junk pile. After that, I couldn't move as fast as I liked without tearing myself open on a hundred sharp and pointing little nightmares. There wasn't much strategy or reflection in my actions in that moment, but I did sort of figure that whatever madness had overtaken the folks in the chapel and some others outside at that point, too, they'd be less careful. Might impale themselves for me, sort of like the first fellow had, only I'd get the hell out of there as soon as they did, unlike earlier.

Like most things in my life, it didn't work out near as good as I'd originally hoped. I shifted one way around a wooden point and then the other to avoid splitting my groin on rusted metal that didn't look like anything useful in life. How the hell did it get rusty out in the middle of the fucking desert anyway? I had nearly died trying to find water, and got sick as hell after I did find it.

Well, my fan club just barreled through and tipped over all that debris and shit, without pause. They mostly did it without adding much to their injuries, too. It's all relative, I guess, but I was relatively good and fucked. Had to pick up the pace a bit more than was safe. Risked circumcising myself late in life, or giving myself a case of lockjaw, from the mystery rust. It was either that or get drawn and quartered by the Insane Six behind me.

I really wished I still had that rifle in one piece right about then. I may be remembering wrong, happens to me all the time these days, but I don't think I got off a single shot from the damn thing. Wasn't even the best club.

A couple of my pursuers managed to dump themselves over a piece of trash that was too heavy or didn't get out of their way fast enough. I think one snapped his neck on landing, for real, because he kept gurgling and gagging, but didn't get up again even when the ones behind him kicked him and stepped on him on their way over. The other tore open her face to the bone, but didn't give up.

By this point, a few blood-caked survivors made their way out the back of the desecrated chapel and squinted against the sun. As their eyes adjusted, they thought something must be good in the junk pile, so they followed the others.

One of them almost got me, but hooked himself on a sheet of barbs and sprung back before he got a hand on. I took the opportunity to keep retreating. The bastard got that hand on the ground and literally peeled himself away from the barbs. Tore away big plugs of meat from his cheek, his shoulder, his ribs, and his thighs. Twang and pop, over and over. Not sure exactly what that was he caught himself on, but any asshole that can tear himself off fishhook barbs like that is a motherfucker you do not want to tangle with.

Wasn't sure where I thought I was going, except away from those savages. Once I got out of the junk, it was just open drylands for what might as well have been forever. It was tempting, even though it was sloped up and I wasn't sure how long I could run. Remembering fleeing from those blackened and bony demon things passed through my head, I think.

I hooked around and ran wide back toward town. Not sure now that might not have been the worst choice, but I thought it was fever madness. Plenty of weird shit had happened to me up to that point, but nothing I would have thought pieced together into any sort of coherent narrative thread. I had no reason to think the rest of the town wasn't sane and might provide some help. I had even sort of forgotten the marshal was out there in that instant.

The fuckers were breaking free of the junk, and then out of the church in some larger numbers. I was already beat. Weaving from side to side. Bounced off the clapboard side of the closest building. Should have had all that running-for-my-life energy, but that stuff wears off fast when you spend too many minutes and days running away from death like that. I heard impacts inside, beating back from the inside of the building. Should have been my first clue I was going the wrong way.

Stepping out into the dusty street in Mainstreet Hell. Blood and filth soaked into the ground. One old cuss swatted away the buzzards that already set upon a body of another fellow that was strung out over about twenty feet of diagonal street. The intestines were gritted over with sand. Burst organs packed with wet horse shit. This old guy wasn't eating any of it, but his yellowed nails clawed through the meat, turning it into pulled pork if he ever let the birds have some again.

The guy looked up at me, maybe more accurate through me, each eye pointing in a different random direction, and I believe he was the first one to speak whether he really saw me, perceived me, or not. "You'll never be as happy as you were before today."

I don't think he was a madman prophet, in truth, or having any sort of oracle possessing him and speaking through his chapped lips. But those words stuck with me. Were they true? Probably, but I wasn't all that happy before the shit hit the fan either.

I turned away and let him get back to processing the shredded human meat to whatever purpose he had in mind.

Another gunshot rocked off and I saw a fellow lift up on the heels of his boots as his scalp, part of his brains, and the escaping bullet kept going for the stratosphere. He fell hard and dead to his back, and the marshal started reloading while his bitch reared up and ready.

Despite everything going on, she spies me and has the nerve to say, "Stand right there. You're done, Wicked."

Like there weren't a mob of crazies coming out into the street that very moment. As they bore down on my back, I made to run for the end of the street. Still no plan, and the bitch decided to open fire on me anyhow, instead of the real killers on my ass. Was point blank almost, and I'd find out she had some accuracy, just not that day.

Real quick, she got the picture that she had bigger problems. Those madmen, covered in blood and hungry for more violence, had been following me back into the heart of town, but they were happy to waylay anyone, including the law. She switched to firing at them with her last few rounds. Don't know what she hit, but must have been one or two of them because I'd burned off most of my hustle, but they didn't get me just then.

The marshal was reloaded, too, but he took her by the collar instead of throwing lead himself, and they fell back to better cover. I was the dumbass still running down the near middle of the street, just in case the ones who could still see and walk had forgotten about me.

Top half of one wall-eyed son of whore still had his gun in his dead grip, for all the good it'd done him. I paused long enough to try to pry it from his cold dead hand. Even though there were only half of him still laying there, he was still pretty warm to the touch, but you get what I'm saying.

His gun wouldn't come to me though. I don't think this was how he did it in life, but he had three fingers jammed into the trigger guard of his revolver. One of them there was snapped off clean through the middle knuckle and I was able to shake that one loose, but couldn't get the gun from him. Trigger wouldn't budge either.

I twisted the dead man's arm around and palmed the hammer. The fucking thing clicked empty after all that trouble. Of course, it did. The guy who owned it got himself torn in half, didn't he?

What little ground I'd gained on the ones still focused on me was lost as a result. Some of them peeled off to chase the law that were chasing me. Others had grown tired of tailing me and tore into each other or some other maddened neighbor still out and about in town. Still had a couple who wanted a piece or two of me, so I ran a little further.

That's when I came upon his bottom half. I assume it was the same guy. Would be a weird coincidence if that pair of legs, in bloody work pants, missing the top portion, went with someone else. Anything is possible in a situation like that, I guess.

There was one firearm still in the holster on the ragged hip opposite the empty holster on the other side. I went for it. Didn't want to come at first, either, from the queer angle I was pulling, but got the weapon loose finally. Must have only been seconds, but felt like forever. Don't know if you've ever been in a situation like that, but you'd understand exactly what I was saying, if you had.

I turned and fired from my knees. Got the last three loads off and missed with all of them. Dropped the iron and forced myself up into a trotting run again.

One of them hit me from the side. I think it was girl. Young woman, I mean, but no telling. Her face was a maroon pool of grease, except for the teeth that stood out ivory-stark in comparison. She had a pretty good grip, considering, and certainly the passion to lay me low, but she was terrible hurt herself. I twisted around and hurled her down, bone-jarring, into the dust.

One of the baddies, that previous had eyes for me, fell on her, but the others kept coming, so I kept going. To her credit, the girl with the maroon face-mask managed to rip into the guy who fell upon her before he could get a piece of her. I was gone and she was out of my life for good though.

The next pile up was pretty disturbing, too. The fellow on his back was kicking and squalling. I would have thought he was a troubled soul, like myself, just trying to find his way to safety, but he kept yelling, "I want your eyes. Give me your god-cursed eyes. I want them. I want to taste them."

Shit like that.

The ladies on him tore at his throat until blood welled from where they pressed into his pliable flesh there. A second employed the same clawing and shredding motion I'd seen the guy talking to me about my lost happiness using. She failed to break the skin, but his pale belly was all scratched up and raw. The third had taken an obsession with his groin. She'd gotten his trousers open and was about twisting and punching his meat. I felt like that might have more to do with his squalling than the fevered madness he shared with them.

Important bit was that there was another gun discarded, just shy of his kicking feet. I took that up. Considered helping the dude out with a few of the bullets to the back of the bitches' heads who were trying to take him apart. At that point, I was getting the picture that he was as crazy as them, and everyone in town had lost their minds all at once.

I whirled around to fire, but my pursuers had gone different directions. Violence surrounded me, but I was temporarily ignored. Almost, anyway.

Marshal Crawford yelled from across the way, "Stone, get over here."

One of the bitches, not his but the ones on the dude whose gun I thought I had, looked up from the old man's battered chest. She spied Crawford first, where he and Annabelle Syne crouched between the side of a wagon and what I think was a livery. Then, she looked up at me like noticing me for the first time.

She stood. She smiled with her mouth closed and her eyes almost clear. She opened her mouth like she might speak, but, then, she showed her claws and came at my face.

I lifted the gun wild up under her chin and pulled off a shot. Thank God there was a round up at the top of the roller. Her throat skin rippled with the blunt force of it, barrel rested up into her gullet and all. The exit had to be almost level at the top of her spine or the base of her skull. The ejecta included bone, white matter, and something black and gooey. Not sure if I got spine or brain, but she twisted as she folded straight down on herself. That fucking smile never slipped her lips, all the way down.

The other two blinked as if coming out of a fugue, but I didn't buy it. Still, seemed like I should wait until they showed their colors. They didn't smile though. One was missing most of one eye and all of one ear.

She lunged for me. And I came around like I was hitting her with the barrel. Fired too soon. Creased her neck. It was a deep groove, but still a crease. As she took my arms, I fought to hold onto my newest gun. Fought to get it around on her for a proper shot, not knowing if I still had another bullet to give her.

As we struggled, I watched a dark bubble swell up out of the furrow I had fired along the side of her neck. It turned into a heavy sagging sack and kept growing. That was the first time I started to think this might be some of the same dark magic I'd experienced in the first couple episodes I'd shared with you in the cursed ranch house and under the black mountain. It reminded me of the horse turning itself inside out from the festering scratch it had gotten from the boney claws of one of those demon devil gods I'd stumbled upon.

The bubble burst and splattered us both. I was sure I'd been infected with whatever it was. Then, more blood squirted out with the last heaving beats of her heart. She held on a moment longer as her knees went, but then let go and had the final decency to leave me alone as she finished dying.

The other one, the third one, now standing over the man they'd ravaged together, just started laughing. It was throaty and uneven, but she was laughing. It shook her shoulders and heaved her withered chest.

It was then that I spotted a small piece of meat in her mouth.

As she laughed, it slithered out over her lip and onto her chin before finally dropping to the ground between her feet. It was a chewed ear, probably the first bitch's ear, I'd guess.

Have I told you this shit before? Well, never mind. We'll move along.

The man under her was no longer assailed, but, apparently, he was spent. He lifted one shaking hand and slapped at the laughing woman's leg over and over, whispering, wheezing, "Your eyes. They're mine. Give them to me, harlot. Hand 'em over now."

If he was interested in ears, he could have had her leftovers right there on the ground, within easy reach.

I lifted the gun at her bobbing face and her glassy dead eyes that I'd swear were seeing nothing at all. If I had one more left to bear, I wanted to silence that hooty, inhuman laughing.

Two men charged in from the side and broke her on her feet as they clobbered her and slammed down on the ground on top of her. Knocked the wind out of her, along with cracking who knows how many bones in the process.

One man forced the fingers of both hands into her mouth. She appeared to bite down, but he ignored it, starting to pull her mouth wider, by the skin, in both lateral directions. Stretched her cheeks. Spread her face as the skin grew thinner and thinner.

The other tackling madman went up her skirts. He didn't claw or fondle or feel his way around. I'm not sure he had a sexual thought left in his head. But he started punching. Right into her cunt like it was a side of beef. He hit her again and again with one meaty thud after another.

By gun, she continued that heaving hooty laugh despite all the destruction.

"Those are my eyes," the fucker on his back said, with no sign of getting up.

It was then I broke open the weapon and saw I had one bullet left in the eye man's gun. I made sure it was rolled to the top before I got ready to close the weapon back up and charged for one more go.

"Wicked!" It was that Syne bitch again, from their cover. I decided I was gunning for her, even if Crawford plugged me the second I did. I was just done with her. Done with all of the madness.

Then, Crawford followed up. "Watch out!"

I got hit from the side, next. The dude caught me high and had no grip on me. If I'd seen him coming, been paying attention at all, I probably could have dodged or gone low and maybe even flipped the fucker right over onto his head. No joy though. I bobbled and twisted. Bent over and went down with him on top of me.

Lost the gun, with one bullet left. Never even closed the damn thing. Nothing ever works out like in the pulp books or the action flicks. Unlike the body being pulled and punched apart a few feet away, I wasn't laughing.

15

I COULD SMELL his sweat and the ammonia aroma of fresh piss as he smothered me under his weight. Like I said, he hit me high and I twisted all over and around, useless, until I ended up buried under him.

He seemed to be working himself around to mount me. I was digging in elbows and shoving up from below, but getting nowhere. I'm not sure he knew what he was doing. Not that I did either.

He did rise up on me, still holding me down under his weight. I brought my arms up over my face to guard my eyes from his fingers and nails. I was aware of the position of my groin, too, hoping no maniac came along to start punching or twisting like I'd seen some of the others doing.

Then, he hammered me. Pain flashed through my forearms, sharp and deep across the bones. I went numb from the shock of the pain, but he kept hitting me. Against all my wishes, my arms fell away from my face for a moment, so I took the butt of the pistol to the forehead, the temple, and the chin in rapid succession. I can't tell you if he knew he was still holding it as he hit me or if it just happened to still be in his hand.

The world got fuzzy, and the only sound was a shrill ringing. A couple more strikes landed, I couldn't tell you where, but they must have been glancing because if he'd kept hitting me square, I couldn't have survived it. The ringing went to the pulsing sound of real bells. Had to be partially the sound of blood pumping through my head near my ears.

A bullet from somewhere passed soundless through his shoulder. I heard nothing over or under the bells, but I saw the fabric shred and soak up red at the entrance and exit of the slug's path. Saw the flesh part and then peak. Watched the droplets trail and spout backward in slow motion.

The gun spun in the air as his fingers folded open of their own accord. My forearms empathized. The open hand came down and slapped me on my left cheek. I felt it shiver with pain all the way down my body, through every dulled nerve, right into my fucking toes. I swear to Christ that dead hand slap was harder than all the crashing metal pistol-whipping I'd taken up until then.

At any rate, the shit woke me up at least. I may be remembering it wrong, but I swear I caught the twirling weapon in the air. The dude was folding down to sink teeth into me, I think. Maybe he did know what he was hitting me with and was pissed I had it now.

I fired off two shots and still managed to miss. I think I'm half deaf today for those shots. The next three didn't miss. Shouldn't have missed the first two. And clicked empty on the last chamber. A misty cloud of blood vapor surrounded us, painted our skin sticky and dark.

That gun was hot as it dug into my sternum when the body's dead weight collapsed on top of me. He exhaled the sour stink of his dying breath into my face and in the pocket of air between us.

I felt myself blacking out from the pressure, making it hard for me to draw the next breath, and the one after that. I was tempted to stay under him. Exhausted. Scared. Couldn't make any sense of my world. All that psycho-babble shit we have so much time for these days. Maybe I had post traumatic stress. Maybe shell shock, like they talked about in the Great War.

Would have loved to turtle up there and wait for everyone to punch themselves out. I just sort of knew that wasn't the case though. That was not how this situation was going to end. Playing dead might have worked. But, then again, I saw their clawing tendencies at work and being dead didn't make you safe. If they got to the dead man on top of me that I was using for cover, they might decide to continue ripping into me and then I'd be trapped under his weight.

No good. No good at all.

I started squirming out from under the body just in time to see another crowd running by on both sides of me. I reconsidered playing dead, but twisted my knee up pretty good as I got out from under him.

Lot of dust got kicked up in the process and I stuck low to the ground to try to get the lay of the land. The crowd growling and scratching at each other, which was sort of their nature, was beset upon the livery. Didn't spot Crawford or little Miss Stop Right There Syne by the wagon. They could have been hiding in it, I thought. They weren't, but could have been. Might have been inside where the crazies were tearing their way through the boards. All I knew for sure was they weren't on me, so I made for the edge of town, wishing I'd taken to the hills when I had the chance, even with the first psychos from the chapel still hot on my trail.

My leg had already been messed up and I was sure giving it a good torque as I got out from under the corpse. It was going to hobble me right when I needed some real speed. But, after a few hopping steps, my gears smoothed out and I got a stride as best I could, as exhausted as I was.

There were a few fires going by that point. No one seemed inclined to put them out, if there was the water to do so. What would a little apocalypse be without raging fires, right?

A lot of folks had fallen. The crazies had bashed open and torn apart each other. The champions of the free-for-all should have been the deadliest ones, mayhap they were, but they had taken some damage as well. They still crept around, looking for trouble in the smoke and dust. If they found none, they were happy enough to rip the dead bodies of previous victims into even smaller pieces.

I got to the edge of town and thought I was clear. But then I saw the doctor. His eyes were wild. His face was a mess of sweat, filth, and what might have been soot, although I didn't feel like everything had been burning long enough for all that.

He had a gun and I didn't. I prepared myself for another whipping, but he raised the weapon up on the run and trained it into my face. He closed the distance pretty fast.

I held up my hands. I think I said, "I'm not one of them."

But I'm not sure he could understand me.

Either way, he veered off. Thank goodness he did it sooner than later because he had company. I'm not sure where he was coming from, but the raging men and women behind him were clearly sick. Everyone in town was stricken with the disease prior to the rush of madness except me, him, the law, and maybe a couple others helping with the burning of bodies, but I suspect most of them were walking around with low grade fevers.

Couple of those guys, with cloths still tied up around their faces, were part of the mob after him. He turned as he reached the edge of the town proper, seeing what was unfolding there. I saw something in his eyes I didn't like. Resolve? Resignation? Regret? Who knows? Didn't get to know him quite well enough to read him under those conditions.

He fired. He emptied his weapon. Dropped a few. Others went after the fallen. Easier prey, I guess. The rest ran into the face of his fire, but he missed the rest. The doc turned to run again, but he looked as spent as I felt.

They caught him out in the open and they made him pay. As far as I could tell, he never made a sound, but my hearing was shot and my brain wasn't processing any of it.

They twisted him. Couldn't have made it any more gruesome if they coordinated it. There was no plan. No reason, beyond the instinct for violence. Even as they attacked each other once they were stopped, they lifted the doctor in the air and pulled him in opposing corkscrew motions. He twisted at the waist. Hips popped first and then all his other joints followed.

I turned my back as his skin broke in long fissures up his sides. He didn't bleed hardly at all, but I was on the run. I'd love to tell you that was the end of the strangeness, but maybe I wouldn't be here at all telling you this much if that were true.

There was more. A hell of a lot more. I set myself mostly north and took my curse with me.

As near as I recall, that day was the first time I killed anyone by direct action, as in me pulling the trigger, and I killed so many I lost count. My body count might be higher if you count indirect killings, like me leaving the Goodall brothers behind, or the grey men after stirring up the boney devils, or so many others I failed to help along the way.

Hell of a day.

You have anymore of that squash casserole, the one with all the cheese melted in? That shit is good.

16

THERE WASN'T MUCH happening in Scully, Alabama before the pandemic geared up a couple months into 2020. It wasn't exactly a wide spot in the highway, as the two lane that ran through it from one state to another was hardly thought of as a highway anymore. The town was a bit of a sprawl between hills and bluffs made of more dirt and clay than stone. The clay was the sticky, staining Georgia red clay that bled out from the corner into the neighboring state where Scully was found.

Driving back and forth from the prison system's lingering old folks facility, with the last old and lingering elderly prisoner, James Fanny scanned the scattered buildings of the town clustered into neighborhoods or around churches and shopping centers. Most houses were squat little structures on a patch of dirt, all alone off the sides of the roads. Junked cars and junk piles decorated the uneven edges of the neglected properties. Deepening tire ruts formed curving traffic routes around the houses or work sheds.

He passed a block letter sign outside of one of the Southern Baptist churches in town on the way. The letters were changed out each week. Sometimes it was announcements or scriptures. Other times they put up phrases meant to be cute, inspiring, or provocative. It was often as much about politics as it was religion.

Right after the rounds of mask mandates spread across the country, they posted: FEAR IS THE LANGUAGE OF THE DEVIL & THE TOOL OF TYRANTS

James was thinking a lot about a little mystery town somewhere in Texas. Not really down by the Rio Grande, not really anywhere. As he drove by those junk piles and church signs, he thought about a man stricken by madness in some long ago Texas town, impaled upon something, but still coming for more in the old man's wild story.

James tried a few times to coax more story out of Stone Wicked. It felt like time was short. Perkins was on his way again and the old man had outdone himself with the action and bloody violence of his latest tall tale.

Garacto. James tried to spell the place a dozen different ways, even though Spanish names were pretty straight forward in both spelling and pronunciation. As far as he could tell, it wasn't really a word at all, not in any language.

Just as Stone had said, there was no sign of this mythical town beset by violence. Not on any map he could pull up in a dozen online searches. Maybe a place like that would be written out if the events that had transpired during Stone's alleged visit went anything like what he described. It also wouldn't be there if this was all an elaborate delusion an aging man concocted from watching too much streaming.

Reinosa. He'd actually forgotten that name until he stumbled across it on a very old map digitally rendered on a Texas history website's archives. It was right on the Texas side of the Rio Grande, like Stone had mentioned. On some map somewhere that James couldn't find, Garacto might be just north of it.

Just might be . . .

One day, he drove past two police officers in black cloth masks, fighting a dirty, naked homeless man wearing red cowboy boots and nothing else. The guy wasn't circumcised and he was trying to bite them. He found the cowboy boots an odd choice. No one wanted to walk the streets barefoot, he supposed. He was surprised to see the local cops wearing masks, too.

James told Stone about the scene when he'd come into work that day. Stone had actually laughed and said, "I've been naked and fighting in nothing but cowboy boots myself, before, too."

"That sounds like a real story, Stone."

"Was the same time that crazy bitch tried to cut my dick off while it was still up inside her."

"Jesus Christ, Stone, are you serious?"

"Quiet up. My show is on."

Fanny had hoped that might lead to more story, but Stone stayed quiet the rest of that day, too.

James scared himself a little as he realized how much he wanted to believe it, how much he wanted Agent Perkins to find out the half of the truth that explained Stone Wicked's time in prison, back to where it started, and how much he wanted the agent to fail in getting Stone transferred away.

He liked his job. Probably wasn't an easier one in the whole prison system, any prison system, really.

This place might be becoming too much of a private mental institution and Orderly James Fanny was starting to believe the patient's delusions. Perkins would not approve. The prison officials he answered to would not approve.

Fanny truly had no idea how much the agent wasn't going to approve today.

Agent John Perkins stormed in like he'd been threatened, maybe his family, too, and was looking to punish the man who had done it. Perkins bypassed the guard as soon as he was let in, not in the mood to suffer fools or the perfunctory check-in policy. This was the type of place where skipping the typical procedures was the procedure.

Perkins' mask was below his nose and uneven on his face. James hated the masks, too, and no one in Scully was really wearing them much. Huge fights broke out over it in businesses that tried to follow mandates or recommendations put out by state houses and centers for this or that, which were so far away as to might as well be on another planet. But he hated when people stuck their big noses over the tops of their little powder blue and white masks.

The single orderly on duty over Stone Wicked thought it best not to bring it up today, but he still hated it.

James stood back a few steps farther than usual from the interview. He kind of wanted to look like he wasn't there as Perkins set up his camera in a hurry, glaring at Stone Wicked the whole time. It reminded Fanny of an umpire waiting for the player to give him a reason to toss him. James didn't like this at all.

Stone started to shift his position on the couch. Just fidgeting or trying to get comfortable, probably. Maybe he was about to try to get up, but that wasn't what Stone usually did. If it was daylight, he was sticking to the couch most days, all day, unless James made him hobble to the toilet.

Perkins was having none of it. "Stay right the hell where you are while I frame you up, old man. Don't move a muscle."

Stone settled in. The agent adjusted the camera one more time and hit record.

Perkins barked, "Tell me about your time in Georgia, inmate."

There was a little motion in his face and shoulders, but Stone sunk into himself. Might have been scared by Perkins laying into him like that.

Perkins pulled his mask off and balled it into his fist. "I asked you a question, inmate. I'm not above seeing that you get punished like any old regular prisoner should for disobeying orders."

Nothing from Stone, except around the eyes. His eyes darted back and forth more than usual.

"Inmate, you're testing my patience."

"Mr. Perkins?"

Agent John Perkins didn't even look at him as he held up a scolding, threatening, warning finger in the orderly's direction. "Didn't ask you a thing, Fanny. Not a damn thing. Do not interfere with my investigation. Do not."

Put your fucking mask back on, Agent.

James stayed silent. He took two steps forward and held his ground, for what that was worth. His attention flicked back and forth from the old man, a prisoner, he tried to remind himself, and Agent Perkins, an authority that held Fanny's job in his hands, he also tried to remind himself.

Stone was his charge, in a daily medical sense, at least. The rest of it was guard's business. Fanny suffered a glance toward the front. Dawes was on duty again, sleepy Dawes. He hadn't even bothered to turn his head around the corner to see what all the fuss was. James was on his own. So was Stone, ultimately.

As Fanny divided his attention, Perkins only had eyes for Wicked.

"Inmate, I'm asking you again. I'm ordering you to answer. And you better for your own good: Georgia. Tell me about your time in Georgia."

"I lived in Georgia a spell," Stone finally offered, without lifting his gaze.

"Now that's how an interview is supposed to work. Tell me about Georgia. I'm all ears, inmate."

"It was in the spring, as I seem to recall."

"To hell with that." Perkins shifted his feet.

James took another step forward, prepared to be yelled at, but Perkins was focused.

Stone wasn't done either. "It got bloody."

"It might be about to."

"That's just how—"

"I know that's what he says, but I got no time for it."

"I'm not sure he can help it, sir. Not always."

"Maybe you go find some other place to help, orderly."

"This is my post, agent."

"Post up in another part of the room. Go fold some sheets or something. And pour yourself a tall glass of decaffeinated silence."

"I'll stay right here, sir."

Perkins afforded the orderly a glance, but then turned his attention to the subject at hand again. Fanny did his best not to wilt. Perkins seemed to reset and lowered his voice. James still didn't like the agent's energy today.

"Anything else you might recall on the subject of Georgia, besides the springtime blood, inmate?" Perkins waited a moment, but then continued. His tone seemed normal if you could discount what had preceded. James couldn't, as he stayed wound tight a few steps away. Perkins was saying, "Those records in Georgia were even harder to find, inmate. We don't even know for sure if Georgia was your state of sentencing or whether you were charged with a federal or state crime. Do you remember your prison assignment from Georgia?"

Stone Wicked sat and stayed stone still and silent this time. His face was turned away, but not at the television. He didn't seem to be focused on anything.

Perkins leaned down, like he was trying to be sure the old man's eyes were still open. They were, but it was impossible to tell if his mind was still with them. Perkins might have also been trying to scare another sentence or two out of the old man. Fanny leaned toward that theory. Knowing Stone Wicked was well capable of talking nonstop for hours about the magical past, hidden somewhere in his head, if the mood took him, didn't help James deal with what he was seeing and feeling.

"The only documents I could find said that you were

transferred from a facility called Blood Mountain. Another hell of a name for a prison. Do you remember that?"

Stone Wicked took a deep breath. It accented all his fragile bones through his thin skin under the white tee shirt he wore today. Perkins was about to go on, it seemed, but Stone said, "There was a lot of outdoor tents when the place got crowded. Lot of nasty shit took place on those 'camping' days. It really was way up in the mountains. Hot as all hell in the summer and bitter cold in the winters."

James nearly swallowed his spit, but managed to hold it to a grunt instead of choking himself into a coughing fit. Perkins might really toss him if he interrupted this sudden burst of coherent response.

Gooseflesh rose visibly on Stone's arms. James thought maybe he should go get a blanket for the old man, but he stayed put instead.

"Glad you're perking up a bit finally. Warms my heart, but the fact that you remember it bothers me a great deal, though," Perkins said, "because for the longest time, I couldn't find it. Not anywhere. The Georgia prison system seemed to have no record of the place. I dug a little deeper and found that it closed in 1929. The closest town was Ringgold, Georgia. The closest prison to Ringgold today is Walker State, some thirty miles away.

"I found the mountain road it was supposed to be on. I even hiked some old trails up there, sure I was going to get shot by a hunter or some sovereign citizen nutjob thinking I was there to steal his guns. I found a few crumbling foundations covered in brush and old growth. Those could have been anything, though. No fences, no signs, no old cellblocks still standing. Not a soul in town I could find, including the local law enforcement, remembers Blood Mountain at all."

Fanny started to relax a little and found himself interested in Perkins' research. If Stone greeted this with another long tale, for Perkins' benefit this time, he wondered if he could get away with sitting down during the telling.

Perkins studied Stone's face on the screen of the camera beside him for a moment before pressing on. "Were you sentenced to prison back in the 1920s, Inmate Wicked? Have you been in one jail or another for nearly 100 years, sir? Really?"

The orderly's eyes were wide again, but this time James leaned forward like this was quite a point of interest. It *was* interesting, but none of the three prison systems Perkins had to bother in order to dig all this detail up liked interesting stories all that much, James suspected. They sure didn't like mysteries. Perkins clearly wasn't amused today, as he returned from his time in the wilderness.

James had heard the year spoken aloud a moment ago, but had not processed the fact that it was a century ago. He'd sat through stranger things than that in this room, but this detail was coming from a respected investigator, someone outside the private asylum this place was becoming.

Wicked gave a crackling laugh-cough. It startled James. Perkins recoiled, too, and nearly bumped the camera. He actually reached to steady it, but it was in place, capturing all of this.

Then, he surprised them again, even though Fanny had been keeping the secret of Stone's storytelling ability for a while. The new bit shut both the other men up. "I was gone before they closed shop for good. The flu ran through that place like fire and took out most of the guards and the prisoners. There were a few days where no one was there to serve us food. Folks just died and got left where they lie. More than once, I could probably have strolled right out, with no one well enough to stop me. I got transferred to The Grinder once all that had passed and they needed to rebuild. Guess they decided wasn't worth putting it back together."

Perkins met eyes with James and then leaned closer to Stone, who looked very sharp and alert now. Fanny considered for the first time that Stone might have been laying low all this time, hiding what he truly remembered and was capable of. Maybe he had been stringing James along with stranger and stranger tales.

You're not supposed to turn your back on them or let your guard down, especially not the harmless looking ones.

Perkins spoke low again, "Are you talking about the Spanish Flu? You're saying you were there at Blood Mountain in 1919 and 1920? Literally, 100 years ago?"

Stone shrugged. "Might have been the cholera, later, that did the place in, now that I think about it."

Perkins tensed up a little. He said, "I wasn't big on history, you know." Fanny wasn't sure if the agent was talking to him now, or mumbling to himself. "This case was the most historic research I've done in an age. If it wasn't for the current pandemic, I'd not know shit about Spanish Flu last century."

Fanny glanced at the camera and wondered if Perkins still remembered it was there and recording. "You should have your mask on, sir."

Perkins acted like he didn't hear it. No yelling. Not a glance. Not even a twitch.

Wicked's eyes gleamed out of his wrinkled face. He apparently wasn't done. "The place was young when I got sent up. I grew old with it and outlived it, too. What do you think about that?"

Perkins tilted his head and narrowed his eyes. Now James tensed as Agent Perkins responded, "I'm not sure what to think, Mr. Wicked. I can't figure out what you did or how long ago that was."

Fanny noted Perkins didn't call him "inmate" this time, a thing the agent had scolded James for not that long ago.

"It was a black judge. That's the right thing to call them now, yes? Wasn't what we called them back then."

"Here we go." Perkins folded his hands together. His balled and folded mask dropped to the floor where it opened a little. "What was the charge, inmate? When were you sentenced?"

Wicked licked his chapped lips and said, "Did you think to find the date that Blood Mountain opened?"

Perkins shook his head slowly. "When were you sentenced by the black judge, Wicked? Was it in Georgia? Tell me."

Now the ancient prisoner was the one to lean forward. Perkins shifted back and adjusted the camera to keep him in frame as the old man said, "I don't recall the date myself, but before I went in, we were riding horses instead of self-driving cars, there was no Netflix to chill to, no TV of any color, no radio neither, as I recall. What does that tell you?"

"If you're telling me the truth," Perkins said, even, but halting, "then you are maybe the oldest man on Earth and not just the oldest guest of the Alabama prison system. Why were you put into that Georgia prison all those years ago? Out with it already."

"It's my brother's fault I got sent up," Stone said.

"What did your brother do?"

"What all rats do. He squeaked."

"So, he turned you in. For what?"

"Trouble out west. Trouble back home. Trouble everywhere."

James shivered just a bit. He thought about a blanket again, but Stone's arms had smoothed out of all the goosebumps. He was the one delivering chills now.

Perkins shook his head and gritted his teeth. "You're a pill, Inmate Wicked, one tough pill. If you're telling the truth, that trouble would be in the cowboy and Indian days, or close to them. I wish you'd just get to the point, answer my questions straight out as they've been asked to you."

"Cowboys and Indians," Stone said.

Perkins rolled his eyes and licked his lips. "Cowboys and Indians, inmate."

James glanced at Perkins, but then down at the floor.

"Those days were longer upon the Earth than most people know." Stone settled back into the couch, but he kept talking. "I don't know what goes on across the West these days, but in my day, there were strange things still lurking in the deserts. Ancient magic. Old curses. Gods older than men, and wilder than any demon mentioned in the Good Book."

"Did you encounter something unexplainable out there, inmate?" Perkins asked.

"Sometimes I found the unexplainable every day."

"What did you do that your brother could tell on you for? Just give me that."

"I got up to some mischief in Georgia. It wasn't enough to involve the law, but it was enough to send me packing to avoid a girl's angry brothers. I got out there where women was loose, but money was tight. Whisky and gambling started out cheap, but the cost stacked up. I ran from that, too, and people started to follow."

He's telling it again, Fanny thought. *He's really going to tell Perkins the whole insane tale.*

"Were any of those people the law?" Perkins asked.

"Not at first, but to pay off some debts, I got mixed up with some bad men. Mostly just petty theft and small robberies. Not banks. There were guys who went for banks and threw enough lead to get away with it, but there were easier targets."

"Were you put in prison for robbery?"

Stone showed a few discolored teeth and said, "You want to hear it or not?"

"I've been trying to get you to tell me this for a while, inmate. My God, you could have saved us all a ton of time."

Then, as Fanny waited to hear the story again, something shifted in Stone's eyes. They lost focus. The brightness he perceived in them a moment before dimmed. It scared him. James braced himself, but he didn't exactly know for what, so he couldn't brace himself well.

Stone Wicked bowed his head and seemed to almost deflate.

Perkins held out his hands. "Well, tell me about how you got in trouble and arrested in Georgia all these God knows how many years ago."

Stone mumbled something. Even James missed it with his practiced ear to Stone's usual grumblings.

"Speak up, inmate. Repeat that."

Stone's eyes shifted to the side and he spoke only a bit louder, but it was loud enough. "It was the spring, as I recall. It got bloody."

"And?" Perkins leaned further forward, but Stone gave him nothing more.

Stone shook his head. "I don't recall."

"No. No, Inmate Wicked. None of that. You went before a black judge and were sentenced because your brother squealed on you. And you've been in prison ever since." Perkins reached out and placed a soft hand on Stone's shoulder. James Fanny took another step and uncrossed his arms. He was within grabbing distance of the agent, but kept his hands to himself. He stared down at the amorphous shape of the discarded mask between Perkins' polished shoes. Perkins spoke close to Stone's face, with both their mouths and noses uncovered. "What was your sentence, inmate? What were you convicted for?"

Stone Wicked lifted his gaze and met that of the agent. The prisoner's eyes were watery, not exactly clear, but he was seeing. They sat focused on one another. "I don't rightly recall. Was in the spring, I seem to—"

It happened fast. James Fanny was in the perfect physical position to have stopped it, but he wasn't mentally prepared. His senses were dulled by too many years of safe, quiet work at the Scully Elder Care Facility.

Perkins had Stone by the throat. Or he seemed to. His hand was on the old man and then seemed to have missed him an instant later. Stone was still seated, but had moved from his skinny butt imprint to James' more pronounced one the next cushion over.

If I could remember how to teleport . . .

Agent John Perkins yanked Stone Wicked up from the couch. The prisoner's feet barely touched the floor. Perkins muscled him around the couch like he was nothing more than a Halloween scarecrow made of loose clothes with no stuffing at all, not even the weight of packing straw.

Stone was whisked away like there wasn't substance and or reality to him at all.

17

THE AGENT HAD Stone partway toward the front door before James got himself unstuck from his spot on the floor next to Perkins' mask. As he circled the couch and tried to catch up, James wished he was in slightly better shape.

What the hell was he going to do when this place closed and he was working in a real prison again?

Stone let out tiny little squeaks of either pain or shocked surprise. The t-shirt ripped along the seam in the back. John Perkins readjusted his grip before hustling the prisoner the rest of the way to the front. That, and the fact the front door was locked from the inside, was how James caught up and slid his bulk between Perkins and the door.

"Open the door, guard. Open the fucking door."

"The hell are you doing?" James demanded, blocking the door even though it was locked.

Dawes blinked and stared on the scene. He looked duller than James, but that was small comfort. Shifting around behind the desk, it appeared that the guard planned to open the door and let Perkins just haul their one prisoner out into the sun, and not out into their little fenced in yard out back that needed mowing.

"Step aside, orderly, or it will be your job. And I said open this damn door right now."

Keys jingled behind the desk. *Oh, for God's sake.*

"Don't you open it, Dawes. This man doesn't have the authority to . . ."

"Open the door now, or it'll be both your jobs."

Fucking Dawes was actually moving. It might be more than just his job if James interfered with Agent Perkins *and* the on-duty guard both.

"What the hell do you think you're doing Perkins? What's your play here?"

"None of your business."

"Inmate Wicked is all my business. Explain yourself and stop manhandling him or I'm reporting you."

"That's rich, Fanny."

"What the hell are you doing? Why are you acting like this?"

"I'm done with this shit. I'm done with one prisoner in his private care facility sitting on his ass, with no record of how or why he's here. I'm tired of him playing the entire system. I'm done running all over God's Green Creation trying to track down his past when he is full capable of just telling us, but won't."

"Perkins, until you make a recommendation and the Alabama prison system sends official orders of—"

"I recommend you get the fuck out of my way, Fanny, or I'm going to have your head. I swear to Christ."

"I'm not moving and you're not dragging him out of here for whatever bullshit you got planned in your hot little head."

"The fuck I won't. He's done with spa treatment. I'm putting him in my car and driving him down to the admin offices to get him reassigned today. This place and Stone Wicked's free ticket are getting punched right now."

"Are you out of your mind? You can't do that."

"Watch me."

"I'm not allowing it, Perkins. I'm not."

"You don't allow shit. You're not shit. Get the fuck out of my way."

"Let him go. You're hurting him."

"I won't. You back off or I'm taking you in, too."

"Taking me in where?"

Another voice broke in. "Stand down, Perkins. You are in a prison facility under my charge, under my watch, and you are out of line."

They both looked at Dawes standing at the corner of the curved built-in counter that he usually slept behind. Dawes held up his cellphone, as if recording video. James used the stunned silence to wrest the torn edge of Stone's shirt away from Perkins. He then moved Stone to the side and braced him back against the wall off to the side of the main doors. He turned his back fully on the prisoner and hid the inmate behind his broad body.

Especially not the quiet ones . . .

Dawes kept his phone up, but took a moment to close a metal drawer behind the counter desk. The keys jingled again.

"Guard, I ordered you to open this door."

Dawes tilted his head out from behind his phone. "I don't seem to remember where you fall in my chain of command. What exactly is your title and position, Perkins? Where are you assigned?"

Perkins stared and his jaw dropped open. Some of his shock would have been hidden if he'd kept his mask on like he was supposed to.

"Consultant," James said. "He's a hired consultant."

Perkins turned on the orderly. James shifted one protective arm behind him, determined not to be taken by surprise again.

"You are overstepping your bounds, Fanny."

"You're one to talk, Perkins. You lost it today."

"I have a right to interview this prisoner."

"You can't take him out of the building. You can't drive him away just because you're pissed about all the driving and hiking you had to do. Are you out of your mind?"

"I'm going to call your bosses. I'm reporting this place and what goes on here."

"Fine," Dawes cut in again. "You tell on us and we'll tell on you, and we'll see who gets in the most trouble."

"This place is shutting down. This whole situation is madness."

Garacto.

Dawes lowered his phone a little, but still held it. "Then go make your recommendations. Advise and consult, Mr. Perkins. But you were out of line today. You're in direct violation of a number of prison system procedures."

Perkins twisted his neck from side to side. He took a couple deep breaths. "I *was* out of line, I suppose. I let my frustrations with this prisoner's behavior get the better of me. It won't happen again. I will be back. Maybe next time I bring the local sheriff with me once the shutdown of this little nuthouse is finalized."

"Chuck?" Dawes asked. "Oh, Chuck and Julia are away at the lake, I believe. He wouldn't come out here for prison business anyway, I wouldn't think. If you did convince one of them you needed an escort, you'd be dealing with Rocky, probably. Chuck appointed him chief deputy when Jimmy retired here recently. We had a big thing. My wife and daughter-in-law coordinated the food. It was a good time. If you need me to call in a favor, I might be able to get Rocky out here to greet you next time."

Perkins held up a halting hand around the time Dawes got to Jimmy's retirement. He was waving him off by the time he ran through the bit about calling in a favor. There wasn't much energy behind it. "I got it. I got it. Open the door and let me go."

Dawes started around the corner, but Perkins moved deeper into the dayroom area. James pivoted to keep himself between the agent and the prisoner.

"Relax, Fanny. I said I'm sorry. I'm just going to get my . . . where the hell is my camera?"

Dawes turned where he had the key inserted in the door lock. "Have it locked up for evidence. It has the incident recorded, along with the phone footage I captured."

"I really am going to get the sheriff if you don't hand my camera over right now, guard. That record is official. It belongs to your bosses."

"Like I said, Chuck is away and we can try Rocky if you really think . . . "

"Enough of the good old boy dance. Hand over the camera."

"The bosses will get it just like you want, Perkins, but it's going up the proper chain. I promise. They'll turn the device back over to you when they're done with it, I'm sure."

"This isn't going to go the way you two think it will. Not a chance, no matter what you think you have to show them."

"You tell; we tell. And we'll see." Dawes shrugged his shoulders and turned the key before opening the door. The air outside smelled dusty and hot, even though it had been chilly when James arrived that morning. "Be sure to sign in next time. And we're going to need word from our bosses that you're allowed to interact with the prisoner before you do show up again. Official word, I'm afraid. You understand."

Perkins turned to James and looked him up and down. "The camera belongs to the prison system. Really. Be sure nothing happens to it. I'll get another. I'm going to head back to Georgia.

See if I can track down a case with a black judge and a defendant named Stone Wicked. I wish I knew how far back I needed to look and if Stone Wicked is his real name."

"Need you to head out," Dawes said, holding the door open not four feet away from their prisoner. "We need to get things back in order here."

"I'm sorry I lost my cool, Fanny. I really am. I like and respect you. I think you want to know the story as much as I do. I'm determined to get it and want you to hear it, too, once I have it, however this plays out."

"Okay. Thank you, Agent Perkins."

Perkins shook his head. "Cowboys, Indians, and a black judge. Here we go."

Stone stuck his head out and said, "The judge was black, as I recall. That's the right word for it now, right? Black folks."

"Close enough." Perkins turned to the door Dawes had open for him.

"Not what they was called back then, anyway." Stone turned his back, as well, and waddled away from the protection of the orderly's mass. "There was a few years there when the federals stood guard on the southern states. That's when I was convicted by a black judge. Those years didn't last and things went back the other way a good long while."

Perkins turned around and James was too busy staring at Stone to step in again.

"What did he say?"

"Time to go. Don't start up again, Perkins," Dawes said.

"Oh, take a fucking nap, guard. You're getting cranky."

"Is he talking about Reconstruction?" James asked.

"Can't be. Fucking can't be," Perkins said.

"Enough." Dawes snapped his fingers a couple times. "Step out, Perkins. Come back with permission. Not before."

"I bet you wish that camera was still rolling," James said.

Perkins turned away without another word and moved toward his car, one of three in the lot. Dawes pushed the door closed and locked it quickly, like he thought John Perkins might storm back in. "Whew. That's more excitement than we're used to."

"Thanks for backing me up, Dawes. That could have gone a lot worse."

"Hell, yeah, Fanny. We're in this together."

James stepped away, wishing he could remember Dawes' first name.

Dawes called after him. "We need to get some pictures of him. Any bruises or scratches. The ripped shirt, too."

"You're right. Let me make sure he's okay first. Some of the bruises might not show up until later."

"We can do two photo sessions."

Stone leaned on the back of the couch, staring down at where he normally sat. James started to reach for the man's shoulder, but then stopped himself. "You all right? Are you hurt?"

"My shirt's tore. It's all stretched out. I don't like it like this."

"I'll get you another. We need to get some pictures. Document what happened. You're not in any trouble."

James thought about that assertion. Stone had a bulldog sniffing out his backtrail all the way to God knew where it began, and with what crimes the black judge from possibly the Reconstruction Era had found out. He might be leaving this elder facility for a real prison again, too. All of that spelled trouble.

"I just want to take a nap."

"Okay, Stone. Let's get you settled then."

They got their pictures. Bruises did darken up, wide and ugly, over one shoulder and his side. And less than a day after that, they were done, like magic. They did not take pictures of the miracle healing. James couldn't help but to think of the story of Garacto again.

James didn't press for any more story. He wanted to, but decided it wasn't best. He waited to hear back from Birmingham on the incident report. He waited to hear or see Perkins again, announced or not. Silence on all fronts.

Then, over a lunch that started silent, Stone perked up again. The storyteller was back. He asked if James wanted to hear more, and he did. They sat over their lunches growing cold and then later moved to the couch.

There was more story to tell than James Fanny could imagine.

18

WHAT WAS THE last place I told you about?

Right, that was hell. That was living hell, for sure. But hell wasn't done. Hell traveled with me.

I made my way up through various encampments, settlements, ranches, and towns without incident. People actually helped me out. Even stayed over in a few forts. Soldiers all around and not a one the wiser that I was a wanted man.

The marshal and his girl were on my tail the whole time. I couldn't know it at the time, but I did know it just the same. And they kept coming. Kept closing the distance. The same people who helped me turned around and helped them, as they dogged me going north.

Nothing out of the ordinary for a while. Almost long enough to convince myself none of it really happened. Almost.

Anyhow, I can't point you on a map where it went bad again, the exact signpost on the next stop on our tour of Hell. I'm sure you're Googling all the places I'm telling you about and are coming up doubting. You don't have to bother convincing me otherwise. I don't give a shit, but I will try to tell you as best I remember.

I know I wasn't anywhere near Fort Leavenworth, even though that was the general direction at first. By then, it was a proper town for out that way. Was no Colorado back then. All that place were Utah, Territory of Kansas and so on, but it was probably right on the edge or corner of that area on a map today.

I wasn't to the Santa Fe Trail on one side, or the Boone's Lick on the other, but closer than Leavenworth at least. I may have those reversed in my head, but never mind.

STONE WICKED

The spot was called Grindfield back then, all one word, I believe. More of a camp in those days than a town. I wasn't there long, but it appeared to be a mining outpost in the early stages of trying to grow into a real place. Not sure what they were mining, but wasn't far from the Colorado River.

Became known as Greyson some time later, just over into Colorado today, I believe. If you held me to it and made me point, I'd pin a little town called Campo today, barely bigger than Grindfield was forever ago. Campo is the Spanish for field, I understand, so may be a piece of the original camp's name. Camp, Campo. Field, Grindfield. You get the lines without me drawing them for you.

If I'd made it that far, I might have been home free. Wouldn't line up to my run of luck in life, but who knows? Doesn't matter because the real trouble landed up with me ahead of the marshal, when I was still on the trail a couple days out.

All because I stopped to help a stranger. Hindsight, should have kept going and let him die in peace. Let the cluster of men in Grindfield to peace, too, whether the bastards deserved it or not. But I'd experienced Christian charity along the way and was starting to really believe the world was better than it was. Hell, even in Garacto I was treated like a man before it turned mad.

Was a man off the road, barely alive, but still breathing at least. Not sure if I were the first to pass him or if the others passed on one side or the other like in the parable. At first, I thought he was befelled by bandits. Turned out, he'd taken a fall, tumbled off the wrong side of the trail and down the rocky slope before his horse run off without him. The animal at least dropped some of the man's supplies in the process, and no one filched them before I came along and he dragged himself back up the incline close enough for me to find him.

I knew his name at the time because he told me, but couldn't tell you now. He'd taken ill from the elements. Got into his lungs and was surely killing him. According to his estimate, we were about two days out from Grindfield, back the way he'd come and the way I was going. With me hauling him and he hobbling along with no energy left, it was closer to three and half or four days.

The morning of that fourth day, he woke me up trying to murder me in my sleep. He just couldn't be quiet about it, though.

He was one of the crazies who could talk, though I was wishing real quick he couldn't.

"I need to see my children one more time. One more time before I burn up in Hell!"

I wasn't sure what he was swinging, but it was coming fast. Not sure if I rolled or sprung in the early morning darkness, but I just cleared getting myself split open. It was a thick branch, dead wood, but solid. He struck the ground hard enough to send a subsonic base note through the dirt under me and into my bones. The end of the crooked limb, big enough to be a tree in its own right, snapped off. That just left him a sharp end on his giant club to use for stabbing or spearing if the notion took him.

I rallied pretty fast and got up to my feet, processing I was in a fight for my life again. Garacto was still fresh in my mind. And getting double-crossed out on the trail was nothing new either. I recognized the madness in his eyes.

"If you could move this well all along, partner, I wish you hadn't made me to drag you for two days."

He laid his big branch across the bent crook of his arm like he'd reconsidered the whole murder game. Lifting the exposed tender underside of his forearm, he ran than skin at an angle down the sheered end of his branch, like he was testing the edge for sharpness. It did cut. Not like a proper knife, but he sliced into himself. When the blood leaked thin along the twisting furrows left by worms and missing bark down the branch, he pressed a little harder and drove the wood under a flap of skin shy of his wrist. The blood painted down one side of the great club then.

The big tab of raised skin in the open bleeding gash on his arm got hung up. He kept trying to pull down, to either increase the size of the fillet or to slice the slab of arm steak right off. Neither happened. That tender bit of untanned skin was tougher than it looked, I guess.

He still bled down the uneven wood, but his eyes started leaking, too. His lips curled and his chin crinkled and he flat out cried. Wept over his inability to flay himself down to the arm bones.

His chest hitched and one heavy sob escaped his throat, followed by some ragged breaths wet with sadness.

His voice shook as he spoke, maybe to me, but looking at his branch and the snagged up skin pulling and sliding along the bone, stretching out down to the elbow without letting go. "I can't ever finish a thing. I can't run far enough to ever be free. I left people I loved, I was supposed to love anyway, back east, so far away. Left them to grow fatherless. To go widowed before I even had the decency to die. I can't even bleed like I'm supposed to. See?"

I did see, but did not understand. Not in the least did I understand. Just like the spiritually blind in the Good Book, I didn't understand a goddamned thing in my life anymore. Certainly, his dilemma and its solution were lost upon me on that trail less than a half day short of the Grindfield camp and whatever help they might provide a sick man hurt upon the road.

I still had a notion to help him, even then. He had the flavor and the stink of the Garacto madness about him obviously. Even a man as dumb and trail weary as I was could see it. He did try to splatter me in my sleep not a breath of time earlier. But he was talking, and seemed more sad than angry. It's a tricky elixir.

"Just calm down a little. We can still get you some help," I said.

He decided to take me up on it, in his own way. My fellow traveler, a man recently too sick to walk under his own power, stretched out his arm to lift his peeled tab of skin up and off the end of the branch. The wound stuck twice. Once, the sharp edge was wedged between the dermal layers and had to pop free. Second, the sticky mat of blood and fat adhered a bit to the wood spear. It made a smacky popping sound as he finally lifted free.

Then, he tipped his hand to me again by warning me, "Hail, friend. You've been so goodly kind to me in my time of greatest need. It'll be an honor to use your skin to blanket God's creation and redeem what was soiled with sin."

"God help us." I backed away, but not fast enough.

He hauled up that branch, swinging the blunt end at me. Through the grunt, he said, "Indeed he will, after we offer up what veils our bloody unbled souls."

I ducked the great stick, but only barely. It may have skinned over my scalp that was already thinning, even in those early days.

He rolled the branch around to the sharp end, caked with his blood and scraped fat, like this was a routine he performed on the regular. I knew he was coming back on me, but didn't have time to turn around for a full on run unless I wanted to lose my head before

I got off a forward step. No, I wheeled backward and with no grace, even if I did manage to keep my feet this time.

Gave my weathered shirt a new rip, a small one considering the mass of the weapon that cut it. Smeared his own blood and gore in a curved stripe over the surviving material running from nipple level down to my liver, at least. The color and curve left me to consider what it would have been like to be opened up by that thing as opposed to near missed.

The fellow gave a low sigh of frustration, like a tough job that should be easier if all the moving parts simply cooperated with what was inevitable, like they should. I kept backing away from our camping clearing toward the narrow trail to Grindfield. And he moved forward with me, faster than the nature of his original illness should have allowed.

He burst into a run and I spun on my heels to get ahead of him. I sort of ducked, but only had my head forward a bit. The sharp end swiped through my hair and his tacky blood stuck and pulled a mite on the way through. I counted myself lucky as I did my best not to trip on roots on my way along the narrow trail. The next swing didn't catch my hair, but was close enough I felt the wind of it. The third struck a tree too close to the trail. Shook it all the way up into the crisp leaves. May have been the only thing to save me.

My old friend growled, choked on something in the back of his throat, tried to clear it, and failed. He stumbled over the roots I navigated and went to his knees. Letting out a moan that rattled with phlegm, he cried, "You're ruining everything. Everything!"

I'm sure I had something cute and smart in mind to say back, but I was focused on putting some distance between us and maybe getting to the next town for help.

I dropped to a trot, but kept going. Then, his steps thundered behind me and he rounded the curve in the trail. His branch was poised above his head and ripping through the low branches above us. Leaves scattered into the faint breeze and a few stuck to the branch to remind me it was a thing of blood.

Picked up my pace until I thought I'd collapse before him. Then, he had to break off. He bent over at first, heaving for breath, cradling his crude weapon. After that, he was shuffling after me, stumbling on roots, but never quite going down again. I probably should have taken advantage and kept running, but I didn't have it in me.

We went on with that terrible seesaw motion of me speeding up when he did, and catching my breath again as he had to let off the pursuit.

The whole time, his throat was crackling with the illness that limited his movement and energy so much in his less mad days after we first met.

"All I want is your skin," he crackled behind me. "That ain't much."

On and on like that.

"Give me what I need and I'll let you be. You know this, friend. Come on, Stone," he pled between coughing fits.

Then, he'd suddenly burst out, loud enough to echo through the hills, "It's for my kids. My bloody kids!"

Finally spotted the signs of the settlement ahead and I was the one to break into a run down the winding slope. My addled buddy joined chase, letting me take lead this time.

"Help! Help me!" I shouted.

The asshole behind me yelled for help, too, like we were in danger together.

I ran into what could barely be called a clearing perched on the side of a hill. Thickets and brambles twisted up on their way down to water, as I recall. A lake? A creek? A proper river? I couldn't tell you today unless I just invented the memory.

At any rate, I had stumbled into a camp and not a town. Not a place of heroes neither. No one was pouring out of their tents to save me. They looked bored. A little startled, but too bored to be scared.

Half of them were naked. Others had their pants off and everything dangling in the sun. If I didn't have a madman trying to skin me alive with a branch, I'd have turned and run the other way at the sight of them. Most were filthy, with dirt over their skin thick enough to change their race and crack apart with the wrinkled folds of their skin. Most had scraggly beards as grey as the layers of dirt would allow. Other were boys, just as dirty, but many too young to shave yet.

That sort of thing was pretty common back then. Orphans and lost boys with no better prospects, seeking cowboy work outside of town. Once most of them were old enough, if they lived that long, sought any other kind of work as quick as they could.

A couple of the boys were buck naked, too. A couple others were wearing ratty dresses. Might have thought they were women or girls, at first, in my rush to get away from trouble and land any sort of help I could get. This bit sticks in my memory for sure because I real quick got the impression that if they did help me with my mad friend, I might find myself overpowered by the grizzly old men who had decided boys worked as well as women in a pinch. Was a lot more of that shit going on out there than the Gene Autry and Roy Rogers songs would have you believe. Hell, I think half the gunslingers out there killing whenever they could were some of them lashing out in anger against what older, stronger men had taken from them just 'cause they could.

Anyway, that's the sort of shit I run into in what I'd guess was a mining camp. I'm guessing the good people of whatever Grindfield calls itself today doesn't mention this in their stories of their founding fathers walking pantsless as they had their way with the boys unfortunate enough to find themselves in camp with no prospects or way of escape through the unforgiving wilderness.

Look, I know boys wear dresses today of their own choosing. I know it ain't like in the West back then or in prison now. I also know you ain't supposed to call them trannys anymore either. What I'm telling you is that ain't what was going on down there in Grindfield.

One of the old buggers who actually had his clothes on reached for me as I passed between the sagging tents spotted and streaked with black mold. I swatted his filthy hand away as I plowed through, but wasn't too proud to beg. "That man's a killer. He's gone mad. Help me."

The men and boys muttered among themselves, trying to make sense of this unlikely intrusion.

I was still backing away, but got distracted by something flowing down the leg and over the bare foot of one of the boys in a dress. At first, I thought he pissed himself. I wouldn't have blamed him, as I was scared enough to cut loose myself probably. It was too thick for urine, so I thought maybe he had the runs. Then, I realized, if it had runny shit mixed in or not, it was mostly blood. I wanted to believe that was bad diet or some bug in the water that did that to him, but intestinal issues don't put you in a dress, so there it was. God knows what I interrupted that mid-morning.

My buddy held up his branch like it was nothing but maybe his walking stick and says, "I just came for what's mine. That's all."

The others turned their backs on him and faced me, ready to set upon me.

One of them addressed him by name and asked, "What'd he take from you?"

I'd forgot he'd come from this camp before I made the mistake of rescuing him from the trail. Maybe before he made the mistake of reaching out for help from a cursed man on the run from the natural law and the evil found under black mountains. Like there weren't enough evil in the world already anyhow.

My old friend was a big guy. It had made him hell to carry and support before his madness turned him loose to walk and chase me. I don't imagine he was made to wear a dress or bend over to hold his ankles. Who knows though? Enough men of any age can force any issue if they take a mind to. If he had been of clearer mind and better health, he might have warned me away from Grindfield. If he'd been of better health, he might have set upon me to have his way.

My faith in humanity and Christian charity was slipping fast that day.

As the crowd advanced on me in various states of undress and uniform condition of filthiness, I didn't like my odds. Even the dress-wearing boys looked like they had some aggression to unleash, some suffering to pass on.

My mad friend took advantage of the distraction and swung straight down into the scalp of a naked old man in the back of the group. Split his head open like a plowed field. Thin blood and brain muck oozed up where hair, skin, and skull plate ruptured into mud. The guy folded to his knees and reached out to catch himself, but still slammed his face to the hard ground of the clearing with a crunch.

The fuckers still didn't turn around as my friend pulled a long knife with the hand not holding the freshly re-bloodied branch.

19

OH, FUCK HIM! I'd been dragging his ass, mile upon mile, back to this place not worth the trouble on a good day and I hadn't seen that knife once. Not once! He'd even used a branch to slice himself as he tried to remove his skin.

Well, the camp of buggers still trekked after me as the big man bent over to use his hidden blade to carve up the facedown naked miner. He made smooth cuts under the sagging butt cheeks to reveal wormy twisting muscle fibers.

"Just need the skin," he says. "You can keep the rest."

His slice thinned out along the dead man's back and the knife slid free. The fellow sighed and cursed under his breath as he held up the cut of flesh that had irregular chunks of muscle and fat still attached to the inside of the skin.

Not sure what he had planned for the skin he kept politely and apologetically requesting. Maybe he wanted to make a suit out of it, or replace his own skin with that of other men. Whatever it was, that incomplete cut wasn't good enough and he flung it aside.

A couple of the miners had turned around to see what their old buddy was going on about. One boy vomited down the front of his faded dress and all over his bare feet between his toes. Don't know what they'd been eating, but it looked like old coffee grounds. There was pearly white mucus mixed in with it. I remember thinking that kid was going to die, and he might welcome it, based on how his life was playing out.

The rest of them were still stalking up on me about as fast as I could shuffle backward. An old guy with deceptively scrawny arms took hold of the front of my shirt with a vice grip. Bunched it all up and lifted me up onto my toes, all off balance. His teeth were yellow to almost being green and his breath was a wet shit in a swampy bog. The way he had me he could have bit me, hit me, headbutted me, or stabbed me with something below my line of sight.

My only saving grace was that he was stark naked. Unless he was palming something, he could only stab me with his ragged discolored nails. He waved a finger in my face, with black filth packed underneath the nail. Brown smears matted down his body hair in patches over his skin. It all looked about like his breath smelled.

He had one open sore I could see just above his collar bone, in the hollow under the bulb of his shoulder joint. Black and crusty around the edges, bruisey green and yellow in and around that, with misshapen pustules in among the rotten crust. The thing was weeping clear in an old stain of disturbed dirt down his chest to the oversized nipple.

Still waving that finger, with its sharp dirty nail coming close to my eye on each down swing. "You don't come in here like that. Not after proving yourself a thief, you crooked corkscrew."

Even though my buddy held the knife, he swung the branch at the back of the crew again.

The ones who got wise to the real threat recoiled after the swing was over. If they'd been the target, they'd have gotten clobbered before they knew they was in trouble. A few of them jostled the backs of the dirty men still fixed on me. Others got out to the sides and wide of the madman finally.

It was the boy barfing bloody coffee grounds and thick cream that caught the sharp wood heavy through his temple. His head was bent down and forward where he was waiting to see if there was anything left of his guts to eject into the harsh puddle over his feet.

A syrupy string of drool dangled and wavered from his chapped lower lip as the boy's ear and face came loose from the bone and split in a half dozen places on the impact. The boy's head whiplashed into his shoulder and rebounded, with all that shredded skin and meat flapping around.

The kid's knees buckled but my buddy balled up the front of the dress and bent the boy backward with his arms out at the sides, stiff and hanging like his ruined head. His good eye rolled in its preserved socket as he looked back at me upside down. Soapy bubbles grew and popped from the foam around his mouth on his exhale.

"Turn around," I said.

The old naked man stopped wagging his finger and swung around to give me a stinging open-handed swat on my ass. Close to me ear, he growled, "I'll turn you around. I'll turn you around and you'll never forget me, cocksucking corkscrew."

He dragged me down and forward, to where I was too close to his speckled sausage poking out from a thick forest of grey hair that almost looked like dreadlocks the way it was all twisted together with dirt and mess. More of those weeping sores marked his angry red sack and the side of his uncut shaft.

I refused to go to my knees, but I couldn't get away from his grip on me either.

My buddy had the boy with his dress bunched up past his waist. His buttocks with scratches all over him. Fresh red and dried-blood brown was swirled all over the cheeks and down the backs of his skinny thighs, like someone had been fingerpainting in the stuff after making him bleed like a faucet back there.

The branch lay on the ground in the coffee ground vomit.

Through those skinny legs, my buddy stabbed the blade up into the boy's taint, about halfway to the hilt. Blood gushed down the blade and over the man's fist. The boy didn't scream like I'd expected. He let out a squeal that was more animal than human. That high sound quickly descended into a guttural groan.

Everyone except the man holding me inches from his junk turned around and stared, frozen, at the real action. I was drawing in the spicy hot stench of this guy's crotch, that was somehow worse than the swampy shit of his breath.

My buddy divided the kid up and forward. The knife was so deep it had to be hitting bone, forcing through the pelvic bone for sure. The guy was strong and each effort lifted the boy off the ground and shook him violent. He made jerking progress through the flesh and bone under that dress.

Sliced through the little sack and dick, in that order. One of the testicles dropped free into the light it was never meant to see, like a little purple plum swinging from a translucent beansprout cord.

Didn't stop there, though. The pelvis grinded together inside the boy as it broke through, changing his shape below the hips that vanished in the open sack of his body. My buddy sawed his way on up through the belly and between the ribs.

One more gush of blood came all in a rush. Never imagined there could be that much blood in a body so slight. It poured out in a floodgate splash that coated the branch, dissipated the vomit, splattered the man's boots, and painted the boy's legs a glistening maroon.

The speckled-cocked asshole finally turned around and, in the process, I could almost stand up straight. Where the boy had been fingerpainted across his ass in blood, the old man was a sculpture of shit. It glued his hairy, pimpled cheeks together. A diaper rash, that stood out in quarter inch high tendrils along the sides of that shit-filled canyon, was all raw and infected.

I needed to get away from this filthy hell I'd stumbled into.

The old man's grip loosened, but didn't release. His voice cracked and wavered as he asked, "What you doing?"

He used my buddy's name, but I still don't recall it. Probably the least striking detail of that day that's burned into my mind, I guess.

My buddy wrested the blade free and started cutting the dress into an open coat. I'd have bet my life that the fabric would slice easier and faster than the body, but I'd have been wrong. It was that same gritted-teeth inch-by-inch effort to get through that stiff material. Finally, he did though, and dropped the boy into the wet pool of what had to be all his blood.

The dress folded open and so did the front of the corpse, split all the way up to the throat and gullet right up to under the chin. It wasn't a body; it was a sheet of guts.

The boy did die, of course, but not from whatever had turned his digestive track to ground up mash, like I'd expected. Might have preferred that death.

My buddy went to delicately trying to carve the outer later of the curtain of skin away from the rest of the mess he had made. Shouldn't have been too hard for him. I'm sure he'd dressed and skinned many animals before he decided human skin was what he needed. I was clumsy with a knife myself, but even I knew how to skin something. He kept slicing it up and ripping through the middle of the boy's skin. Maybe skinning a human is harder than other animals. No way I could know.

The others kept staring, like they thought maybe it would make more sense if they just gave it a minute. They were no strangers to violations of the flesh, so this could be something if my buddy would just explain himself.

He got frustrated and let out a little whine before he started hacking and stabbing down into the exposed organs, mincing them up, bursting them open to the various biles inside. Not that I expected it to look great, but the deeper he dug into the boy's guts, the less healthy he looked. Everything in there was a sickly off-color and runny. More than a few wormy parasites got exposed in that short tantrum.

"Will you just hold still and let me get this thing done? Would you now?"

The boy didn't answer, but I can't imagine he could have held any stiller than he already was, being butchered up and staring dead blank up the slope like he was.

The man still held the knife, but hoisted up the unwieldy, blood-soaked branch like maybe that was the fine tool he needed for the job. Probably wouldn't have worked anyway, but the arm with the deep gouge under the flap of flesh was going a little ham handed on him.

I tried to pull away a few times, but the dumbfounded filthy bastard, caked in his own fermenting shit and spotted with rotting sores, still held my shirt tight enough to arrest my escape. As my buddy finally gave up on the branch and let it tumble heavy into the scattered and ruined guts of the most unlucky boy in all the world, I decided I needed to vacate sooner than later. I threw a punch into the old naked man's ear. If I had his attention, he probably could have deflected it or taken the punch with a laugh before he turned me into one of his dress boys, but this time it staggered him and was enough I could pull my bunched and smeared shirt out of his grip. He covered his offended ear with one scrawny arm, but still watched the butcher of Grindfield.

My buddy's gashed arm hung limp down at his side. He stared down longingly at the flayed boy and the branch across him. "Why won't you just cooperate? This could have been so beautiful."

Beautiful? The boy? The branch? His arm? Didn't know and

didn't care. I set to run again. Grindfield wasn't my salvation. I might have brought the curse to that place, or just walked into it. If I had to guess, that town today probably has a hell of a run of bad luck. Tiny population, but can't seem to stop attracting the worst lot. Maybe one of those places where kids keep disappearing, or cults keep taking up residence out in the deep woods where mining camps used to be. Crops grow bleached white with alien fungus, and stray litters are deformed beyond saving. That ground was fouled beyond redemption long before the oldest citizens of the little village there were ever born.

My buddy was up and moving with one arm and one knife in it. Whipped through one fellow's throat deep enough to scrape his spine and all but decapitate him. He stood longer than should have been possible after that, with his shaking hands trying to find his gushing throat and failing. The next cut folded open a shirtless man's side all along the ribs. It must have been the cleanest cut my buddy got all day, but he didn't take time to appreciate it before he hacked open a balding man's skull. Scalped him a quarter of the way into his brain. Those two fell before the fellow with nothing much holding his head on anymore.

Others got to moving. Whatever ailed many of them, they didn't move as fast as me, which might have been all that saved me that day. My legs and side still burned with acid and I hadn't recovered from my previous run, but I got away. Right out the bloody ass end of Camp Grindfield.

My buddy was shouting at all our backs for us to be reasonable. He just needed our skins. He didn't need the rest of us, just the skin.

We all scattered into the surrounding woods, but my guess is most didn't survive to the next morning. Was a long day and an even longer night, but my butcher buddy wasn't done with me, either.

20

THE CAT AND mouse bullshit continued through the day and into the night. I wanted to stick to the trail. I wanted to run. I didn't have the energy to run forever. No one does, no matter what is after you. The trail was switching back and forth as it wound up and down over the hills. It'd take me right for a good while and then twice as far back to the left, undoing any real progress.

So, my butcher buddy kept crossing over my path as he entered and exited the woods, sometimes carrying the evidence of his plunder and mayhem. I'm not sure if he moved on from his mission to just collect the skins at that point or what, but in addition to the slabs of meat and the poorly prepped human hides he had dripping over his shoulders as he hunted back and forth through the hills, he carried other goodies, too.

At one point he had a head each in his grasps. One he held by its thinning hair. Its eyes rolled up to the white and its jaw hanging open and jutted crooked. A few vertebrae worth of spine still hung out from the base of the skull like a frozen snake. The other head swung back and forth upside down, because my buddy was holding the decapitated skull by its beard. The teeth clacked together at the end of each swing. That was his injured arm, so even though he held onto that beard and the bowling ball weight of that head, the arm seemed to just sort of flop dead by his side with each step. No real control over the motion.

I know there are horror movies everywhere with stuff as gross as that in the first reel, but we weren't inoculated with that sort of gruesome shit back then. We'd seen plenty of real life horrors, and I was racking up my own library of terrible images burned into my memory forever, but that was still beyond the pale of my experience.

I ran away.

As I was looking for the trail again, he passed within spitting distance of me and I crouched down behind a fallen log as best I could. Don't know what he decided to do with the heads or a lot of the meat that had been over his shoulders, but most of that was gone, save for the sticky stains, at that point. This time he had a fist full of dicks. Couldn't get a count on them, but a lot more dicks than one would expect to run across a fellow carrying. Couple of them still had flaps of sack meat attached.

The guy was chewing on one piece of meat. It bobbed around just outside his lips. Could have been a dick. Hard to say. See lots of people saying, "Eat a dick" or "Eat a bag of dicks." If those fuckers had been there in the woods with me that day, they wouldn't ask for that shit anymore. Was terrifying.

I was lost as hell by that point. Just trying to stay away and ahead of that lumbering monster of a man. Kept thinking I'd found the trail again, only to discover I was still in the thick of the wilderness. Seems like it would have been hard to miss, you know? We were hemmed in by hills. Couldn't climb the sheer rock faces, and didn't want to step off a fucking cliff. Trail had to be in the middle. I ran away uphill, so the trail had to be downhill. Then, I'd nearly step off a sheer drop, or come sure I'd gone too far and start back up the other way. Find myself at the base of another stone wall or a drop off in the other direction.

I was lost.

Got exhausted. Got hungry, despite everything I'd seen. And it started setting dark. Figured I might be able to hunker down and wait until light, let that bloody fucker wander off on his own. But then I'd hear him, crashing through the brush and mumbling to himself. I'd hear screams long after I thought there couldn't be anyone left to kill but me. Then, he'd be stomping back through in my direction all over again.

I tried to keep moving and out ahead of him for a while, but then was so dark I was just making a bunch of noise trying to move and could step right off a drop and be halfway to dead before I knew what I'd done.

So, took all my will to just sit still.

He kept passing real close to me, like he was sniffing me out or toying with me. And he kept blabbering his mad, heartbroken, murderous nonsense to me. Reasoning with me. Begging me.

"Come on, Stone. I need this. I can't never see my boy again without your help. I need your face. I need your cock. I need to size up your feet and hands. If you'll help me out, I'll take what I need and give you the rest. I'm so close to finishing him. A couple more things and I'll have him back."

On like that. All fucking night. I might have passed out from exhaustion, but not for long with him squealing and crying out to me the whole time. At some point in the wee hours of morning, way too far from sun up still, I realized that madman was trying to rebuild his son from the spare parts he was taking off the men and boys he'd slaughtered. Not just the skin, but every part he thought he needed to remake his boy. Maybe chewing on each dick he cut off until he found the right one.

All fucking night. Took me a while to realize the sun was breaking up between the hills and revealing that endless woods again. I didn't want to, was scared to, but I had to move again. Still exhausted. Still hungry. But I had no choice, unless I wanted to wait to be found, which I did not.

Got my ass going again. Still lost, but going one step in front of the other. I didn't want to be found by that butcher man, but I really, really didn't want to run across the meat sculpture of his son he was crafting out there in the middle of nowhere.

Turned out, there was worse than that still ahead of me.

21

CAN'T TELL YOU for sure how long or far I wandered. Not sure if I heard him begging me for my face, my feet, and my dick for several nights following, or if I just imagined it in my fear. I kept going though.

I came up on another town, a more proper town than Grindfield, at least by a little. I think I could tell you the name, if I thought on it some, but hardly matters as there wasn't a soul left alive by the time I got there.

My curse preceded me that time. Or it had spread out faster than I was wandering and hooked ahead of me.

At any rate, I walked through abandoned buildings and a fucking boneyard. Literally bones, human bones, scattered every which where. I read some books when I first got locked up, and over the many years inside. They take all the good stuff out of jailhouse libraries on account that they think murder stories and sexy stuff will get us all worked up and dangerous. Maybe they're right. I found a history book years back that had stuff about Ganghas Kahn, Kubla Kahn, or Shacka Kahn. Whatever his name was. Anyhow, some missionaries or warriors were approaching his land and saw a snow-covered mountain. As they got closer, they realized it was a mound of bones from where they had just stacked the bodies. The bones in that next town I ran into wasn't really anything like that, but I thought about that stretch of my journey when I read that piece about Kahn's bone pile. I think I knew how those poor fuckers felt when they realized what they'd walked into. No Chinaman's bone pile there, but if all those bones, and the ones I'd run across later with my hands tied in the miles ahead, were all put together in one spot, then I don't know. It might have looked something like a snowcap from the right distance in the wrong light.

I wanted to believe was an animal that did it. Well, back up a second. First, I wanted to believe they were animal bones of some herd of something that got slaughtered and picked clean before or after the town was abandoned. There weren't as many skulls as there were broken up skeletons, which is its own kind of terror, but the couple that were left were clearly human.

After that, I wanted to believe it was an animal that did it. I'd seen human madness and butchery. I wasn't excited to deal with a man-eating bear that could level a whole town, even a small one, like this grouping of shacks, but if my butcher buddy or someone else infected with his craving to collect dicks and skins had gotten ahead of me, that was somehow worse in my mind.

The bones had been scraped clean. Looked to me like from knives and not teeth — human, bear, or otherwise. The marks in the bone are different. It's not worth explaining. Just trust me on that. These people had been taken apart and carved clean by someone who could wield a blade. I was sure of it. Sure at the time, anyway.

What else? Didn't see a lot of hands or feet left around. Kind of scarce, like skulls. Of course, dicks don't leave fossils, far as I know, no bones anyway, so who knows how many of those might have been collected?

I didn't get much from the buildings. Could have been a struggle, obviously. Could have been people leaving in a hurry as their fellow townsfolk, trappers, or miners were taken apart. There wasn't enough furniture to get a feel for what had happened in there. Looked like maybe some old stains and something dragged through them, but all that had time to dry up or been licked up before I got there. One of the doors hung partially pulled off its leather strap hinges.

At the time, I might have also considered it was savages. That was a constant worry of folks out there back then, sure. Knowing what I know now, and everything I told you leading up to this point of the story, I can't recall if that was a possibility in my mind at that point. I just needed to get out of there and away.

Heard something scraping down in the wood line, way down

the rocky slope. Trees were big, but spread out down there before they thickened up deeper in the gullies. The echoes of that scratchy noise made it sound close, like I should have been able to easily spot the source between those first trees, unless whatever it was hid itself strategically behind one trunk to block my view. Then, why make the noise, right?

If I'd learned anything, whatever was overtaking everyone out in that endless wilderness, stealth wasn't a priority for it.

Could have been teeth against bone I was hearing. Could have been a well-used blade taking care of the last bit of flesh on a bone as I stumbled upon the end of whatever this was. Very briefly, I considered hiding in one of the shacks for some shelter. I'd already run through the night before and wasn't excited about repeating it. But it was clear these structures had provided no safety from whatever was out there.

So, I moved on. Still heard the scraping for longer than made sense. Looked over my shoulder often as I negotiated that rocky rise. Saw nothing and tripped on my face more than once. Drew blood. Left stains of my own for something to follow. Maybe a scent of the stuff on the air for whatever was hungry for it.

Heard footsteps, too. Knew I was being followed. Paranoia, for sure, and probably hearing things that weren't there on top of all else, but turned out I was being followed, tracked by more than one party that wished me ill.

It was a delirious journey. Eating what I could find. Cooking over low fires and snuffing them out as quick as I could. Everything going in me was half raw. Everything coming out was soupy and full of blood. Was sure as Christmas I was dying of something. Pictured my insides turning into coffee grounds.

Saw another town in the distance some days later, bigger than the previous two. Proper buildings, with top floors and real slanted roofs. Nearly turned my ankle more than once working my way diagonally through the brush and down the slope toward the civilization.

Rock dust kicked up with each step as I met the bowl of the trail and weaved down into the midst of the town. No signs of life. Quiet unto death. I sort of knew what I was going to find before I saw the first of it.

More bones.

God, help me, these bones were carved down, broken apart, and scattered in a manner that resembled the previous town, and had me thinking of my buddy butcher. These weren't as clean. The bones weren't as picked over, and the meat still attached to them in bits and pieces was still fresh, still bloody.

Doors hung open. Furniture might have been askew inside a couple places, but not really ransacked. Flies, though. The flies were thick, like clouds of living smog. Smears of blood and filth dragged the floors out over the stoops and across the white rock ground a little ways. The white dust in those spots had caked into a bloody mashed paste. Nothing had licked up or dried yet. The flies were feasting, though.

Plops of horse shit still marked the main passthrough of town, in the thick of the buildings. They weren't steaming in the cool of the day, but they were wet enough that, if I chose to, I could have sliced into them with the soft rounded blade of my hand.

Whatever had happened here, it had gone down in recent days, probably recent hours. The butcher and his kind that might have caught the spreading madness, too, could still be close at hand. He might just wander over my path at any moment, with a fist full of dicks or holding some miner's severed head by the beard with the teeth still clicking together.

I wandered out to the far edge of town. There was a mill with a waterwheel down on the river in the middle distance. The wheel was still functioning. I remember thinking that's where I needed to go next. That would be where survivors were. Not sure why and I never got a chance to test that assumption, not on my own.

A few horses, and one still wearing a saddle, stood out on the trail just before where it bent off into the hills and away. They stared back at me where I stood still in the dead town. Nothing but wind and flies and the smell of rotting blood and guts. Couldn't hear anything else. Maybe the waterwheel if I concentrated and looked right at it.

I needed to search for supplies, too. Wouldn't think that would be a top priority walking up on the slaughter of a whole town skinned to the bone and scattered, but you still got to eat soon as your stomach settles again. I thought the mill might be a good place for that, too. Might be able to wash the horror off of me a little if the water was cold enough, as it tended to be most times out that way.

I stared down at the shape in the ground in front of me, though, right there before the buildings started to break up where the little ghost town petered out. I couldn't tell if it was drawn there or coincidence. It was the drag pattern of the blood, same as leading out of the open doorways behind me. Couldn't tell where these curved smears started or why they ended. No sign of where the bloody bodies that made them were carried off too, neither, except for the bones scattered about in no discernible pattern. There were no drips of the painters hauling the meat away either, but with that much blood on the white ground, anything that bled that much on a drag would have to drip from a carry. Had to. Couldn't figure it out.

I guess you call it a star pattern or a spiral. Blood and gore in the center of the design pooled up thick enough to have elevation as the stuff coagulated and hardened into a gel. The smears curved out from that center, about as wide as a dragged body, and those painted arms or spokes faded into rough points. Sort of looked like claws. I used to know, but can't recall now how many of those spiral blood marks hooked out from that ripe berry-red center. I'm picturing five right now, like the fingers on a hand, but could have been six or more. Maybe less.

Not a fly on it, either. Buildings were swarming with them and the fuckers were all up in my ears and eyes, driving me mad, but not when I stood as close to that star blood smear spire as I dared. They couldn't get enough of the stuff. Felt like every fly in the West as I tried to swat them away from me, over and over, but not there. They wanted no part of whatever this was.

Walked wide around it and flies were on me again as I put my back to the thing and hooked around toward the mill below. I stole a glance to the horses, wondering if one would let me ride. One of them bobbed its head, but the whole herd of forgotten animals stood close together, like for warmth, but wasn't that sort of day. Just stared at me like they were watching or waiting for something specific. It creeped me out as much as everything else in that terrible place.

I stopped short again and stared down at a pelvic bone. Was more bone than meat left behind, but it certainly wasn't skinned as clean as the others. A little bit of joint and cartilage jutted down in ragged knobs where the legs would have been. A big lump of flesh off center, but still, where the groin would have been was topped with a healthy bush of hair, matted and glistening with blood though. There was an opening there below the hair, right about where you'd expected. It, too, looked bloody and abused. Nasty cuts. Gooey mess. If you pressed me, to this day, I'd guess it had belonged to a female. Betting my life on it? No way. Could have been the bloody site of a collected cock, too. Whoever, whatever done it, had poked around with a knife or some other tools, I dare say. Too curious to leave the hole alone, even in their madness.

And the flies liked it, too. They crawled all through the gore-greased hair, in and out the mutilated fuckhole.

I swallowed down on acidic bile trying to crawl up my throat. Managed not to add anything to the sick scene.

Did start to wonder, with all this slaughter, if my butcher buddy might not be trying to rebuild his whole family from all the stolen parts he seemed to be collecting.

Glanced over at one of the more distant buildings trailing out from the main part of town. I just wanted to look at anything else. It was a small building. Almost too small to be a house even. At its base, the rough board sign was broken apart and splintered. Could have been hanging over the place. Might have been the name of the business that had been packed into that shack or the name of the town itself. I saw an "H" and a "R" in the clutter. Even took a step toward it, maybe in hopes of figuring out where I was.

A click sound popped out and echoed somewhere behind me. Would have thought nothing of it, even being so jumpy, surrounded by horrible death as I was, but a gurgly trill of clicks and pops followed the first before tapering off.

I whirled around and saw nothing I hadn't already witnessed on my tour through hell the first time. The swarming flies made the clear space around the blood star stand out as a void between the undulating clouds of insects. I saw nothing that made the sound, but the buildings blocked my view of some of the distance beyond town.

More clicking. Some hissing that sort of got lost in the wind, but not enough. Seemed loud to me, out on that white ground, but wasn't enough to clear the flies. I thought of the noise of gas leaving a dead body left out too long. Such a thing might fit in a place like that, but every remain in the area was nothing more than isolated bone and clinging flesh.

Some rocks shifted and ground together. Then, another click. Just one. A metallic noise, but could have also been a noise created by a mouth.

I moved sideways, trying to keep one of the bigger structures between me and whatever was out there with me. Tried to peer through the windows as I passed, looking for any movement, but seeing none except what your brain will try to fool you into seeing when you move past rough glass reflecting and refracting shadows.

Drew closer to the wall as I approached the corner. I was looking straight down at that mill. It was too far away if my goal was to get away from something. I had in my head that was the place to go. I'd ascribed some sort of omen magic upon the place, and I was full of fear and superstition by that point.

I also felt in my bones, which I hoped to keep in my body, that something, the clicking thing no doubt, was waiting right around that corner for me like the bogeyman it was. If I stuck my head around, it would take my eyes, skin the face right off me to the rich red underneath, and chop my head clean from my neck to carry around the woods for a while. If I sprinted out and down toward that magic mill, it would have me and rip my bones out in rapid order while I still screamed for no one to hear but my butcher. At that point, had to be music to him, I'd imagined.

True or not, I believed I need to go. So, I went. Pushed off my back foot and broke into a run, without daring to glance to the side. Might have even had my eyes closed tight. I don't recall. Felt like tempting the fates, which I then believed to be monsters crawling through the dark under the Earth, who you never wanted to disturb or let know you'd seen them.

I just ran. May have gotten a second or third step in, but no more than that.

They grabbed me and dragged me down to the rocky white ground. Skinned my chin and added my blood to the pristine rocks half buried all through the area.

Then, growled my name into my own ear as the full weight pressed down on top of me.

22

"STONE WICKED." I think I pissed myself then. If not then, it was shortly after, but we'll get there.

"Bind his hands."

I tried to fight my way free, but couldn't even really draw a breath at that point.

"No. No. Roll him. Need him to walk behind the horse. Get his hands in front."

"What about his feet?"

"Said he needs to walk."

"Just until we get him secured?"

"He is not going anywhere. Roll him."

He didn't say "ain't", he said "is not", all articulated out like that.

They did roll me and, of course, I looked up into the faces of the marshal and his girlfriend.

Marshal Elliot Mother Fucking Crawford.

And that bitch Annabelle Syne. She's the one I think about whenever Joe Exotic there starts going on about Carole Baskins, you know. Maybe we all have a woman like that in our lives at some point.

I was too surprised to say anything or to resist, for whatever that would be worth. I don't know that I was relieved. Better than getting my bones cut out and my dick carved away into a fresh hole, sure. And, thinking on it now, better than those sodomite miners picking up on my trail for anything they had planned. No better assailants to fall prey to in that moment, I'll admit, but I was in shock and I felt like a hunted man who had finally been hunted down.

With my hands bound, they hauled me up to my feet between them. First time I'd been up close to either of them longer than it took to run past them in a dark cave chased by hell monsters, or through a town stricken by bloodthirsty madness.

They were both taller than me. Him by a lot. Her not by much, but still taller. They were both stockier, better fed. Healthier. I mean, look at me. I'm tougher than most folks think on first glance, and I've withered a bit with age, but this is about the size I've always been. Hadn't been starving along the trail since things had turned ugly again, but just getting by. Didn't have a lot of fight in me at that point, mental or physical.

"Don't try to run, Stone. You're caught," Syne said. Or something to that effect. We talked a lot, so I'm probably mashing all those memories together, but I'll do my best to parse it out where it matters. It's a story. You get how this goes.

I do remember she waved a finger in my face like she was scolding me. It bothered me. I think I remembered the butcher buddy doing that at one point. I didn't like her already, either.

I just shook my head and said back, "Why don't you shove your scolding finger up your bloody fuck hole, soiled dove mouthpiece."

Crawford clocked me across the jaw and staggered me. Even after insulting her, it was Syne who took my shoulder and kept me from falling to the rocks again. Thought he hit me with the butt of his pistol because it hurt so bad, but appeared to just be his hand.

"You best get a hold of your tongue, you yellow dog," Crawford said to me. "You put us through a lot of hard trail to track you, so testing my patience further would be a mistake. You can apologize for what you said or see how hard I can punch the second and third time."

I want to tell you I told him to go fuck himself, but I snapped out a sorry before I licked the blood from the corner of my mouth.

"Not to me," he said. "To her."

You know how tough guys do.

I turned to her. Stared into her eyes until she looked away. Wasn't much of a victory, but I took it. "Sorry."

"Just behave yourself from here on out," she said. "We have a long way to go."

She started to lead me away by my bound hands, but Marshal Crawford took me by my shoulder and jerked me around to face him again. I braced to be hit again, but he instead got close to my face and said, "What did you have to do with all the godless business we've been seeing along the trail, Wicked?"

I think I took longer to answer than he liked because he got closer to my face and growled at me some more. "You don't want to test me. No judge out here to see and any bruises I put on you will be healed before we get you back to face up."

I stammered a bit and then said, "I don't know what you mean. What business?"

Crawford drew back his fist and I flinched.

Annabelle Syne spoke up and said, "The bodies, the bones, the bloodshed. There's no one out here but the three of us, and we know the two of us weren't involved."

"How do you think I was involved?"

"We're trailing you," Crawford said, "and there is bloodshed everywhere you walked. We've passed through four towns behind you, and every one looks like this."

"Four?"

Syne took Crawford by the fist and lowered it for him. "Lying isn't going to get you out of all this, and we aren't going down like all those poor people."

I looked back and forth between them. "You think I killed and skinned all those folks?"

"A moment ago you didn't even know what business I was referring to," Crawford said.

I shook my head. "I didn't even go to four towns. I went through a camp called Grindfield and I stumbled in here not a moment ago. When I got to Grindfield . . . wait . . . "

"Wait nothing," Crawford said. "We're supposed to believe you were there for two massacres, but not the other two?"

"Well, three of them, counting Grindfield. I forgot about the last one," I said. "No, wait, you were there, too."

"I know I didn't kill anyone, Wicked. Her either, so who are you trying to fool?"

"You were there at Garacto. The both of you. You were there at the black mountain and saw those things."

"This isn't about that," Syne tried to say.

"The hell it isn't. Excuse my vulgarity," I said. I was still afraid of Crawford hitting me again. "You saw the people there go mad. You saw what they did, how they took each other apart. I was helping a guy along the trail. He got sick and turned mad himself. Started carving on himself and then came after me. He chased me into Grindfield and started slaughtering everyone. Horrendous stuff. Like this. I've been fleeing through the woods ever since. This was the next town I came upon, not long before you got me."

"So, your friend, who you were helping along the trail, went crazy and just started cutting people up, leaving bones laying ever which where?"

"Probably not just him."

"So, you're saying he recruited a team of men to do this? Civilized white men did this?"

"You saw Garacto," I said. "You saw the things under the mountain. Don't pretend we live in a normal world anymore, marshal. Don't pretend you can't imagine what happened here and why. Wait, there was another town between Grindfield and here."

Something clicked down the slope, and then clicked again. I disinvested from defending myself in that moment and tried to lean out to see what it was.

"I can't imagine it, Wicked. I've been following you for a while and I have seen with my own eyes the trail you left behind and . . . " On and on and on he went for a while.

I tried to lean out further, but Syne made to pull me back upright and into place. I shook her off and took a full step and a half sideways. She sprung like I was trying to go. Crawford didn't act like he thought I was trying to escape. He sort of trailed off in his lectures and accusations. I don't know if he saw it in my face or eyes, but he turned to follow my line of sight to whatever had me spooked, and maybe stole all the color from my face as the blood ran out of it.

Don't recall exactly what he said, but it was a string of curses worse than anything he'd just smacked me for. There was no denying our shared experiences anymore, because another party of things chasing me had arrived.

The trees were further away, across the river and beyond the mill. In among those shadows were where they stood and scratched at the ground, raising up white dust on the wind in contrast to the dark knots of flesh around their bony bodies and joints, knobs of flesh and twisted sinew over the exposed bone to hold it all together. A couple of them had their black skin robes. All of them had the blood red eyes sunken in their awful skulls.

Straight from under the black mountain, from across a desert, and too many miles away, the bone devils were back. They had found us. They had found me. It was quite the fucking reunion.

"Let me go. Let me go. Let me go!"

"Quiet down, Wicked," Crawford said. "Just close your mouth and let me think."

"What's to think about?" I asked. "We need to get out of here. You remember how fast those things move?"

"You tried to leave us out there with them. I remember," Crawford said. "Annie, go get the horses."

She moved away along the side of the building I'd slunk along, but then in a different direction from the horses I'd seen down the trail, the way I wanted to be going just then.

"We all need to go, marshal. Are you daft?"

"Enough of your babbling, Wicked. Enough. You ever try to run from a wild animal before? You seen what they do? We're going to hold steady and quiet. Then, we'll get out of here once we have horses to flee on again. Don't suppose you still have the horse you stole from us, do you?"

I couldn't quite recall what he was talking about. In my mind, I'd ridden out on the horse I stole from Frank and the old crew. Hardly seemed worth arguing over with those seething things down there staring back at us in red from their black pitted skull sockets. The creatures shifted from side to side, giving a scraping sound over the rocky ground, but they hadn't advanced just yet.

"Horse got scratched by one of those devils," I said. "Got infected and the animal literally turned itself inside out. I mean, it really, actually—"

"Don't care, Wicked. Don't tell me a story. The answer is no. That's all I need from you, scoundrel."

"We need to go right now, marshal. Waiting here is death. You see what happened to everyone in town, and you see what done it right down there sizing us up."

"I told you to quiet down. No more noise. I mean it."

"Those aren't wild animals. No earthly beings at all. Can't you see? Those are monsters. Demons straight out of Hell. You didn't get a chance to see their chamber, the place where they kept all those dirty grey slaves that came pouring out the cave with us. They are torturing spirits, marshal. They are here to steal us and consume our souls. You can't stare them down like an angry raccoon. Please, let me go or take me out of here right now."

"I swear if you can't close your flappy lips, Wicked, I'll feed you to them my own self. You got that?"

I didn't get a chance to answer.

Those things lurched forward. Not all at once, but they moved out of the trees in a rush when they did. The almost invisible flow of the river down there frothed up as a couple of them planted their front claws into the rocks and eddies there.

Boards peeled off the side wall of the mill and scattered, some getting carried downstream, others clearing our side of the bank. Another monster bounded up onto the roof, put its claws through the rough-hued shingles, and tore one of the beams out into view in a giant splinter. To its credit, the building stayed standing.

Marshal Crawford shifted backward a little and pulled me along with him by my bound hands. We didn't even make it far enough to touch the building where they'd nabbed me.

"Keep going. Keep going . . . " I muttered it under my breath because I had no breath left, seeing these things again and the reality that they had us. They had us dead to rights, on essentially open ground. "Keep going!"

The one that ripped up the side of the building sprung forward again and this time hung itself up in the outer rim of the water wheel. As it twisted off true, the wheel gouged the building side facing us and then ripped away entirely. Out from the interior, the arms and connectors tore through a widening hole in the side of the structure. I don't know how familiar you are with mills. You probably seen a few modern replicas that don't do the same things the ones in the past did. It's not important, I guess, except to say that the inner workings of an old mill could be heavy as fuck, and the sort of thing you'd need construction equipment to tear out in one motion. None of that existed back then.

The monster screamed in a high growl and shook off the wheel, sending it tipping and crashing into the deeper water there by the mill. It splashed down and diverted the water a little, in a swell.

The beast waded out and then up onto the rocky lip on our side of things. Still a good ways away, but it wasn't much distance when facing down something like that. Still had the cow-bone face and dark horns. Tendons connected all that exposed bone, stretching taut enough to make sounds of their own. Water sheeted out of the joints and unnatural knots of flesh where it didn't seem any living organs could function. If nothing else, I thought the beasts must have stomachs, but couldn't figure out where one would go. After the water, a thicker effusion of dark blood seeped out between the rubbing connections of the knots, like lubricant.

Most had white tongues, but the one up on the bank stuck out a purple tongue.

They all started hooting, popping, scratching at the ground like bulls getting ready to charge, and screeching. The fucking screeching was madness itself, and it would nearly drive me mad before these things were done with me.

Steam started rising off their flesh and exposed bone frames all around. The ones wading into the water fared a little better, but not by much. The blood and water sizzled around the surface of their horrible bodies, like spit on a hot pan. They backed away into the scant shade of the trees for what protection it provided. Most of them anyway. The rest still snapped and screeched at us, marking us again.

Marshal Crawford eased me a few more steps backward, but didn't seem to have taken the full message that it was time for us to go anywhere but here.

Then, something started moving around in what was left of the mill.

"Annabelle, how are the horses coming?"

"Yes, Annabelle, please, for Christ's sake," I added.

He didn't slap me again, but he did give my bonds a yank and nearly shuffled me off my boots for it.

The last of the bone demons that was still in the water, boiling in the sun, the one that came out the farthest, the one with the purple tongue I thought I remembered from the desert, turned back and emerged on the opposite bank again. Its attention focused on the mill. The beast started clawing at the crumbling hole where the wheel had been ripped away, breaking away the powdery edges.

"Jiminy Christmas," Annabelle Syne piped up from the dusty, rocky main street of bone town behind us and well beyond the building we were lallygagging at as we watched the lords of Hell prepare to run us down as they'd likely done every dismantled corpse in town. "Let's make haste, Elliot."

I turned to run where she sat on one horseback, holding the reins of the other, but he pulled me up short and spun me back around to face the monsters, like he wanted to make me watch.

"Easy," he said to me, as if I was one of his animals. "We're going to do this slow so as not to spook them. One step at a time, nice and slow."

"They're the spooks, marshal."

"Just keep your mouth closed and move with me, Wicked. My lead."

So, we walked backward, step by step along the side of that building, like we were sneaking away from creatures, evil spirits really, that possibly tracked us for hundreds of miles, maybe, from out of the desert into the mountains. *Make hay while there's daylight*, I thought then and still think now, but I'd let him drop on me and tie my hands, so I was at his mercy for the moment. Him and the monsters from under the black mountain.

The stubborn devil that had been last out of the water and lingered at the mill, burrowing his way inside, was really cooking at that point. Smoke poured off of him at several points like he was a leaking furnace chimney. He was the kindling the moment before it heats up enough to erupt with the rising campfire. The exposed bone, which was most of their body, blackened as I watched. And fuck me, I couldn't help but watch, the way Crawford had us scooting backward in scared polecat fashion.

On the purple-tongued thing's back, where all that sooty carbon black was changing the monster to charcoal, lighter lines and shapes showed up in the gnarled flesh and exposed bone through those scorch marks. Most notably, the rough and ragged shape of an upside down cross showed pretty clear in its back. It was a crooked, twisted shape, and it was off to a diagonally, but clear as day. Another shape, on the back of its skull through the blackened bone, was more red than bone white. It was sort of a circle, with thick lines spiring out of it. It looked purposeful to me at the time, and I've seen the same thing here and there from time to time since, but I had no reference for it at the time. And you understand I was scared shitless, looking for a way to escape instead of divining symbols from the tealeaves of burning monsters.

I did think at the time that I couldn't figure out why they were able to chase us part way through a desert in blazing sunlight, but seemed to be cooking alive in overcast mountain daylight. I only pondered it briefly, as the bone devil with its sacrilegious body art and purple giraffe's tongue yanked a screaming woman from the wide hole in the wall of the mill. He slammed her to the ground hard enough to silence her from the lost wind, and then plunged its front fangs into her belly where he tore her open with a single ripping bite. Her blood spattered his long arms and misshapen chest, where it sizzled and popped.

The others roared and charged back out of the trees to fight each other over the opening. They pulled out more women and some children, too. All screaming, but not for long. It didn't take the black mountain beasts long to rip them open and then to tear them apart. The one with the devil cross on its back fed there in the sun as it crisped, but some of the others dragged the remains of their prey along the ground and into the trees. They stripped the bones fast, chewed on them as they scraped every bit of meat they could take, and then cast the bones through the air in all directions.

We finally made it to the damn horses. Crawford mounted the empty saddle deftly and claimed the reins from his partner. He pulled me up by my bonds and nearly dislocated my shoulders in the awkward process. Hurt like hell and plagued me with pain for days, but I bit the inside of my cheeks until I tasted blood to keep from screaming out. I had no desire to draw the attention of the hellspawn that already had my scent, especially if they were already lathered up in a fit of bloodlust. So, best I could, I pumped my legs and worked my knees in the awkward struggle as the horse sniffed and snorted, shifting from side to side, with Crawford giving me half-assed help, at best, to get up on the animal's rump.

Didn't get it. They had run from these same monsters, too, so what was up with the delays?

I got up there behind him, with my hands bound and not much saddle to hold onto. They finally kicked into motion and we headed out of town. I didn't want to look, but I turned my head back anyway. Saw the damage, but didn't spy the monsters anymore.

We got almost all the way along the trail to where the horses from town cowered in fear. They finally bolted and spread out as they left the trail and us in a hurry. Wanted to suggest that maybe we might rope up the one that still had a saddle. We could escape better and faster on three horses instead of two. From the looks of things, the mount was in need of an owner. But I stayed quiet. The law dogs had shown they had no interest in taking suggestions from me. Even the completely sane suggestion that we get the hell away from the killing field feeding frenzy of the desert demons. Now that I finally had them in motion, I decided to stay quiet.

If you hadn't guessed all on your own, that was another terrible night.

23

BEING HUNTED BY my butcher buddy with the skin obsession was bad enough. I still half expected him to be out there. Still wasn't sure if he hadn't played along with the bone devils in stripping the town of life, even after the harvesting they did at the mill. Hell, I sometimes dream him up some nights, here in the safety of my little room. But knowing those desert-dwelling devils from under the black mountain had somehow trailed me out to the wooded wilderness, where there was no one to help, was far worse.

They didn't trail me exactly. They got ahead of me and were there waiting. If I had gotten there at night, without the sun to help, I can't imagine I would have lived long enough to think on all the implications much. You and Perkins and Crawford and the rest would have either never heard of me, nor never found out what happened to me. Of course, those poor people from the mill lived longer than you'd think with how much those monsters tore into them. Long enough to really suffer.

Then again, maybe there was purpose behind their choices on that count, based on what happened later. It's hard to tell. I was still discovering that the world was full of powers and principalities. Everything answers to something, it turns out. There's always a larger god above the darker and lesser ones.

That night, we stuck closer to the trail than I thought we should. Why make it easy to be found? I wonder if Crawford was still in denial about what was really going on. I couldn't explain what any of these things were or meant, but I had no illusions that we were dealing with anything other than unnatural evil from a hell worse than the fiery pit preachers imagined for us.

The noises started from a distance while the light was still dying in the west. I don't know if you've been out in the woods, far from any city lights, at that time before night sets in full. Not sure a place that far removed really exists anymore, but down in the trees, it'll get deep dark. You stare into that blade of light along the horizon and can almost convince yourself it's still day. But then you look anywhere else and see that a dark deeper than shadows rules. Add in mountains to that and better stop moving for the night, if you know what's good for you.

Were it a natural night, you'd generally want a fire to ward off nighttime predators. Even then, it serves to have someone alert because animals can get hungry enough to dare to come at your firelight. At least Crawford had wit enough to know we didn't want light. Those devils might be allergic to sunlight, in the vampire sense of things, but I believe I recalled plenty of fire in the black mountain chambers.

I don't remember perfectly now. Maybe there was no fire down there and the glowing stones were enough. Crawford might have thought a fire was just the thing and it was Syne who talked him out of it. Certainly wasn't me. He had no interest in anything I had to say at that point. Later, he wanted to talk all the time.

Those things were following the trail because that hooting, screeching, banshee wailing drew closer, echoing through the gullies and piercing the night. The horses weren't far enough removed to keep from being scented or even spotted, depending on how good those things saw in the dark from their empty sockets. Or if they had some other sense that traveled and searched the ether. How else had they circled in on me?

We weren't far enough, either. They dragged me farther off and up a hill through thick brush. Too dark to see shit and loud as you want. We found a piss-poor little cave overlooking the bend in the trail below, although I don't think any of us had the eyes to point it out at night.

My hands were still tied in front of me, so I was tripping, spilling, and cutting myself the whole way. I wanted to complain, but hated to make a sound with those things drawing ever closer. Not to mention I was bleeding a little, to add to the stink of fear we were all sweating off.

We pushed through cobwebs and rubbed our scalps through

the mud on the low ceiling of the cave. Couldn't do more than crouch, and Crawford was a big fella. Syne wasn't slight either. I was fine having them between me and the death out there. I was sure from the mill that plucking the three of us out, one after the other, was no big deal for those creatures, if they still had an appetite.

Something slithered over my hand. Wait, my hands were tied. So, something slithered over my tied hands, but I didn't have the room or flexibility to pull them away. I believed the disrupted spider got a bite or two of poison into my back and side as well.

I couldn't hear well enough to tell, but I think those things circled us all night. I can't believe they were incapable of finding us. Not after making it all the way out there from the desert. If God has his mysterious ways, maybe his lower counterparts do, too.

Thought for sure that would be the worst hole I'd ever find myself in again, but the hidden dirt cave with the dead man stored inside was still in my future. Come to think of it, the monsters didn't find me there either. It was that woman Avalon I should have been careful of then.

But I'm getting ahead of my story. This was the first awful dirt cave I was stuck in at that point.

No way any of us slept. Not like that, with all that. I lost time, though, as the night seemed to be forever, and then the muddy law dragged me out of that warren cave backward into the light of morning before it seemed possible. Morning creatures chirped and carried on like there wasn't evil stalking the close world, lying in wait.

I was too exhausted to move, but Elliot Crawford and Annabelle Syne planned to make me march all the way back to whatever courthouse had a taste for me. I was going to say Georgia, but that came later. Doesn't matter, because we never made it.

We started up the trail with every intention of cutting across at the next proper town and back into civilization. Like Moses and God's lost children, we had a hell of a lot more wilderness to wander through first.

24

THEY LEFT MY hands tied, but then attached a cord off the back of Marshal Crawford's saddle. I stumbled along behind their horses, getting jerked and dragged by the trotting animal, breathing in farts and dodging fresh plops of shit as soon as they fell on the trail.

"Come on. I can't keep this up. Let me ride, or slow it down at least."

"After all the horses you stole and God knows what else you've done, walking will be good for your soul," Crawford said, without turning around.

So, with my feet and calves cramping up on me and putting in every effort to keep from falling to me knees tied behind their horses there, I kept going, one foot in front of the other, long after my legs had gone numb.

I kept snatching a look over my shoulder whenever the animals faltered enough to put some slack in the rope. I knew we were being followed. Didn't hear it. Didn't see anything. The nights were scary, tied to some tree while the two of them took turns watching me instead of paying attention to what might be hunting us.

We made it to another town, bigger than the previous, but still a frontier, slapped-together gathering of outcasts. It still had people in it, instead of flies breeding in their dirty bones like the settlements leading up.

Place was called something like Sugar Brush or Honey Brush or something like that. Don't quote me. Was a long time ago and I was delirious from being hustled along the trail behind them for days on end.

There was no mill, at least not in sight. The river was further away and concealed in hills and trees where the town and its dirt road cut through a narrow, pitted valley between.

The marshal came to a stop and tied off in front of some establishment. He left Syne to guard me where we'd managed to stop in the one spot in that cut in the earth with no shade. Not sure what she expected me to do, but she stood by their horses with her hand on the butt of her pistol like she expected something. Or hoped for something.

As Crawford went in to have a word with whoever about whatever, I dropped to my knees and cried out in pain. Annabelle Syne laughed at me, with her hand parked on her gun like that. I took a breath to tell her to go bugger herself, but needed all that air just to keep my brain going. I rolled to my side, right there in the dirt.

The shit wagons and the boys paid to roll along and collect all the paddies kept going and shoveling, not too many feet away from me. They even collected a fresh offering from Crawford's horse, who shit and farted more than any creature in God's green creation as far as I could tell from my point of view all those days.

"That man all right?" one of the boys asked.

"He'll rally fine," Syne said. "He's working out his penance on the way to the hangman."

As far as I knew, they had me on a little thievery was all. Horse-thieving could get you strung up back then, sure. Horse thieves sat somewhere below murderers and the smear of green wet shit on the bottom of your boot, but hanging wasn't an automatic. I wondered if they had me for more than I'd done, maybe mistaken some of the old gangs' doings for my own.

Tried to ask as much, but still needed all that breath to catch up with my fluttering heart, so I left it to later, letting my eyes slide closed. Smelled that burnt smell of sun-heated stall dirt, stronger than the shit wagons still working around me.

Crawford came back out. Could have been a minute. Could have been an hour. I was no more rested.

Crawford said, "There's some trouble."

"What sort of trouble?" Syne asked.

He kicked the toe of his boot against the ground a bit. Floated some dust into my teeth in the process before he answered. "The sort that has people disappearing up in the hills to and from town. A few animals vanishing from the stock of some of the outlying holds. Mining camps have taken some losses, too."

"Any idea who's behind it?"

I managed to grumble from the ground finally. "How you two still not know what's going on here?"

They didn't hear me, or opted to ignore me. Usually, Crawford couldn't help but to bark back at me whenever I had something to say. Couldn't seem to help himself. Had that effect on him back then, I guess. I don't think he had many friends.

"They think it's savages. Things had been quiet up until recently. There was even talk of trade at one point. Contact with the tribes cut off recent, and then the disappearances started up."

"What are your thoughts on heading southeast, like we had planned?"

"A few hours of daylight left. Might need to bed down and start fresh. Cover more miles than usual to get clear of whatever this is."

"Sounds best. You springing for a room?"

"I think camping within the valley will do us fine."

So, that's what we did. They walked the horses and dragged me to me feet. He pulled me along, but had to support most of my weight as we found a grassy spot on the east end of the cluster of buildings. At least there was some shade.

I tried to collapse again, but Crawford had me go ahead and relieve myself, like I was his dog on a leash, and then tied me off to a tree, sitting up.

"I'm surprised they didn't try to recruit us to take out every tribe and Indian in the territory," Syne said.

"They tried," Crawford said. "They only barely bought that I had a dangerous prisoner I needed to deliver. Our problem versus their problems."

"They didn't believe it because it's not true," I barked from my dry throat.

"You just a poor, misunderstood soul, Wicked? Falsely accused on all counts and persecuted for the sins of other men? That sort of thing?"

"I don't know what you've accused me of because you hadn't said," I retorted. "I know I didn't slaughter a string of towns through the hills. I know you shot dead more madmen down in

Garacto than I did. I know you saw those monsters that chased us out from under the mountain, and saw them again on the mill side of the last abandoned town where you caught me distracted. I also know it ain't savages that are snatching people out of the night in this town, neither. If the tribes have gone silent, they're probably being eaten up, too, like we saw happen to those souls at the mill."

"That's quite a tale you weaved together." Crawford sneered at me and then looked away. "I like how you managed to leave out your thieving and killing that set us upon your trail in the first place, like all is forgiven if you somehow find more trouble while you're fleeing."

"I didn't kill no one. Anyone that tells you I did is a liar."

"World is packed full of liars then. In my line, we call them witnesses. We got a lot of them that identified you and the rest of the Goodall Gang. Robberies, nights gambling turned deadly violent and, of course, the horse thieving. We also have witnesses from the Haunted Ranch who say you stole a small fortune and came out on top of a shootout with the rest of the gang. Good riddance, I say, but they're still men and it's still murder."

He didn't call it the Haunted Ranch, but I don't remember the name of it just now. It was the one I'd mentioned at the beginning of this story. I might have said the name then, but I don't know. Turns out he was on a partial bluff himself. He should have been the gambler betwixt us.

"They killed the other boys. That kid and the . . . "

"Go on, Wicked. I want to hear this."

"I didn't kill anyone."

"So you say. So they all say. Never a guilty man alive that could admit it once he was dead to rights."

"Where are the bodies?"

"You tell me, Wicked."

"No, you tell me, marshal. You got witnesses that saw me take out my whole gang, single-handed, after some big score. If they witnessed a killing, they should be able to identify the bodies by location, but I know they didn't because they hauled them off while I escaped."

"That so?"

"Funny they couldn't point out the bodies to this supposed killing spree. Funny you don't consider the other boys are still alive when you couldn't locate a body."

Syne jumped in then. “Are they still alive?”

“Annie.” Crawford waved her off. “So, tell me what happened.”

“Those people . . . ” I was about to spill it. That first round of dark magic that preceded the mountain and everything that followed. Crawford wasn’t ready to yet admit what he had seen with his own eyes was real. There was no way I was going to sell him on two pockets of evil. “There was no fortune in that house, but we found a funny little room hidden in the walls behind the bedroom upstairs. You go back in there and you’ll find all the bodies you ever wanted and more.”

“That’s where you put them?” Crawford asked me, all straight-faced and serious.

I shook my head and looked away. “You can’t make a blind man or a fool see what’s right in front of them.”

“I see you fine, sir. I see you clear.”

“Tell me what you saw under the mountain that chased us across the desert.” I glared right into his face. “Tell me what you saw at the mill. You seem to have some need to pretend none of that really happened. Why is that, marshal?”

He wouldn’t look at me. I knew I’d hit some kind of nerve, but couldn’t decide if I wanted to dig at it or not. The man had already hit me once, and I was at his mercy for food and water.

Crawford waved me off. “You’ve already admitted being in the house. You’ve admitted the rest of the gang is dead. That’s enough to assume the rest.”

“You’re a fool,” I breathed out.

Don’t know if I said yet, but Crawford told me later that he never went to the ranch, nor talked to the strange bone-collecting family of the dark magic boy. Never saw the house with the hidden room holding a pack of grey shit-covered blind slave men. He got a little secondhand report from local law on his way through, but moved on after me quick. Still after me for lightweight stuff I’d done before the gang and all their bullshit that got pinned on me as the only survivor.

So, he was bluffing his knowledge of any of that. Was getting me to tell on myself the way lawmen have always done with dumb crooks like me since time out of mind. Like every other stupid prisoner before me and after me, I almost just kept talking until I spilled everything.

He'd be super surprised when all the shit I didn't tell him came crashing back down on top of us all. Hell, I knew every bit of it, and I was still surprised.

Crawford and Syne prepared a supper from supplies they'd picked up in town. Cheaper than a room plus meals, I suppose. Made me eat there, back tied to a tree and my hands bound together where my wrists were starting to get raw.

And then we were interrupted.

Preacher came to see us and didn't look so good. Yellow in the skin and the eye whites. Face had a waxy glisten to it. Shiny and flat at the same time, it made him look less than human, lower, somehow.

When he spoke, saliva strung from his top and bottom jaws or palates or whatever the hell you call them. Stuck to his teeth. Slimed over his tongue, which was thrush white.

"I want to pray with you," he said. "The Lord has warned me about you in a vision. Your path is dark and beset by demons from Hell."

"Sure is," I said.

"We appreciate it, Reverend," Marshal Crawford said. His hand rested on the butt of his iron at his hip. I found myself appreciating him a little bit for that move. Maybe he had a scent for danger after all. The preacher smelled pretty sour, too, though. "We can always use prayers, but I might ask you keep your distance from our prisoner. He's a dangerous sort, so remote prayer might be best here."

The preacher tottered forward and then back again. "Oh, but we all need redemption and forgiveness. We all need grace and a chance to repent and a warm cunny from time to time. Let me bow the knee with the prisoner and the stranger, dear knight."

Blood dribbled dark from one nostril. The preacher swiped the back of one hand through it and smeared it over his grizzled cheek, almost to the earlobe. Looked like a shit stain and was almost the same color, even while the smeared blood was still wet.

"No, he's right," I said, tied to my tree with my hands bound in front of me. "I'm awful dangerous, a real desperado. A bandito not quite ready for the Savior's touch. Best to pray me up from the church for now."

"Everyone is a sinner." The preacher's yellow eyes rolled and his bloody lip twitched in a rapid quiver, almost like it was ecstasy he was feeling instead of holy revulsion. Phlegm rattled in the back of his throat until I almost wanted to punch him to get him to finally clear it. "All wet with it from bloody birth. Hell, people wouldn't sin except that it feels so good. Right? The Savior is ready for your dirty, filthy, scum-soaked heart. Pray with me, son."

Crawford placed a palm against the hollow of the preacher's chest and stunted the holy man's forward progress. All I could do was cower against my tree prison.

At the time, I thought the preacher might have drank himself yellow. Bad liver is what it is, but we didn't know those fine details back in that day. Thinking back, could have been yellow fever. It sprouted up from time to time back then out there. Would fit with the theme of the curse I've been telling you about. Can't swear to it, though, as we had nowhere to process stool or snot samples like you can do for me today.

The preacher's shirt bunched up and flapped against him as he pushed back and Crawford planted to hold his ground. It served to show how skinny the guy was, or had gotten.

Preacher looked down at Crawford's offending hand and then back up at the marshal, like he was spoiling for a fight. Annabelle moved around flank and behind the preacher a bit. Looked like she was preparing in case it come to that.

"You standing in the way of the Lord, cocksucker?" the preacher growled from between his teeth.

Crawford actually laughed out loud. It was somewhere between a fuck-you laugh and legitimate good-natured amusement. Caught the addled preacher off guard and he eyed the lawman, more confused than fevered angry anymore. The marshal said, "Don't think that's what this is about, friend. How about you and I take a walk? I could use a little holy counsel with the things I've seen out here lately."

"Yes?"

The preacher started to go along. Allowed himself to be turned and even made a couple steps away from our half-assed camp.

Annabelle Syne circled back between me and them. They'd been working together a while, I could tell. Had their little dance and unspoken language down. I remember, in that moment, when I almost forgot the preacher, started to believe that business with the preacher was done, I thought it was inevitable this pair was going to catch me. They had their shit together and I was just bumble-fucking my way through life, from one disaster to another. As long as they wanted me, they were going to catch me in time. Time was always going to be on their side. If I really learned that lesson then, I might have saved myself a ton of trouble.

Might have lost that train of thought because the preacher roared out a string of nonsense that might have been curses. He threw his arm and rolled Crawford's hand off his elbow. I'm not sure if it caught him by surprise, if the preacher was stronger in his anger, or if Crawford decided it was best to create some distance once the preacher made it clear he was going to escalate.

"Settle it down, mister," Syne said, with her hand on her weapon.

"I'm going to pray for that man. I'm going to see his soul home to the Heavenly Father's blood-stained hands. Christ himself will wipe the ass of his bandit's heart clean of all the shit of sin. He will be clean and forgiven through spilled blood. You can't stop the spill, you bastards. It's already spilled for you and me, you rat-bastard cock-licking Philistine whoremongers."

"Maybe we just let him kneel down and pray from where he is," Syne said, "to have it over with."

"Keep that crazy coot away from me," I said. "I'd rather kneel in prayer under the black mountain with the grey men."

"I kneel for no man. I'm God's messenger and I stand in his stead." The preacher was slobbering and swinging wild, as Crawford stood back out of range. Crawford did draw his weapon and I braced myself to see the marshal shoot a preacher dead. The guy was batshit, of course, but killing a preacher was a hell of a thing, even under those conditions. Preacher man wasn't done, though, and a modest crowd was forming up the dirt street to see what all the commotion was about. "I am God. I will wave my holy cock and deliver my communion scum onto the lips and over the tongue of every child of the Most High. I'll cover you with it for the forgiveness of sins until you all glisten with my sticky grace. See if I don't, cock-licker."

The preacher started undoing his trousers and staggered forward. Crawford lifted the gun and then brought the grip down hard into the center of the preacher's forehead with a mighty crunch. The man wavered on his feet a moment, his hand still clawing at his crotch and partially undone britches. Blood leaked thick down between his eyes, dripping heavy off the pointy tip of his nose and then, as the flow picked up, other trails ran down over his lips.

The man parted his lips a little and flicked his tongue out a couple times, all reptilian. He tilted his wounded head back and gazed up into the skies above the sharp bowl of valley the frontier town occupied. That clear blue sky must have looked apocalyptic red through all that mess staining his face and running through his eyes at that point.

He whispered like a man in the throes of passion, "Which is shed for you."

The preacher staggered backward. He bobbled about, trying to keep his feet under him in the street. His knees tried their best to unhinge under him, but never quite brought him down at first. He had the chicken dance going, like those UFC fighters when they catch one hard across the chin, you know what I mean? There'd be a whole lot more chicken legs in the octagon if marshals could take their irons across a guy's forehead like that, believe you me.

The guy vomited up a toxic yellow paste, many shades worse than the hue of his skin. It mixed all rancid down the front of his shirt with that wash of blood from a bitch of a headwound Crawford delivered on the profane pastor.

Then, the fucker finally fell hard on his left side in the middle of the way and was out cold. His eyes were half open, but he was still breathing. Snoring, really, like he was choking on blood, but he couldn't have swallowed or inhaled all that much. Must have been a preexisting thing.

Well, the fucking town of Sugar Brush or Honey Brush, or wherever the hell we were, lost its collective shit. Those people poured out of every door like they was packed in there clown-car style, just waiting for an excuse to mob up.

They had an excuse now, it seemed. They were out for blood and the preacher's split skull wasn't enough for them.

25

CRAWFORD AND SYNE backed away, both with their guns at the ready, but they weren't standing between me and the danger anymore. It almost looked like they were ready to jump on their horses and make a run for it. Not sure what that would have meant for me.

The voices overlapped each other. The horses snorted and sidestepped. Hell, the animals were more spooked by the energy of the mob than I recall them being by the fucking bone devils.

They might as well have been saying nothing because I couldn't make out a word of it.

"Hold the horses," Crawford said, down and to the side.

Their dance was a little off at that moment because Syne held her weapon out and down to her side, she had her boots spread a bit wider under her for a better base, and there was space between her and him, but she made no move to follow his order, no indication she even heard it.

Her eyes were on the crowd that was lathering up by the second, advancing in slow little shuffled steps, making sure the others had the same idea before anyone rushed forward all alone. There were a few guns in the crowd, but not a lot. One rifle I could see held across a dude's chest near the back. He didn't have a clear shot from there, but you never know in a situation like that if it's going to matter to him. There may have been a shotgun someone else held down low back there, too, but couldn't see that clearly from where I was on my ass tied to that tree.

More blades, for sure, I remember that. Knives, but also a guy in a leather apron shook one of those butcher chopper things. What are they called? Shit, I know this. Give me a . . . chef's dirk? No, a cleaver! He had one of those.

"Annie, wake up, lady! Hold the horses. Now, please."

She sort of woke up from whatever had a hold of her then. Blinked herself back into the moment. Pulled her eyes away from the crowd and looked on her boss man. Her eyes were still wide and darty. Lips opened in a sex doll 'oh' before she closed them tight. And they were blue. Her lips were thin and blue with bloodless fear.

Like I said before, it seems like I got a lot of detail on certain things before I blank out on stuff most other times. When I'm in the flow, though, there are certain moments and certain details that hooked onto a deep emotion at the time and rode that memory hook hard and wet all the way up until now. I can fill in and figure out the rest as needed.

I remember her fear and her blue lips well, because I lost respect for her. I went from seeing her and him as inevitable, to seeing her as his liability, Crawford's Achilles heel. I'd pay for that miscalculation in time, but that was my takeaway after glimpsing the truth right before, when it was just the preacher they was dancing around.

"The horses, Annabelle. Get them by the reins, please."

She sort of came back into herself the rest of the way and took firm grip on the horses' leather, like he'd told her three times before she did it once.

Crawford faced full forward, took a couple steps into the mobs' faces, and the bastards in the front actually backed up a step. I don't know whether they over or underestimated their odds in that moment, but that was when they lost. He brought the business end of his sidearm up only but a hair and fired thunder into the town's dirt street. He punched a dark hole into Hell between his boots and theirs. They skittered and danced back and to the sides, like he was doing the Mexican bullet dance with them.

I know that's not kosher to say anymore. Pretend I didn't, if it offends you. I'm just used to telling it that way the few times I did over the years. I usually only got to talk to the other whites in the prisons I been in.

I think it's interesting he fired into the ground. Folks don't do warning shots very often for real, not now or back then. Again, that's a lot of TV and pulp western stuff. I hear cops aim down when they hold their weapons ready these days. I know what I know from TV. They used to hold them up in the old cop shows, as I recall, aiming up on God and Heaven as they snuck about and peeked around corners when shows were still black and white. When people did fire off guns in the old days, they did tend to fire into the sky. More dramatic. Of course, all those fucking bullets come back down eventually. There might have been more space between folks back then, but there are stories about innocent people taking dead from a bullet coming down some miles away after some yahoo took a notion to shoot into the sky for effect.

But Crawford fired his free shot into the ground. Might have been advanced lawman instinct. Could have been he was ahead of his time. Not all marshals were worth a shit, but I had the combination of fortune and misfortune to catch the one that seemed to know best before most other folks figured it out. That was just one example, I guess.

Didn't seem like great instinct to me at the time, firing a shot when a mob, some of them armed with lead themselves, were wilding and strung high like that. I expected that to set off a massacre of flying bullets. I was low, but also tied to the wrong side of the tree for it to protect me from any strays.

But the crowd got quiet and the guns in play stayed at bay for the time being. Solid instincts, like I said. Just couldn't get his rational brain around the irrational realities of the situation we were in.

"You need to get this man some treatment and stop acting the fools like this," Crawford said with authority, as if stating the obvious to children. He motioned at the bleeding preacher on the ground with his unarmed hand.

A few folks, including some women who came out with knives ready for action, moved to comply.

The man with the cleaver pointed it at Crawford. "You hit him. I saw you. He never did ill to any man and you opened up his head, a man of God."

The crew moving to help hesitated, and the crowd started to accuse the marshal of foul play again. Crawford's gun hand twisted and turned at his side, ever so slightly. Might have been indecision, a moment of it, anyway. I don't believe another shot into the ground would've been received the same way as the first. Unless he was going to plug one of the ringleaders, maybe the loudmouthed butcher, then his next bullet was going to be wasted effort. And shooting one of them wouldn't have done much for his case of self-defense.

"The preacher ain't himself," Crawford shouted.

"Not after you took after him," one woman said. I think she might have been a whore by trade, as I recall the look of her.

The crowd actually laughed a little at that. Whores are generally funny, I find, from my limited experience.

"Look at him," Crawford ordered. Again, a few of them did. "Not the red of his unfortunate injury. I'm talking the hue of his skin. The pallor of his face. He's sick with something, and it has him behaving in a manner that would embarrass him in his normal, lucid state. He tried to force himself upon us and our prisoner in his confusion. He wouldn't be swayed and had to be dissuaded. This isn't about us. It's about him, and he needs our help now until he returns to health. Not just from his bloodied scalp, but the fever that got him that."

"I don't know what all those words mean," someone said.

"He's saying the preacher was addled with fever," someone else answered. "Sick. Or possessed. You saying our pastor's possessed?"

"No," Crawford said, with an air of barely restrained patience, "not possessed. Sick with some fever and delusions."

"Big words again."

I was leaning toward possession. I also got a notion in my head. Wasn't a proud moment, but I wanted out.

"He's lying," I yelled from the tree where everyone had mostly forgotten me. "Untie me. They aren't law. They're lunatics, robbing and killing all up and down the countryside. They took me captive from my own church and have done all manner of unspeakable things to me. They are attacking preachers all across the country because they're crazy."

"What'd he say?"

Crawford cut his eyes at Syne and that's all the signal she needed as she moved around behind him and toward me.

"What's going on here?" the man with the cleaver wanted to know.

"Does this man have family?" Crawford demanded.

Everyone seemed taken aback by that, caught off their guard.

Someone finally answered, "He has a son from his widow back east, and a new wife about to give him another one any day now."

As Syne knelt in front of me and glared at me, I got off one more barb. "He just wanted to pray with me. That's all. And the marshal hit him."

She covered my mouth and nose with one gloved hand. It smelled more like ass than leather. Tasted like shit, too. I tried to lick and bite her through it, but failed.

Looking back, I probably screwed up my ploy to undermine them when I called him a marshal right there at the end. I forgot the story I was weaving off the top of my head.

The crowd was ignoring me again as the bitch tried to smother me one-handed.

"He needs to be cared for now." Crawford pitched his voice low. The crowd nearly leaned forward to hear him better. "For the town's sake, for his sake, but most of all for his dear family's sake. Tend his wound, please. Nurse past this fever that has him acting so unlike himself. I'll, of course, help pay for his care, but please, just get him off the street, would you?"

I tried to use my double fists tied together in front of me to hit her or shove her away as my vision got spotty, but she pushed my hands down and away from her chest. She was a lot stronger than she might appear at first glance.

The crowd moved slow. As the preacher was carried away bodily and his head wound compressed, the group finally broke up.

Syne let me breathe and I gasped wet oxygen past my slobbery lips. "Trying to kill me."

She braced herself on the tree above my head and brought her knee into my gut as she stood. I barked out in pain and was a couple more seconds before I could suck in painful air again.

"That was a jackass thing to try at a time like that," Crawford said.

"You expected me to behave myself when you keep hitting me?" I demanded.

"You're lucky I didn't let that preacher make good on his offer to baptize you in his scum," Crawford said.

"Was the fever that had him acting so, you think?" Syne asked.

"No other explanation I care to consider," Crawford said. "We best make it through the night and leave ahead of the sun in the morning."

I wanted out of town, too, even if it meant dragged behind the horses again. I didn't care for the idea of leaving in the dark.

Crawford did the best he could with that situation, but he would regret sending that sick preacher back to his family.

26

I SNAPPED AWAKE feeling like my chest was crushed, knowing I was in the claws of those fucking bone monsters. No more poison scratches turning horses inside out. They were going to rip into me and harvest out ivory, taking what they wanted from the choice bits, and leaving the rest in the open for the flies, and eventually the vultures. Or worse, they would tear out my eyes, pack the holes with shit, and make me their grey man.

"I can't breathe. Let me breathe," I begged, before I realized I was begging the lifeless ropes around me that had me tied to the tree.

I tried to settle down a little, but the night was all commotion and the sleepy mob had roused into shouting again. I was still in Sugar/ Honey Brush and the beasts that haunted the land, out from under the mountain where I'd disturbed them, were free to come get me whenever they pleased.

"Untie me. Don't leave me here to die."

I still hadn't spied Crawford or his girl since waking up to chaos.

People ran past the patch where I was tied and continued past my view, toward the heart of town, such as it was, behind me. I tried to squint into the darkness to see what might be chasing them past me. I knew it was out there, but I couldn't see the hills the road passed up and over that cut this valley so deep and sharp. It was too dark for that and the little bit of light from lanterns behind was not close, but was still enough to make the night tougher to see through. Wasn't like today, where towns are high lit through the night with bottomless electricity.

More folks ran back the other way and out into the deep dark my eyes couldn't penetrate, like they was looking for death and he couldn't get here fast enough for them with his bone demons in tow. I couldn't see the part of town these new folks came from behind as they vanished into the darkness ahead.

It didn't occur to me the first folks running into town were running toward something instead of away from a thing. That was that fatal goodness that people still had in them after all the bad in the world. Might have been sick curiosity, too. That night might have cured them of any running-toward-trouble instincts of helpfulness.

The hollering hit a crescendo at that point. People tripped and bumbled by in a scatter.

A woman ran past from the direction of town and the chaos. Her dress was barely on her. She was covered in blood, drenched in it. Her run turned into a stagger because she kept tripping on a gory rope of meat that dangled out of her and tangled around her feet. She didn't fall, not just then, but she got turned around not far up the road from my assigned seat.

That's when I saw her holding her ghost of a belly, the place where her belly used to be. It took me a while to figure out what she was doing and why, like trying to pick out the hillsides in the dark beyond the lights of town. It wasn't a belly, see? It was a gouged-out hole, through her dress, through her flesh, through her womb. She held her sticky hands in front of that open, barren cavern carved into her middle. It was a phantom thing, a habit of supporting the expectation of coming life for all those months, and the confused horror of it all being gone in a way she couldn't possibly imagine, not in her right mind, certainly not after her husband the preacher hit her so many times, hard enough to dent in her head, and stabbed her enough to disfigure her face with the same razor he used to sterilize her.

See, I forgot the townsfolk said the preacher's wife was pregnant. And this bloody visage of a woman in front of me certainly wasn't with child any longer, had she ever been. The excavated fetus would be coming along shortly, I would discover.

The next horror in this visceral parade was the boy the preacher had by another marriage, if I remember the story right. He was tall for his age, but lanky and wiry in a way that made him look fragile. Maybe it would have been different if his clothes weren't cut almost off of him, and his skin weren't flayed to the bone in so many places. I'll never know what either of them looked like in life, before the bloodletting.

The boy reached for his mother with hands missing a few fingers. Those would be coming along shortly as well. She waved him off and backed away, still trying to shield her phantom womb from him. Her knees tried to buckle twice on her, but despite being gored out almost to her spine, she kept moving.

Dropping his butchered hands down by his sides again, in a gesture that looked so much like childish disappointment, he made sort of a quarter turn away from her retreat and toward my captivity. His face was all carved to hell. Looked like his father was trying to create a pattern of cuts at first, but then got impatient and sloppy, or the boy started struggling. There was a bloody slice across one of his eyeballs that continued into the cheek and around to the ear. The other cuts varied in depth, but were not as long or quite as jarring as that one that left the scrawny preacher's kid half blinded.

"Why's this happening to me?" he whispered. Wasn't sure if he was looking at me because his eye was hidden by that long slash, but I didn't have an answer for him anyway. Maybe because we went under the black mountain and violated some treaty we didn't know we were observing. Maybe because my stupid-ass gang decided a ranch house in the middle of nowhere was a soft target.

I could tell he was the preacher's kid. Even all carved up like that, being mostly skin and bones, and years off from being a man, he had that haunted look about him. Not the recent madness of his father, but the sort of desperate distant look that men who hear God in a biblical way get. Like prophets sent to wander in a desert turning donkey wild, I mean. This kid might have grown up to be a decent god-fearing man, even with his father wound up in frontier evangelism, but that wasn't in the cards for him anymore.

His father, the town preacher, bolted into view with striking force. He only held a fold open straight razor, but swept it through like a broadsword. All the skin around the boy's neck and throat turned loose at once, contracted, and wrinkled up with all the pressure off. Seemed like too much skin for a boy his size. Everything inside his throat, cords, pipes, and sub-dermal insulation broke up in a series of pops. Strings of flesh and gristle, that hadn't quite severed with the initial force of the partial beheading, stretched to their breaking points and let loose, too.

The boy's arteries gave one mighty gush into the night air and then they quit on him, too. I saw his wet vertebrae, stacked neat between his skull and the rest of his skeleton, getting a breath of fresh air through the new vent through his neck stump. I saw the root of his tongue from the underside twitch, as he maybe considered speaking, but no longer had the ability or will. Watched him fold to the ground with a look of terrible shock and surprise in his one good eye.

In the untold time it took him to fall, couldn't have been long, but everything was fear-stretched in that moment, the humidity changed around me. I took a light misting that I only later on realized might have been the spread out moisture in the night air from all that blood that got power ejected out of him on one violent pump. I smelled the minerals of it.

The woman, the preacher's wife, kept one hand defending what had been lost within her already, and the other out in a warding gesture. That bloody hand shook and curled into the fingers of a witch losing her battle. "You stay away. You've done enough. You've done enough!"

The preacher was a sheen of fever sweat. The bandage around his head had yellowed with the effusions of his wounded forehead, dark in the center and spreading thinner out from there.

He'd managed to not get a speck of his boy's humid blood on him, even after all that butchery, on and off the scene, even after turning his son into a geyser of blood before dropping him the final time. Of course, it was dark, so maybe I missed it, but they were close enough for me to spy the root of his son's tongue, so there was that. I could see his skin had yellowed a bit more, made him look like old wet parchment in the night. If his son's blood provided the extra moisture and swampy metallic stink in the air, the burn of fever in the preacher exuded off of him like a blast furnace to add the heat to the humidity.

Then, I spotted his hand. Heard it before I saw it. Was making a smacking, squishing sound. It was the hand not holding the razor, the one down by his side, all covered in gore and leaking each time he flexed his knuckles through the nastiness caked there.

Got a little something on him after all. Wasn't from his son, not the born one anyway.

He mumbled at first, but then loose fingers dropped out from between his teeth and lips. They pattered to the grassy ground around his bare feet. There were his son's missing fingers. "It's as much mine as it is yours, you dirty harlot."

He held up the gory hand to show her. He showed her what he had taken out of her. I'd seen babies before. I'd even seen dead ones, including a stillborn, all purple and cold. This was something different. Greasy with the clear fluids from the womb, it wasn't enough to wash out the scarlet gore the preacher had to raze and claw through to dig out their preborn child. Was still an impossibly small thing, less than a doll, but formed along enough for me to recognize a head, sealed eyes, a pooched mouth, and the fetal curl of what would have been a body in the making, if the father's fingers hadn't been forced through the goo of its back and chest, mushing it all around as he kept wiggling his fingers, making its alien form quiver and dance like a profane puppet.

She backed away from him, but her legs were finally starting to give. She still warded and protected as if the unborn still dwelled within her, instead of breaking apart on her husband's squishing fingers. One stub of an arm fell into the grass amongst the larger fingers of the fetus' dead brother. Chunks of unformed flesh, that included curled legs, broke off from the body. Then, the head rolled away and bounced along the ground, almost to the born son's open throat. The preacher kept twiddling those fingers in the mush long after the aborted fetus was minced away all around the grass.

Her legs buckled and she hugged herself around her missing belly on the way down into her own fetal position. He charged and caught her head in both his hands, as if to cradle her fall. One hand still held the razor. The other was covered in primordial dead baby guts.

He gave a deep growl and twisted her head around backward with a snap. The razor might have helped the process, but he kept twisting, pulling, and tearing with brute force, first stretching her neck and then ripping it away, with all the connections pulling up out of her body with it.

I swear she was dead before she hit the ground and he caught her. She had to be dead when he separated her head from her body.

But I still heard that endless shrill screaming echoing all through the valley.

No one was sleeping anymore, no one for miles. I'd seen them running hither and yon, leading up to this family massacre, all through the street in both directions, but now there wasn't a soul in sight as the preacher turned his attention on me at me tree. He let his wife's head roll out of his grasp, and from his mind and heart, like he'd let his unborn child break apart between his fingers.

The sick preacher approached me at my tree for the second time that day. This time, no marshal or lady assistant to intervene on my behalf. This time, he bore a well-used razor before him. With it, he could cut me free or cut me open. I didn't like my chances.

The portion of his bandage over the wound was glued in place by the seepage there, but a loop of bandage drooped down over the top of one wild eye.

He wasn't close yet, but too close for my liking, and close enough that I could see he had specks of gore on his lips and in his teeth.

As he shuffled forward, he said to me, "I see you for what you are. You are the darkness. It clings to you. No mere sinner, you. You are the sickness. You did all of this with my hand. I don't need to pray for you. I need to cast you out. Send your soul into a drowning pig. Rid the world of you to make room for the light again. What say you, dark man?"

"You killed your wife and son," I said. "Worse than any animals ever were. Don't blame me for that. I wasn't even there."

"You were there. You were the shadows in the corner of my room, and the corners of my head. You are the darkness, but I get your meaning. I'm not forgiven, so let's go back into Hell together. You can show me the way."

He knelt down with his heavy knees pressing into my thigh muscles with agony. I braced myself to feel the bite of the razor he used with surgical accuracy and barbaric force. It was his clean and sticky hands, both, that I felt instead though. One side of my face smeared with fetal blood and tissue. The other slid slick with my own sweat and his rough grip. He breathed into my face and it smelled of a slaughter house. Maybe that slaughter poured down a spoiled well and allowed to fester in the moist mineral stink down there. I'd seen him spit out the fingers, but I wondered how much of that he had swallowed. He was just as likely to bite off my nose and lips as he was to slice through me with his practiced blade.

Before I could try to come up with any clever words to try to save my soul from the bloodthirsty preacher, the first shots whizzed by, without stinging anything along the way. The next ones punching into or past the tree. Bark sheered off one side and scattered into the blood-humid wind. Bullets that planted into the trunk near my head, instead of passing through into my brains, kicked off larger chunks of bark that scraped my scalp and bounced off of his face, shoulders, and chest.

The preacher recoiled and sliced through my shirt and skin at my bicep on his way off me. He spit out something onto my shirt and maneuvered just a bit to keep the tree between him and the unseen posse of shooters. That kept me in the line, too.

"I'm not looking for any trouble," he said. "You run on now, and let me handle God's business here in the wilderness. I forgive you, but get your sorry asses away from me, brothers."

They responded with another volley. At least one was a shotgun blast, but I think it might have been two or three of those. My other shoulder, that hadn't felt the razor, took the hornet stings of buck. If I'd taken those pellets straight on, they'd have chewed me apart. It might have been on a graze, but still hurt like a motherfucker. One of the wraps of rope on that side busted loose and whipped around to pop me on the face, right beside my nose. Made my eye water and hurt almost as much as my abused shoulders.

"Heathen whores!"

Another lone shot winged him and staggered him out to the side a half dozen steps, like he was shucking and shuffling a dance move exit from the stage. In a way, he was. They unleashed on him at that moment, wasting lead and buckshot a plenty. They hit him several times, popping holes into him and tearing his flesh with his clothes. They missed a bunch, too, and ripped the pulp out of the tree just above my head where they'd previously stripped it of bark.

I think I might have been screaming for them to stop, but I don't remember. I know my throat hurt after and didn't stop until I left that wild-folk cabin up in the mountains.

The preacher still held the razor as he finally pitched back with his arms spread in a dead man's cross. Fell just so to have one boot propped up on his dead son's hip, and his neck cocked to catch pillowed on his wife's corpse's bosom. Didn't realize exactly how tall he was until that moment, where he stretched from one body to another. If his head had rolled a little the other way, his entire skull could have vanished inside her split-open belly. They formed quite the family portrait from the last ring of Hell.

I'd say all went quiet then, but it wasn't so. The shrill screaming continued unabated, so I realized it couldn't be coming from her.

Before I could process what that meant, the cracking noise started above my head and then turned into a groaning collapse. The top of the tree fell where the timber had been broken away too far by passing bullets. It missed crushing my head or legs, but a sharp spit of wood cut my shoulder long ways on the way down past my arm. It cut perpendicular to the razor wound on that same arm. Formed a bloody cross symbol on me, but the standing post section of the cross was proportioned wrong, so it looked to be upside down.

I was the darkness, right? A soul only worthy of casting into the drowning pig.

A few more loops of my rope broke loose in the process, giving me a little more slack to breathe deeper, which I needed in that moment.

"Marshal Crawford? Syne? Where are you?" My voice was all froggy and burned with my cries for help.

And I don't know if I could be heard over the screech and screams coming down from the hills. Coming down and getting closer, once I had time to focus in. Awful and familiar, they were.

"Oh, shit," I croaked to myself.

27

I WOULDN'T HAVE seen them at all, except that their motion was so jagged and exaggerated. I don't know. Maybe they found us because they smelled the blood our presence had inspired. I also saw them because the exposed bone that formed their skulled faces and their impossible limbs stood out from the rest of the darkness. They screeched up at the stars the way a wolf would bay at the moon.

The bone demons struck a few trees on their way down into the valley, shaking the tops and tearing a few out of the ground by the roots with sliding crashes, despite the size of some of them. They weren't sticking to the winding trails that people had formed, but were coming straight on.

In the darkness of this bloody night, there was no direct sunlight to heat them up and cause them to smoke. We were caught in their hour, their time of power.

Then, they fucking stopped again. Like they had down with the mill at the river, they pulled up short, making all sorts of noise as they tore at the ground with frantic energy. Did they want to kill me or just torture me from now on?

There was another motion. Not jagged, like the flailing bone monsters, but flitting, flashing from one location to another. It was weird and unreal enough for me to believe I was seeing things out of my shock and fear, but my recent experiences had taught me that what was real was not limited to what should be possible in the natural world anymore.

Where the hell was Crawford? That bastard tied me to a tree and then left me in the night for killer preachers, the bone devils hunting us, and whatever these new spirits were. They weren't all that new, it turned out. I knew them all along.

These appearing and disappearing figures flashed their way down into the valley and the town beyond, where the bone monsters had stopped short. As they did, the devils I knew lowered themselves to the ground. They stuck out their sharp bony snouts like they were sniffing out the air, or waiting for something in particular. A few pale tongues flicked out, tasting the violence on the breeze. In that moment, in that posture, they looked more like animals to me than the malevolent devil masters of the realm under the black mountain that I knew them to be. At least they stopped screeching and screaming for a while, but the townspeople I couldn't see from my place of captivity started up screaming in horror anew.

"God help me," I begged from my raw throat.

The first one appeared close enough for me to see clearly. Well, as clearly as I could focus on whatever they were. It was humanoid, I guess that word is for something that isn't quite us, but bears some markers of resemblance. Tan-grey skin and they wore drab suits, like proper gentleman on their way to church or some show. Kind of appropriate as the tall figure of the not-quite-man thing stood over the dead preacher and his slaughtered family in the blood-matted grass not far from me.

He tilted his head and examined the scene with his colorless dark eyes before raising those terrible eyes onto me in my helpless state. His hair was pitch black and greased down flat against his head, like the grass greased flat under his dress shoes.

His arms dangled long and unmoving down by his side. The thin fingers didn't shift at all. Maybe that wasn't entirely true, though. In one sense, maybe in one plane of existence, he didn't move at all. But around his edges, there was a static energy that crackled silently and made his outline waver in jerky motion.

He stared at me a moment longer before he flashed out of existence and instantly reappeared a few feet to the left, beyond the pile of bodies. He vanished and materialized on the road, several feet to the right. There his head was turned to the side so he could still stare at me on my tree.

Then, he vanished completely. I'm sure he probably reappeared somewhere deeper into town and accounted for some of that human screaming and panic going down outside my range of sight.

I started to remember then. I recognized who that flitty spirit reminded me of. Didn't think anything could scare me in the night more than the bladed preacher or the return of the bone devils, but then I remembered my terror in barely escaping the ranch house from the beginning of this tale, and all the dark evil that swirled inside there. It had flowed like black oil down the inside of the windows and dripped out of the broken glass onto the porch.

Crawford didn't bring me to them, but he held me up long enough for them to find me on their own. The whole evil family had arrived, it seemed.

I started making an effort to get my ass free of that tree finally. I'd even managed to push my feet back for a little leverage. The roping further down the trunk was still tight and cut into my gut as I applied upward pressure, but where the tree had broken off above me, I started forcing the top few loops up and over. I started to gain more slack and was able to push upward a little harder.

The figures continued to stutter flash through the town. I saw one grey-tan woman in a black dress and high boots, like she was dressed to mourn, manifest off to my side. She lifted an ornate handgun with an impossibly long barrel. She vanished again, but I assumed she hadn't left town. Shooting started up once more and screams followed.

Then, the boy appeared in front of me. He wore his little suit and had a four-barreled rifle rested over his shoulder and behind his neck, pointing absently over the buildings and up the valley wall. He stared right into my face with his dark and sunken eyes. His little mouth was a colorless somber line.

The dark, cold well smell now had its source.

This was the same kid from the ranch who had laid waste to those other boys in my gang. The same one I had barely escaped out into the sun as he tried to flash out there with me and failed. Now, it was night and he'd followed me up into these mountains. The marshal had tied me down for him, and with Crawford nowhere around, I started to draw the paranoid notion that this was the rendezvous point. This was where the preset meeting had been arranged to hand me back over for their grey man room behind the master bedroom of the ranch. The preacher had just been a coincidental inconvenience to this moment.

It was still a long time to morning, but I wasn't sure the sun would save me anymore, even if it was a deterrent to these creatures.

The boy reached out to me with one hand. Unlike the older spirits still flitting in and out of existence through the town, this boy had planted himself solid in front of me. I tried to twist away from his touch, but it was no use. Even in my attempt to free myself, I'd just managed to jam myself up into a half squat, with less room to shift myself one way or the other.

He took hold of my throat, as if to choke me. At first, the cold felt healing, and I started to think that was his purpose. Then, the cold turned to burning and I did feel choked. I closed my eyes against the pain.

The only thing I wanted in that moment was to be anywhere but there. I squeezed my eyes shut and wished for it to all be over. In my fear, I felt like I was drifting out of my body. I could almost feel the ropes vanishing around me. Instead of rising up out of my body, I felt like I was pulling sideways.

From a distance, I heard the spirit boy give a small gasp. His terrible touch had left my throat and I pulled some air to celebrate.

I opened my eyes and looked into his terrible face as I crashed hard back into my body and the tight pain of my ropes.

He whispered in his childish voice, "You son of a bitch. You stole that from us."

I had no idea what he was talking about. We'd left with nothing from their haunted ranch. Well, I left with nothing. The rest of the gang never left.

His icy hand palmed my forehead. Gave me an instant ice cream headache. Wasn't but a second or two before the inside of my skull started to burn hot instead of cooling down from that still cold touch. He was going to cook my brain inside my head, and there was nothing I could do about it. Based on how we'd performed back at the ranch, I wasn't sure there was much I could do alone if I was free.

"Please, stop," I begged. "Please."

The boy's voice. My God. In that moment of confusion and burning pain, I thought I hadn't heard him speak before. As the words came out of him in that lisp, I remembered he had spoken to us in the house as he made short work of us. He had been talking about the prizes back then, those bones we uncovered in a trunk we had hoped contained treasure. I hated his voice.

"You will eat the sickness. You will go down with it. You will no longer use our power to spread your mayhem. It will all come back on you. Once you descend, we will feed on your energy and take back what is ours."

The prizes.

A tall man in a suit flashed into place, standing just behind the boy, where the man announced, "The hangman comes. Let's be gone for it."

Then, he was gone.

There was a guy at one of the prisons I found myself in later. Might have been Blood Mountain, now that I think on it. He fed crows with bits of his food. Drove the guards crazy. Once he had them trusting him, he'd use a pair of clippers or pliers, I don't remember exactly, and he'd fork the birds' tongues. Don't know if that was necessary or not, but then he taught them to speak. Not in a squawky parrot voice, but in a rough old man's husk. That's what that man sounded like with all his "hangman" and "let's be gone" bullshit.

The boy seemed to ignore whatever that man was about. He still worked to melt my brain with his dark magic, to punish me for invading his house and not staying to be captured like the others.

"You are a part of this now, and there is no escape for you. Only descent. So, you will go down for all you've done. You'll pay back the balance of the stolen energy. Traitors and deserters are always hated. We don't accept your desertion from our numbers, Stone. You'll come home one day."

Was something like that. He might have said some of that to me another time.

I cut my eyes to the side, sure I was going to die like he was prophesying, like he was demanding of me. I spied those bone devils up on the slopes, crouching like trained animals. I thought about them under their mountain, being attended by their blind slaves. I thought about them stopping across the water at the mill after they'd come all the way to find us. I thought it was the sun that stopped their pursuit but, at that moment, I wasn't so sure. Here in this valley, where they'd had me dead to rights, they'd stopped short yet again. They heeled like trained dogs and waited for the ghouls from the ranch house to arrive and go forward.

I turned my watering eyes back on the boy's sunken ones that couldn't have looked more disinterested and passionless as he cursed me in lispy tones and cooked my brains with his dead cold hand.

I'd still held fear in my heart for this boy, and now the adults that surrounded him in a dark magic tribe, but I had largely dismissed him into my past for the bone devils. I'd been distracted by all the cannibal bloody madness dogging us along the trails. Then, the return of the bone devils out in the open had me fixated on them as the gods of night set upon us. It never occurred to me until that moment, still tied to a stump in front of that boy, that these strange spirits might be the masters of the realms I'd uncovered, and the bony devils were a servant to them, the grey men being below all.

If the bone devils from under the black mountain sniffed us out and tracked us, it was for him, this terrible thing in the form of a boy, and for the others like him, but larger. I had the order of things wrong in my head, so here we were.

The funeral woman, with her long-barreled pistol smoking out the bore, popped into place off to the side, blocking my view of the patient bone devils up the slope. She didn't even bother to regard me as she spoke in a low, drawn, reverberating tone that made her sound out of time with what we'd always thought of as the real world.

"You linger too long. That is how we found ourselves here in the first place."

I had no idea what it meant, or what it had to do with me and all that happened, but I recognized it as a scolding. He looked away from me, but she and her obnoxious gun were gone from sight before he could engage her.

He pulled his hand away from my head and my head cooled off very, very slowly. The four-barreled rifle I had forgotten about swung off his shoulder and now aimed absently down at my crotch.

The boy reached down and I clenched up. He pulled with force and snapped the rest of my ropes. The crush pressure hurt through my chest and ribs. More bark peeled and shed off of what remained of the stump. I fell to my side in the matted grass, unsupported.

My hands were still bound separately as I struggled to get up. He leaned down close to me and I cowered. He took my wrists and used a single fingernail to slash through those ropes. The abused skin around my wrists stung and seeped from all the abrasion they had taken. I pulled my stinging but freed hands into my chest as the boy still leered over me.

"Your time is coming to an end." He stood back up and turned away. "Your days will be short and you will serve us, blind and empty, through the dark of endless night."

As he walked away, I was thankful to no longer have the barrels of his weapon trained on me, but I was most happy to no longer be under his empty, evil gaze. He strolled away with his strange gun down by his side, held by the stock. A leather strap with silver buckles dragged the dirt and grass.

The boy stood over the preacher's body and those of his family, head cocked and considering. He knelt again and palmed the dead preacher's forehead. I half expected the body to twitch, but it didn't.

The boy used the pad of his thumb to lift the loose strip of bandage, and one eyelid of the dead preacher with it.

After a long moment, more lingering, I guess, he disengaged the man and ran his finger through the inside surface of the dead woman's open womb. The boy brought that dark finger to his lips and sucked on it. There was a popping smacking noise as he pulled his fingers back out clean.

He reached down, yet again, and I expected him to go for a second taste. Instead, he picked up two of the son's severed and discarded fingers, the same ones that had been in the preacher's mouth not that long ago. The dark magic boy stuffed those in one of his pockets as a souvenir, a prize.

He just started to unbend his knees to stand and then he finally vanished. Him, his gun, and his prize fingers were finally away.

I stood slowly, looking for trouble. The spirits didn't appear anywhere I could see. The waiting bone devils weren't within sight either. Weeping spread through the town, but most of the lights had been extinguished, hiding the rest of the night's havoc from me. I'd seen enough of it from my tree which no longer held me.

I started walking. My legs were watery under me, but I made it to the dirt path that served as a street and kept walking with my back to town. I walked past the bodies and Crawford's gear. No idea where he was, and I didn't care.

Why had the boy cursed me and declared my days short and all that, but then cut me loose? Had to be toying with me, I decided. They laid in wait to take me down just as I believed I was free, but I kept walking.

Horse hooves pounded behind me and I staggered off to the side. The rider, a woman, raced past me and up the trail out of the valley. Any fears she had of savages had evaporated to the heat of the horror here in town.

My head was still hot from the boy's touch. I rubbed the raw skin of my wrists even though they stung like hell. I kept walking.

Another posse of four horses thundered by, the men fleeing the same direction as the woman.

I finally started up the incline of the trail and through the switchback pattern it cut up the valley wall. Where was I going? Anywhere but there.

You son of a bitch. You stole that from us.

Some more horses pounded up the slope and I stepped off to the side to let them pass. I was grabbed from my belt and under my jaw. Before I could think how badly I should be scared, Crawford hauled me bodily up onto his horse behind him.

He growled out at me, "You try anything more than to hold on tight, I'll club you addled and tie you to the horse's rump the rest of the night."

I held on tight. Wasn't thrilled about still being in custody, but I liked the idea of escaping on a horse better than trying to out-walk the monsters that had found us here.

The motion rose up through the high grasses to our right, and then above us on the left of the switchback. Those bony bastards were still on us. They galloped along beside us in a pincer move as they navigated the steep slope. We were not going nearly fast enough, nowhere near the speed we'd employed that allowed us to barely escape these creatures in the open desert.

Opened their skeletal snouts and screeched. Narrow black and white tongues, with needle points and whipping snake motion, flailed and vibrated right beside me on both sides. Then, they went from galloping to running hunched over. Reaching with terribly long clawed fingers, devoid of flesh, too many knuckles, I pulled my legs up under me behind the marshal as I clung to his coat.

I was all coiled together, trying to make myself as small as possible. I'd have vanished out of the world entirely at that moment, given the option, and probably the world would be a better place if I had. I was positioned as if I planned to leap off the back of the horse. In a movie, I'd land and roll, and without a scratch on me, but in the real world, I'd more likely snap my fucking neck. That might have been okay in that moment, too, but I was afraid I'd live and then the bone devils would have me as their reward for tracking me down for their dark-spirited teleporting masters.

I got that same queasy sideways out-of-body feeling again. The illness of that feeling was ultimately what made me not try anything.

The boy had told me my days were numbered, essentially, and at the time I believed him. This was it, I thought.

The devils clawed into the horses' sides and haunches. They weren't deep wounds, but I still remembered the animal turning itself inside out in the desert. I knew they were doomed and we were next.

The monsters didn't go back to galloping and they didn't reach out in time to snag us off the back of our rides. They stood up closer to their full heights, towering over us, even on horseback, and screamed up into the night sky. The animals spooked and almost threw me, hunched up on its back, so I dropped my legs back on both sides of it and held on tighter.

Marshal Crawford barked at me, "Stop messing around. I've had enough of you."

I think he'd had enough of being pursued by evils in the world that he couldn't explain and that his mind still didn't want to accept. I let it go, though.

I think the horses were slowing down as we topped the valley, but the bone devils had fallen behind and their incorporeal masters, as I now believed the unnatural family from the ranch house to be, were nowhere to be seen. At least that night, they had departed us.

28

THE HORSES DIDN'T turn themselves inside out this time, but they died horribly. Crawford and maybe Syne, too, might have suffered from those infections as well, if I hadn't already seen this happen and stepped in to warn them. Syne had a lot more sense about her than I gave her credit for most times, and even though her animal suffered, she kept her distance. If I'd kept quiet, everything that followed might have gone different a few possible ways. That was a long time ago, though, and we got no way of knowing beyond imagination and speculation. That's the work of fiction writers and I got no time for it. Hell, I guess I've had nothing but time in my life, but we'll move it along anyway.

The wounds were long and angry with infectious heat along the animals' sides where they lay on their sides beside the trail, heaving for air. The flesh, muscle, and fat under the scars pulsed out of time with each other. They swelled and diminished in patterns that had nothing to do with the rhythm of a heartbeat. It was like something was alive under there and trying to fight its way out. Maybe it was. Who the fuck knows? I'm no scientist or wizard.

I said, "Marshal Crawford, you're going to want to get back out of range. I seen this happen before and it gets messy, sir."

He ignored me. My raw wrists were still free and my tired head already ached, so I didn't want to push my luck too much.

Annabelle Syne said, real quiet like, "Elliot?"

He ignored her, too, and drew his weapon. He paced around his poor horse's back and aimed down on its head. One dark eye rolled up at him and then away, probably not seeing him at all. He fired and put the first out of its misery. I startled in a jolt, but Syne stayed rocksteady. Her horse gave a kick from the ground that almost caught Crawford's ankle, but missed him.

"You want to do yours?" he asked.

She shook her head.

"It needs to be done."

"I understand. I don't want to do it though."

He walked around to get position on the last horse's head.

The wounds on the dead animal were still pulsing. I wasn't surprised.

He blasted through the head of Syne's horse. She did flinch at that. I jolted, too, of course. I don't think her reaction had as much to do with the sound itself though.

The wounds started pulsing faster and more pronounced. I backed away and further up the trail from the cursed bodies, even though Crawford had told me to stay perfectly still if I knew what was good for me. Syne glanced at my slow retreat, but made no move to stop me. She backed up a step-and-a-half herself.

"Marshal," I said, "you're going to want to get back away from there in a hurry, believe me."

"Elliot, listen to him. Come away."

Crawford glanced between us and then back at the horses. He'd been convinced. He gave a half-hearted run out to where we were on the trail just before the ass end of his dead horse exploded, blasting black muck down the trail away from us several feet. A yellowish pus oozed out of the ruptured half and the front end of the horse deflated before our eyes.

"Father in Heaven," he said.

Her horse blew up in a series of a half dozen bursts, running from back to front, not leaving much of the body left. Green and yellow fluid geysered upward. We backed away a little more as that foul-smelling ejecta splattered in front of us near our feet. It sizzled and popped and spread There wasn't enough of the second carcass left to deflate.

"It's probably not over," I said quietly. "We should leave and keep going for a while at least."

Syne turned heel to take me up on my suggestion.

I turned to follow, but Crawford had me by the scruff of the neck. He hauled one saddle up onto my left shoulder. He then placed the weight of the second saddle, along with the bags, onto my other shoulder. I dropped to my knees and then my ass under the weight.

"Get up and walk, scoundrel."

"It's too heavy."

"Get up!"

"I've been walking for days. I'm beat. I can't carry that much," I said. "I just can't."

He took me by my shirt and either planned to haul me back up to my feet or to haul off and hit me again.

Syne stilled his hands, God bless her for that much, I guess. "I'll carry one, Elliot."

"He'll get himself up and carry what I tell him to carry, Annabelle."

This whole time, those globs of off-colored infection were popping and bubbling behind us, spreading slowly toward us.

"Marshal," she said, "we just need to go."

She hauled her saddle with her heavy bags onto her own shoulder and stepped away like that was settled.

He dragged me up to my feet with me holding his saddle, which was still a lot for me at that point. Crawford held out the leather reins in his grasp. "Put your wrists together and hold them out in front of you."

"I won't," I said.

"You'll do so on your own or after I make you bleed to convince you."

"My wrists are raw already. You need to let them heal. Just let me walk, sir. I got nowhere to go, even if I took a mind to."

"I'll tan your hide raw, if you make me ask again."

"Elliot," she said.

"Enough from you on this," he let her have a little of his verbal wrath, too. "You don't seem to appreciate your situation here, Mr. Wicked. Not one bit, I think."

"I understand plenty," I said. "You can't make sense of all the darkness you've seen on this trail, so you're being harder on me than you would as a result. There is no natural explanation for all this, but your eyes and mind don't want to buy into what you've seen. You're angry and I'm the only one here to take it out on. My wrists are ruined from your rope, and now your ropes and horses are gone from the monsters that dog us through the wilderness.

Tying me up isn't going to fix that. My wrists need to heal. Just let me walk and we'll get to wherever you think we're going some time."

"Stop your blabbing, Wicked." Crawford looped the leather over my head and fashioned it into a collar around my throat. "Have it your way. Now if you fall behind or try anything, you can choke for your trouble."

He gave the reins a yank and I gagged. We started up the trail again, leaving the awfulness of the dead, infected animals behind us. He paced beside me and a step ahead, with my leather leash hanging slack in his fist. I knew if I dropped back, he'd take the opportunity to yank a choke out of me. Syne carried a saddle and bags, too, on my other side and a half step back.

So, that's how we negotiated the rest of our time together. Plenty of bad nights and long days, with the unnatural screams of bony devils always within hearing in the depth of the night. We saw no one for a good while, but we were never alone out there.

And as if the mad preacher who shaved his family to death, including the unborn tissue he carved out of the lady of the house's belly, weren't a bad enough spiritual experience, the real religious nuts were still ahead of us, waiting.

29

I WASN'T FULLY awake when the first devil sunk its teeth into Syne. It lifted her, shook her, and swept her away into the forest. At least that's how it looked to me at the time. Seeing what had happened to the animals from just a scratch from those things, I figured a bite was the end of her.

I think she got her gun out of its holster and into her hand before the creature shook it loose from her grip. It might have flown right out of her holster from the violence of it all. Either way, I saw it land not far from me, but I didn't go for it. I just tried to get the reins off from around my neck.

Crawford mumbled out something. I think he was awake, but I didn't catch the words and I wasn't sure if he was talking to me, Syne, or the monster. He was on his feet over me, but not for long.

One of the monsters wrapped its long bony fingers around the marshal's ankles through his boots, wrapped his feet together, and yanked them out from under the man, dropping him to his face.

His eyes were wide with shock as he looked up at me without his hate, leaves in his hair, and just said, "Stone?"

The screech from the devil who had him raked all other sound out of the world. The thing took off in a one-armed gallop that was very primate-like. I didn't know a thing about chimpanzees back then, but that's what that thing was like, tearing through the forest in a mad dash frenzy.

Crawford zipped away from me, dragging along the ground on his face. Thought that was the last I'd see of either of them and figured I was next. My days were numbered, I'd been told.

Oh, shit, I kind of started in the middle of things there, didn't

I? There were a lot of terrible nights out on the trails after things started to go bad for me following the ranch house. Getting woke up by the devils, after they final took a notion to lay into us, was sure one of the worst.

Anyway, they had Syne and just took Crawford, leaving me. That's what I thought had happened.

But I didn't get my head loose of the leather fast enough and Crawford had been sleeping with the other end of the reins wrapped tight around his fist. So, as he was spirited away, the leather pulled taut and cut off my airway entirely. Felt like the top of my head got torn off as I jerked sideways off my feet and I dragged across the ground, too.

I looked for anything to hold onto. I clawed at the grass and dirt, rolling to one side and then the other, but it was no use. Wasn't getting a whiff of air through my pipes either. I had to try to claw at the straps around my neck, but those leather cords were dug in deep to the soft tissue around my throat and neck. I could barely feel it in the furrows imprinted in my flesh. Couldn't get my fingertips or nails between the leather and myself. I was fading fast.

Rocks tore at my clothes and cut into my skin after ripping through those. Crawford and I crashed through a fallen log, taking it apart with our bodies. Slamming trees and bouncing through ditches, there was no relief. The monster had Crawford, and me by proxy. It wasn't letting up. He was going to drag the skin right off of us and shred us down to bones before he stopped. I was going to be choked to death long before that, for whatever consolation that was. Then what? I don't know. Add us to a bone collection under the black mountain, or in the hidden trunk of treasures under the floor of the black magic ranch house of angry boy spirits.

I had no choice but to get myself loose. I started pulling the straps up and over my chin. Really had to dig those reins over my Adam's apple. I tasted blood, even though I couldn't breathe. My eyes would be a smear of blood from the broken vessels. Felt like I tore my lips and nose off getting them over my head.

I caught one gulp of air and then the remaining loops of leather tightened my throat back closed. I had to repeat the process again. The whole time I was being dragged through the woods and cut to pieces on the rough terrain.

Before I finished, I think I blacked out. More likely, I finished getting myself free, but the lack of oxygen stole the memory.

Either way, I finally got myself loose of my leash and I tumbled to a stop, watching Crawford vanish into the darkness of the night without me. He was facedown as he left, and probably not conscious anymore.

I hurt like a motherfucker, bleeding from everywhere, oxygen starved down to the cellular level, my throat raw and bleeding. I just lay there, swallowing over and over between gasps for air. Felt like I was swallowing fire and gargling blood.

My ears rang, but I could still hear the screeching. It sounded distant, but not gone. Not sure if they were farther away in that moment, or if it was my fucked hearing from the damage I'd taken. They were still there though.

I got to my feet and just picked a direction to flee. I could have been going in circles or back the way we came, for all I knew. I was bleeding from everywhere. My clothes were in shreds. I just staggered from tree to tree all through the night. I barely made it to the next place to lean before I would have fallen on my face. Kept going like that.

The night lasted forever and I was going at no speed at all, but the screeching died off around me. They'd left for now, happy with what they had taken in those two law dogs, or they was saving me for later.

I just kept going, almost mindless at that point. Not even sure you could call it survival instinct anymore.

It wasn't morning yet, wasn't light in the least that I noticed, when I finally heard the voice address me off to my left.

"Are you the one I seek, or should I wait for another?"

30

I WAS SCARED SHITLESS. I pissed myself and my ragged clothes, I know because it burned as it leaked out, like pissing razorblades. I was all fucked up inside from getting dragged.

That wasn't no man's voice. I turned my head, expecting to see the spirit boy back to harangue me one more time. Playtime was finally over and he was here to collect me for grey man duty.

It was a woman, though. Her hair was fluffy and wild, dark and tangled. The remains of a forgotten braid still wound up in the impossible nest of her hair. Dirt and old dried mud cracked through the flakes of her own dry skin ringed around her face, up under the edge of her scalp, and down her arms and legs.

She wore bear skins and nothing else. It was a time I didn't see many women at all, clean or otherwise, and they didn't show much skin when they did. Even most of the whores covered up when they were out where the public could see.

She smelled, of course. It was a wild, dirty smell, but had a musty quality over it. Powerful stuff, like she had slathered herself with animal fat to keep the insects off of her.

"What?" I said, as I held onto a tree with small gnatty insects crawling over me and my freshly clotted cuts. I stunk, too, mind you. No deodorants to speak of back then, you know. I'd been dragged behind a horse's ass for days since my last bath. I was foul with ball sweat and body odor stink. Of course, I'd added a little bit of a piss smell into what was left of my clothes, too.

"Are you the one I should expect, or am I waiting on another, dear sir?"

I still just stared at her, dumbfounded. "I don't know what . . .

I'm . . . I don't know what you're expecting or not. I'm lost. Chased by monsters not of this world. I'm probably going to die out here, one way or the other."

"If you live somewheres long enough, you'll surely die there, too."

"I . . . well, I meant I was on my way to dying before my time."

"We can't have that. You need tending to keep that from happening."

I didn't know if she was asking me or telling me. Running into a lone woman in the middle of the woods was about as strange as anything else I've told you up to this point, you understand. I was exhausted and half out of my mind from overexertion and coming down off a fear high.

"I don't know where I am or what I'm supposed to do," I said. I was on the verge of tears.

She reached out to me and I recoiled. Actually hit the side of my head on the tree I was holding. She paused, but then placed her hand against my forehead. It was rough and calloused, like the hand of a working man. I shivered under her touch because it reminded me a bit of the burning cold touch of the spirit boy who had marked me and found me again, not that many days past at that point.

I let my eyes slide closed and almost fell to sleep standing up there.

"You burn with fever," she said. "You have taken ill while being lost, dear man."

"I've been exposed to a lot lately."

"My name is Avalon," she said. "My cabin is a hike from here, but it's the closest thing. You'll never survive trying to make it anywhere else."

"I'm Stone Wicked," I said, with my eyes still closed. Now that she mentioned a fever, it was all I could feel, like she had conjured it. I considered whether she might be a witch. If she were, it would still be the least surprising thing I'd run into in a long time.

She pulled me away from my tree and took my weight against her side and shoulder. We bumbled along, step by step, up the slope of the hill I didn't realize I was on. I could feel the skins she wore slide loose back and forth over the curves of her body underneath.

We reached her cabin which was built into a shallow gully in the side of the hill that kept going upward beyond us. There was a short bridge of bound sticks that felt rickety under my boots, but held us as she lugged me over a gap and onto the raised log floor of her cabin. I'm not that tall of a man, as you can see, but if I had another inch on me or the soles of my boots, I'd have had to duck. A fire smoldered in the mud and stone cooking fireplace off to one side. The slanted roof was packed with mud and sod, only letting through light in a couple spots where the roofing met the tied stick walls or the dirt side of the hill that formed the back of the cabin.

I went to my knees on the rough flooring and bowed my head. I leaned toward some bedding opposite the fire in one slanted corner of the wall. Avalon took my shoulders firm and held me upright.

I drifted in and out, there on my knees, as she first braided my hair up away from my face. Everything hurt and she wasn't being terribly gentle. From a bucket of that fatty grease that she herself smelled of, she smeared little gobs of the stuff into the cuts around my scalp. Stripping me of the rags I wore, she tended all my wounds down my body.

I remember asking, "Should I wash some of these cuts?"

She said, "Washing the body is the foolish practice of sinners. You need only worry about washing the spirit once and then never again."

Didn't make a lick of sense to me, but I had nothing left in me for arguing.

Avalon moved me, naked, over to her bedding on the log floor. She opened her bear skins and wrapped me up in them with her. You might think that would be the moment I'd have been turned on to her, being the only woman I'd been naked with for quite some time, but all I did was sleep, and I slept the sleep of the dead. Might have just been exhausted, and I was, but I also felt safe with her. That's how I felt at the time, anyhow. And I'd gotten sick as hell for the last time in my life.

I startled awake a few times, but she whispered in my ear everything would be fine.

The last time I woke back up, I heard voices outside. She did her comforting whispering thing again, but this time I was thinking about vanishing spirits and their pet bone devils that already took the marshal and his girl, so still had to be hungry for me, too.

I broke free of her hold and her bear skins to run to the door. My bare feet hurt on the logs. Looked around and didn't see my ragged clothes or my boots. Not sure when or how she spirited them away, but I was sleeping pretty hard.

My eyes burned and watered. My head was hot and I shivered in the stale heat of the rough cabin.

The door's hinge was one long stick on one end of the woven door. It fit in a carved hole at the top and bottom of the opening for the structure, filled with lubricating grease and fat. It turned smooth and silent as I peeked outside.

More than a dozen more people moved about out there in the grasses between the trees. They'd woven sticks together in the shape of dreamcatchers strung from trees and on the ground. They wore nothing but bearskin wraps as well.

How many fucking bears did these people kill?

As they came and went, I saw my first assessment had been wrong. This wasn't a proper village, but the lean-to survival cabins were nestled back into the trees and contours of the land. Mud and sod roofs concealed some of them. Vine screens served to camouflage them further.

I was so startled to be in the midst of people again that the giant cross, made of two bleached logs lashed together and supported up between two larger trees, was the last thing I noticed and the last implication I figured out later, only after it was too late.

One hairy and barefooted man, tall by the standards of the time, a regular white boy afro of curly hair bushed up over his head, wearing a small kilt of bearskin like Tarzan, if the character had existed at the time, turned toward me where I was peeking out of Avalon's cabin raised up on the hill above the scene. As he stopped and gave me a broad smile, others took notice and turned toward me, too.

Avalon whispered from behind me, "Fear not."

It was a Bible phrase. Was the thing angels said when they blasted into existence, all fearful and terrifying like with dark pronouncements about the future. Angels appeared and vanished at will, like the dark spirits of the haunted ranch. And, probably like the characters in the Bible who had to witness unnatural events and beings, I feared plenty.

The man held out his broad, hairy arms to me in my poor hiding spot. His furry kilt slipped a little down his furry happy trail.

He called out, “Peek-a-boo, Bo-peep. Come forth and join the sheep.”

“Like hell,” I whispered.

Avalon reached past me and shoved the door. It swung wide and exposed me to everyone there. She was mostly naked, too, wearing her skins casually over one shoulder like a drape, showing more than she covered, but that was little comfort to me there among strangers.

31

"**I'M SICK WITH** something," I told the hairy mountain man as he led me and sat me bare-assed on a fallen log as bleach white as the bars of the massive cross suspended behind me. I was chilled from my fever, so sitting on that twisted log in front of a fire felt good.

A couple of the others wrapped me in a spotted tan and white deerskin that I couldn't quite wrap around me like a blanket or robe. It was better than nothing, but not much better. My little wrap stood out in contrast to their darker, bushy fur coverings.

The whole encampment smelled of unwashed bodies and animal fat. I think I smelled the same from the treatment of my cuts.

"You might want to be rid of me." At the time I said it, I thought of it as sending me on my way, as opposed to sacrificing me to some ancient animalism deity of the forest, or whatever these people might be into. I hadn't had a lot of experience with cults back then. I knew about Mormons and Shakers, too, I think. Hadn't heard about some of the weirder ones that came out of Vermont and New York. Back then, New England was like California in spawning weirdos and the people who would follow them. I believe this group was an offshoot of one of those groups that traveled west and outlived the parent organization by a bit.

"It won't come to that yet, friend," he said to me.

He told me the history of their group after he introduced himself. I wasn't paying close attention, or simply forgot over the years. Maybe I lost the details because of how it all ended. I did have a pretty bad fever at the time. Even if they had let me leave right then, I'd have not made it far before collapsing in the woods. Who knows what would have gotten a hold of me then? Probably not bears, since it looked like the group had cleaned out the woods of them for all their hides.

His name was Malcolm Blank. I remember it because it struck me as funny at the time. Couldn't tell you what the fuck I found so funny now, but I laughed and laughed until my chest burned and my head throbbed. Old Malcolm laughed right along with me, like we were old friends.

Avalon snuggled up beside me with her bear skins loose around her hips and her grimy breasts hanging out low and heavy. Malcolm looked her up and down as the laughter died off finally. I had swooned against her from the dizziness of all that exertion. She bore my weight as he licked his lips. I got angry seeing him do that, like she was something that belonged to me after a long walk, a short nap, and some animal grease more likely to infect my cuts than to heal them. The bugs were leaving me alone at least.

She said, "We need to baptize him before tonight."

Malcolm's tongue slipped away and he considered her. "You think he's worthy, do you, dear?"

"None of us is worthy. Forgiveness is for the unworthy, brother."

"You learn your lessons well," he said, as he stared at her titties some more. "You learn quickly, I know that about you."

I tried to get up, to stand between her and his leering eyes over his licking lips, but my legs wouldn't take me all on their own. I don't think they even noticed I tried.

"Time is short and our days are numbered on this Earth," she said.

My chest got tight at those words, so like the curse uttered by the spirit boy who still hunted me, as far as I knew. That boy had given me this fever, I believed, although, it was probably the mad preacher back in Honey Brush who sneezed in my fucking face after misting me with his family's humid blood.

"We should take it to the group first, don't you think?"

She mumbled something I didn't catch, even with my burning head lying against her mat of hair and her cool shoulder. Then, she spoke up for the rest, "Salvation as voted on by people. That would be a proud thing, if we did."

"Wisdom from the mouth of a babe. Your lips drip holy nectar."

I closed my eyes and snapped my teeth out of some fevered animalistic instinct.

"Will you join us, Stone Wicked?" Her voice was not smooth and sweet, but it was beautiful in my ear at that moment. "Will you be baptized into eternal life?"

I know what you're probably thinking. You'd have resisted or begged off joining the cult so easy. Maybe wait to get better and then cut out. I know everyone has a strong opinion of what they think they would do under pressure, how they would always stand and never fold. I'm here to tell you that I've been around a while and, from my experience, there are a lot more people who fold when the time to stand is thrust upon them.

I was sick. I was tired. I had been chased by the law and by monsters of different kinds all across the wilderness. I'd been dragged bloody by that law and those monsters, too. I'd been in the heart of madness, with sick and cursed minds ripping each other asunder. I was a broken man at that point. I had nothing left in me to fight or to stand against and, to be honest, I wasn't much of a fighter or man of iron before all that turmoil and testing. I was a knockabout guy, like they say in all the crime shows.

Crawford liked to call me a scoundrel, but I was far less than that. I was a tagalong bandit with no real direction or ambition of my own. I did not hold even a finger on the wheel of my destiny. My life's story happened to me. I didn't move it at all. I ran away from plenty, but I was never running toward a thing. I was a side character in other folks' lives from the beginning. I'm only the main character now because I'm the last one left to tell it.

Isn't that some shit?

So, I agreed to let myself be baptized into the cult of bear skins and stinky grease. They were happy with me and I wasn't used to that sort of thing, having folks happy with me or my choices, being accepted.

Even in that moment, I didn't know if they were going to baptize me in greasy bear guts and set me on fire, or use real water. They weren't much for bathing the body, I think I told you. If it was water, this might be my last chance for a bath, for a while.

I had no concept of forever or for life, at that point. I didn't consider whether I was signing on for life. I just wasn't surviving well alone. I wanted to be fed and held by Avalon as I slept off my fever.

Turned out it was water. Water, and a bit more.

32

I'M NOT SURE how far the river or water source was from their little encampment. Maybe they'd been trapping rainwater up there somewhere. They dug a hole, lined it with skins, heated the water and poured it in.

I was stripped down of my deerskin and lowered into the warm waist-deep baptism pool. I was fever chilled and wanted to submerge, but they forced me to remain standing as the men and women cupped water over my braided head and my aching shoulders. They wiped me down with their bare hands and reached under the water to scrub on me and paw at me under there.

Clearly not descended from the tradition of Baptists.

The water beaded on the grease over my cuts. My wounds stung from the water and from them smearing the salve, but it resisted the water and the pressure of their wet hands.

They spoke their pseudo-holy words. I parroted back everything. Don't clearly remember a word of anything much spoken during the ceremony. I asserted this and agreed to that. I renounced one thing and disavowed myself of another. On and on this went as I got handwashed and hand jobbed under the water.

The dirty scummy cult members, who didn't bathe their bodies anymore after bathing their spirits, starting touching and undressing each other. The women paid special attention to Malcom and the other men slipped their pokes in wherever they could find an unattended hole. I'd never seen people use their mouths like that, and for that, before.

Malcolm broke away for a moment and offered me a slurp of his manhood. I've been offered similar before and since, with varying levels of politeness and insistence. That time I declined and he shrugged off my rejection as there were others willing to take him up on it.

He was circumcised, so I wondered if he was Jewish. That sort of thing wasn't as common among us Gentiles back then as it is now. Still wasn't interested in a helping, either way.

Avalon and a couple other curvy women pulled me up and out of my baptism hole. I was freezing in the afternoon air. They laid me out on the skin side of a bear hide that would become mine. The other men didn't come over to stick themselves in this time. The other women attending to Malcolm had to do double and triple duty for a while.

They worked me up and worked me over with their hands, mouths, and every gritty fold of flesh they had to them, undoing the progress the warm water had made in cleaning me up a little.

Now, if it was anyone but you I was telling this to, I'd be tempted to exaggerate my exploits that day. Didn't have an opportunity like it at any other point in my life. Definitely the sort of thing a guy should brag about every chance he got. If this wasn't a story of horror, I might indulge in a little dirty romance fantasy, like I'd come upon some woodland nymphs ready to please me instead of a bunch of unbathed cultist hermits playing tug and tickle.

I was young, so I had that energy and dumb endurance going for me, if you get my meaning. I'd also been through hell and was in rough shape. I hadn't been with a woman in a while, so I was motivated. I had a pretty severe fever that was only getting worse, too.

In the end, all of that together led to an ebb and flow in my energy. In the bragging version of this side tale, I'd have been doing those broads all at once, over and over. In reality, it was mostly Avalon, and it was sort of a half-hard bumbling effort most of the time. If it wasn't for the other two poking at me and flicking life back into me from time to time, not sure much would have happened at all. It took me so long they got bored and went back to finishing off the other men and each other. I got there, finally using my hand more than her, but she still did most of the work.

I got up and wrapped myself in a bear skin matted with leaves.

I didn't ask whether I had permission, but I prepared to leave and go sleep off my fever in Avalon's shelter.

But it was apparently time to crucify Malcolm Blank upon the twisted beams of the bleached wood cross I'd been mostly ignoring up until then.

33

IT'S A LITTLE less dramatic than it sounds, but only a little. These ropes made of hemp and vine were flung up over the bars of the cross. Then, Malcolm willingly let them tie him, not just at the wrists, but in this sort of S&M net of knots down his arms and across his chest. Real kinky stuff. People pay good money for that stuff these days.

He was willing, but still screamed when they took their knives to him. They had metal weapons and tools in their camp I'd seen, but they used stone blades to carve into his palms and his ankles. They took a spear and didn't exactly stab him, but they twisted and abraised the point into his ribs until they broke the skin. He bled. The bruising spread all up and down his side while I watched.

They adorned him with a weaved headband of smoothed river stones on his head. No harm there, but then they used their Stone Age knives to cut his forehead and scalp at intervals all the way around his head. They cut him pretty deep on that last bit, masking his face and pasting the hair on his head, chest, and back with blood.

He became a little less willing at that point, and tried to fight back. A few of the men pulled the ropes to bring his arms out on both sides of him and to stand him up straight as they finished. The women did most of the cutting. Even with his bleeding ankles bound together in their crucifixion harness, he managed to horse kick a few of the woman hard enough to nearly knock them out. They got back up and kept cutting.

Everyone spoke words of encouragement.

"You can do this, brother."

That sort of thing.

Last, they took off his bearskin wrap. Some of the blood flowing down his neck and chest had clotted in his pubic hair. His rod was rock hard, more so than when he offered me a taste. Malcolm was screaming and crying about how he changed his mind.

One of the women grabbed him there and squeezed hard, swelling the head of it up fat and purple, like an overripe fruit ready to burst. Despite all his kicking and protesting, she ran than stone edge nice and slow through the groove of his pee hole, like she was trying to widen it.

I forgot about all the cock stuff until just now. I guess I might have been wrong. This crucifixion might have been as bad or worse than you might have imagined.

Anyway, Malcolm Blank screamed to high heaven. He bled a lot. The woman working on giving him a second circumcision gave him a couple vigorous pumps with her fist. She took him into her mouth and drank down the fount of many blessings bleeding off the end.

A few of the other women took turns giving him a blood-lubed jack and drinking the blood off the end there. Avalon did not. None of the men did either. I was glad, because I didn't want to find out this was their way of taking communion or something. He stayed hard long enough that someone would call the hospital these days.

I don't think they went to work on Jesus' dick like that in the Bible, so if that's who they were imitating, they'd gone off script a little.

They hauled him up high. He wasn't exactly attached to the cross, but they positioned him over where he would be nailed. Malcolm swaying in the wind, but stayed pretty close to true over the cross.

It might have been worse for him strung up like that because he couldn't use his legs to lift up for breath. His breathing got ragged, too, as he spent the early part of the evening begging to be let down.

Blood dripped fat, dark, and heavy to the ground under Malcolm. Everyone except for me kind of walked through the drizzle, letting it drip into their hair, on their faces, and down their bodies. They used their hands to smear the blood the way they had done with the water during my baptism.

It was just starting to get dark at that point. We'd eaten at some point during the process, but I barely remembered it.

I heard the screeches that I no longer mistook for mountain lions or any other natural creature. They were here, the bone devils, and they could surely smell the blood.

"Those are monsters," I explained. "We're not safe here."

They went on about the wards and the protection of God and his angels. As near as I could tell, the wards were wreath-like concoctions scattered around the camp. Many of them had the spire shapes curling out from the middle that I'd been seeing around the countryside quite a bit, and a few times since.

I started trying to tell them what these monster things were and what they had done. At first, I thought I had their attention, with their eyes wide and the dripped blood smeared over their soiled skin.

Then, I realized I was seeing something else on their faces. There was ecstasy, bloodlust, anticipation, excitement. Whether they believed my warnings or not, they wanted it all to be true. A world of nighttime demons and devils crawling through their forest was exactly the world they wanted to live in.

Avalon took my shoulder. Her hand was sticky with Malcolm's blood she had painted herself in, staining those same tits he had been staring at as he licked his lips. I didn't pull away.

She said, "The darkness must come before the veil can be torn."

"I don't even know what that means," I said. "We're all going to die here."

"As the Faces of God wills it," said another.

Everyone grumbled their agreement while Malcolm cried above us and the bone devils drew closer with their endless screams.

"I don't want to be out here when they come. I'm tired. I want to lay down."

Avalon took me to her cabin, like a lost puppy seeking shelter. For what it was worth, the others didn't want to be outside in the open, either, it turned out.

So, the bone devils came and accepted the blood sacrifice offered to them. They wanted more though.

34

I WASN'T CONSCIOUS for the entire night, I don't think, but I sure wasn't sleeping through that invasion.

Malcolm screamed for the monsters to get away from him, over and over. I peeked between the sticks in the walls. They crouched and leapt up in the air, snapping at the cross, coming short of snapping at him. They didn't seem to understand he wasn't attached to it and didn't find the ropes tied off either. Eventually they tore that bleached cross down in splinters. Then, they started working over the trees.

I'm not sure if the wards of twisted sticks they placed around helped or not, but the monsters seemed lost and confused to a degree.

It didn't stop them from hunting out and tearing into the cabins around the rough perimeter of the settlement. The victims screamed and begged. Their passion and lust for the monsters was lost in the violent reality. Like bears, the bone devils eat their prey alive. And, half the time, they seemed more interested in extracting bone than consuming flesh, but they certainly did both.

Eventually, they turned on Avalon's shelter. They shattered the short bridge between the cabin's slope and the land leading into the village now spotted in bloodshed, carnage, and slaughter. They tore at the door, not breaking it off completely, but breaking it askew, exposing us inside. They reached over with their long limbs and clawed away the layers of her roof. It was packed tougher and stronger than it looked, but they were relentless, digging their way inside.

My days really were numbered, it seemed.

She cast aside a few items she had stacked along the natural back wall of the structure, even as the monsters slowly tore their way through to get to us. She found the edge to a false portion of the wall, caked with mud to blend in well in the low light. She folded that hatch away, as well, and took a body by the feet to drag it out over the log floor from the hidden storage area dug out into the hill itself.

My boots tumbled out of that opening, but I did not spy the rest of my clothes in there. I was focused on the corpse she was wrestling out into the small space with us.

"Help me," she grunted.

"Help you with what?!" I demanded over the den of noise around us.

"Help me offer them another sacrifice before it's too late."

I had the idea of what her scheme was here, without understanding at all who this body was or why she was storing it. The somewhat fresh stink of it was a stronger exposure of the smell I was apparently already ignoring in there.

He was naked and decomposing. There was a festering black hole above his scrotum where the rest of his piece should have been. Didn't want to think on that too much.

"Who was he?"

"Nevermind that now. Help me."

I did help, but I minded it. "Were you planning to do this to me next?"

She didn't answer as we hauled the body to the skewed door. The flesh was cold and slimy. Our fingers dug in deep and the impressions in the moist flesh remained.

She kicked at the ruined door. It was the third attempt that knocked an opening we could pass through. One set of claws swiped by, very close to her face. A long bony snout snapped behind those, but she pulled away.

The bridge was gone, so I wasn't sure if we were going to dump the body off the broken edge. Then what? Were they going to be under us? Better this guy than me, even if it was just for a short reprieve, I figured. So, I kept pushing him out into that opening, even as the wood under us kept catching on and pinching the body.

As the weight started to go over, the devils snatched the body across the gap and tore into it on the dirt edge, not that far from the doorway. The door itself twirled away completely. They sliced through the dead flesh and flung fetid organs everywhere. Some landed on top of the shelter and dripped toxins through where the sod and mud insulation had been removed. They tore and scratched until they gripped the bones inside the limbs and then cracked them loudly as they levered the bones out of the body entirely. One of them buried its snout inside the open torso. A moment later, it lifted the ribcage of the dead man out whole, like extracting a nut from a husk. A couple of them fought over the ribs.

Avalon took my hand and squeezed it hard. She spoke close to my ear and said, "If this is the moment we are delivered beyond this world, I want you to . . . "

There was a gunshot. Then, a couple more. I hadn't seen a single gun the whole time I'd been there. I wondered why they hadn't tried shooting them before now.

The creatures outside gave a piercing chorus of grating screams before charging out into the growing dark. They were moving away from our shelter, but weren't truly running away from anything. They were going after something.

Avalon dropped my hand and backed away a few crawling steps. I moved forward, into the opening. I heard more shots and saw the flashes. I focused out on Crawford and Syne, pinned down in a small divot near where the fire had been. The devils had them trapped as they furrowed the ground, circling them. The bullets tore through the bodies and took chunks of flesh out of the dark lumps of the devils' bodies, but the monsters weren't going down.

"The hell are they doing here?"

Avalon had no answer for me. I don't know what possessed me, but I retrieved and pulled on my boots. I shed my bearskin and leapt, naked, across the gap. My hands planted in the eviscerated corpse the monsters had abandoned. The putrid flesh separated and squeezed between my fingers like cold clay. I thought of the preacher's fetus and vomited up whatever I had eaten into the deboned body cavity.

I desperately clawed my hands through the dirt and moss, trying to clear the grey mash from my fingers and nails. In the process, I came up with a broken stick with a sharp point. Must have been part of the bridge. A piss poor weapon if there ever was one, but I ran down the hill with it anyway, wearing nothing but a pair of boots.

I guess maybe I decided, despite everything, Crawford was worthy of saving. I had a moment of brave clarity and maybe saw into the future at the type of friends we could be. Even a scoundrel like me was capable of a moment of redemptive bravery and . . . Wait. Is that what happened?

I can't remember clearly. Doesn't matter my reasons, I guess.

So, I was all covered in blood and I charged at them with a sharpened stick, like a knight trying to slay a dragon. Only, in this case . . . Hold on. Back up. I fucked this up, I think. Okay, Malcolm was still alive at first. I think the plan was for him to suffer through the night and then be let down. Some kind of scapegoat ritual. I think charging with the stick happened after the sex and the knife thing. That's right. Had to be because I was covered in blood, soaked in the stuff. The order of things is all mixed up in my head.

I think there were gunshots, and I think the monsters ran off from the body they were eating and deboning, but I didn't go out there at first. Why would I?

Okay, sorry. I'm an old man, it was a bad night, and everything was happening at once.

So, back up to the shelter with me and Avalon still inside. The door has been torn off. The place was compromised, but where the hell else are we supposed to go with those things outside raising hell?

She pulled at my arm as I tried to go to the door to see what was going on. Were those really gunshots? I hadn't seen any guns and, if they had them, why weren't they shooting earlier? Right?

I was weak, though, and she had a grip on me.

"Come with me. Come with me."

She pulled me backward. I tripped over my boots, but I kept coming. She entered the opening for that dugout storage area. The corpse stink was thick in there and I resisted.

"Come on," she said again.

I thought maybe there was an escape tunnel. An escape tunnel would have been good right about then. I was in rough shape, though, and barely felt like standing at all. How far away did the tunnel open? Would it be far enough for us to flee through the night undiscovered?

There was no tunnel, though. Just a confined room where the gasses from that dead body had accumulated. Maybe it was better cover back in there, but Jesus Christ, that stink crawled into everything. It's not a smell that you encounter much anymore in the civilized world. I'm telling you, it digs deep into your sinuses and you can't unsmell it. The memory of it locks in. I'm probably ruining my dinner revisiting this shit, but what the hell? We've come this far, haven't we?

She pushed me to my back and stripped the bearskins off of both of us.

"Who was he? Did you kill him?"

She covered my mouth and started working my junk with an unsympathetic intensity. Hand and mouth, back and forth, she was relentless. I had already spent myself earlier that day, and was in a rough medical state, but she didn't take any limp excuses.

I twisted my head up and away to try to breathe. I only freed my nostrils, which forced me to take in more of the smell of the previous occupant. That didn't help the mood much either. I was staring out of that tight rectangular opening, through the shelter, toward the screams and cries of the nighttime attack still going on out there.

She hit and slapped me down there, making me cry out under her hand. She started biting. I struggled, but she just got rougher with me. I'm not even sure I recognized that she was trying to have sex with me. I just felt like I was being attacked.

It must have worked well enough for her because she finally mounted up and I got the picture. She was wet and ready. It was almost too hot inside her, like an oven. She bucked and ground on top of me. A couple times I felt myself bend painfully, but she kept going. Her head and shoulders scraped the low roof a couple times, and dirt rained down over us. I brushed it away and spit it out. The stuff was between my teeth.

Against all odds, I finished and I finished hard. It hurt, but it still was what it was and I lost myself in it. It was powerful enough of a finish that she felt it, too, and finally came to a stop.

I didn't notice her take up the knife. It was one of the stone ones. A metal one might have been faster and then I wouldn't be here, but it was still sharp.

She raised up just enough to give her access to the base of my dick and started cutting with it still inside her.

35

SHE REALLY CUT ME. I don't know what you call the position, but she was straddled on top of me and facing me, so she cut at the back of it, near the root. If she'd cut into that thick vein underneath, I think I might have bled out.

I realized what was up, even if I couldn't quite believe it. Unlike that fucking Malcolm Blank, getting my dick cut didn't give me a chubby, so I shriveled up real fast and slipped right out of her scummy snatch. Probably saved me from getting it cut clean off.

I twisted and scrambled out from under her. She came forward to slice into me. I hit the back of my head hard on the top of the opening and scattered chunks of packed dirt and rock on my way out. She was out after me and on me again. I crossed my arms over my head and face and tried to fend her off, but she pushed against my shaky arms and sliced my cheek, then opened my forehead. Just a few more cuts to the many I already had.

The rocks sliced up and dug into my back and ass as I kept trying to retreat backward. She stayed on me. I knew the bridge was gone and if I got to the door, I'd fall out backward and probably break my neck.

She was stronger than me when I was sick. Hell, she was probably stronger than me healthy, too. I bit her. I bit her hard. I chewed at her wrist, then I drew blood from her cheek, just under one eye, and then I closed my teeth on her throat, but didn't quite break the skin there.

She got pissed and started punching me in the face and the ribs, over and over. I managed to get the knife away from her and was going to plunge it into her side when those fucking bone devils crashed through the front of her shelter. Broken logs scattered to the wind and the monsters grabbed for us, but we fell into the hollow underneath the ruined shelter and landed hard.

Her cured mud and stone fireplace shattered on impact and scattered bright orange coals around the dirt and debris under the ruined cabin. Some hot coals burned at one of my bare hips.

Some of the structure remained in place above us, for whatever that was worth.

Even with those things climbing down in there with us, she kept fighting. She was screaming, punching, and she started biting me, too. I pushed her head away from me with my palm up under her chin and then I stabbed her in the side, between the ribs. I pulled out and stabbed again a few times.

A set of bony claws swept through and tore her head clean off. One minute I was holding her face away from me up under the jaw, the next her decapitated body collapsed over my bare chest and spewed gallons of hot blood out of her open neck, over my chest, across my face, and up my nose. I was drowning in blood. It couldn't have been, but I swear that blood was hotter than the scattered coals from her fireplace.

I struggled to get her off of me, but we were slippery as hell. Every time I lifted her up, she slipped through my grasp and fell back down on top of me. The last time, I got a double handful of her breasts and lifted her up again. The bone devils accepted my offering and snatched her up and off of me to dig into up on the edge of the hollow. Unfortunately, the knife was still in her side, so they took that away, too, leaving me naked, covered in blood, and unarmed.

In the lull, I saw my boots in among the broken pieces of the shelter. I shuffled down and managed to pull them on. No real plan, they were just mine, so I put them back on.

I would have been content to stay hidden down there in the pit, surrounded by debris, but one of the monsters decided to try to get down in there with me. It wiggled and reached as it made its way. Its purple tongue slithered out from between its fangs and I swore I recognized its markings.

I rolled over and struggled up away from it. I knew there were more of them up there, working over the bodies, but I'd just avoided getting my dick cut off and I was in no mood to lay around waiting to be eaten or to get my bones torn out of my body.

I got up over the top and moved to the side to avoid where the group of them were feasting on what was left of Avalon's body. I ended up planting my hand straight into the decaying guts of the man she'd cut the dick off of before me. Grey mash. Mashed up corpse on my hands and my last fuck's blood all over me, I threw up in the body cavity of the man before me. Tried to wipe all that gunk off my hands into the grass, dirt, and moss, like I told you before, and came up with a pointy stick.

The monsters turned their attention on me, with the two bodies out there and me covered in decay and fresh blood both. They came at me and I stabbed up into the black mass of flesh between exposed bones that formed a chest. It seemed unimpressed and screamed down at me as the others circled around me. One of them was still jammed up under the surviving portion of the shelter, squirming and screaming, but the others had me.

I heard more of those gunshots. They punched through the fleshy bits of the monsters around me. It didn't take them down, but it pissed them off. They lifted their heads and let out a shrieking chorus of screams. Left me and the bodies and charged down the hill.

That's when I spotted Crawford and Syne aiming up on the monsters trying to eat me. They retreated into a little dip in the land that wasn't much shelter at all. They kept plugging the monsters with a few shots that sent splatters of their black flesh flying out behind them, but the bone devils didn't let up on circling them.

"What the hell are those two doing here?"

The stuck monster behind me unstuck himself. He took down a little more of the shelter with him and crawled up out of that pit behind me. Had no choice but to run.

That fucking Malcolm Blank was still alive and dangling from his ropes high above. He called out to me, "Please, Stone. Brother Stone, save me. Help me down." On and on like that.

I had a bone devil on my ass. Was charging naked down the hill, covered in blood, with nothing but a pointy stick and my boots. The one behind me wouldn't let up until I was almost on the pack of them circling Crawford and Syne in front of me. It wasn't courage or a moment of redemption. I was running for my life and just happened to stab one of them as I was trying to get away.

It turned and threw me, with the stick still in it. The stabbed bone devil lashed out at the one chasing me. The pack started screaming and kind of broke apart from their attention on Crawford and Syne.

"We need to get out of here," she said.

"We'll never outrun them," I said. "They're always after us."

I hadn't decided I was teaming up with the two of them. I was just expressing the futility of trying to outrun them through the night.

"Jesus Christ, Stone, are you hurt?"

I looked down at myself covered in my blood, covered in cuts, my injured dick stinging from someone else's blood getting in the cut there. I actually laughed, but it quickly diminished in hitching crying.

"No time for that," Crawford told me. "We need to move."

"I'm hurt bad," I said, "and I'm sick as hell."

"Let's go before we're dead as hell," Syne said.

I looked back toward Avalon's shelter, what was left of it. I thought about the hole in the hillside. I thought about the bone devils clawing people out of the mill. Maybe no shelter was good enough, but I thought running through the woods at night was a mistake. I also thought it would be funny for the two of them to have to be trapped in there with the open tomb stink of the place. Let them get a little bit of the filth on them, too.

"Come on," I said. "I know a place we can hide."

I ran and they followed. I stumbled once, as dizziness started to overtake me. Crawford propped me up and finally let me go as we kept going.

Syne reached out and pulled me up short as one of the devils tore through our path. It made a wide galloping turn and came back on us. We scattered and separated, just avoiding being ripped apart.

I started running again and only realized I was approaching the bashed-up shelter alone once I was almost there. Crawford and Syne climbed into another cabin off to the right and two bone devils started taking it apart with them inside.

Oh, well, I tried my best.

I saw Malcolm was missing all himself below the waist. His top half was slumped on his ropes and silent, finally. A couple monsters clawed their way up the big trees trying to get to the rest of him.

I ran between the two corpses and jumped from the edge of the ground without thinking. It was only in the air that I remembered I was naked and likely to impale myself on something in the landing. I tumbled into the back half of the shelter, scuffing my boots and hitting myself in the nuts, but otherwise intact.

Crawling back into that stinking hole in the hill, I took hold of the hatch and pulled it closed into place behind me. I must have passed out in the darkness.

I had fevered dreams all through the rest of the night. Kept waking up to darkness and not knowing I was awake or even alive.

At one point, I heard commotion outside and light spilled through a crack along the top of the hatch. I opened it just enough with shaky hands to see a pair of naked men out in the sunlight, fighting each other tooth and nail. I thought of the towns we'd passed through on the way there, and the madness that ensued.

The rest of Avalon's shelter had been ripped away from the hillside, but I'd gone undiscovered in the secret storage room, by the bone devils or the lawmen.

I was starving and thirsty and still weak with fever, but I closed myself back into the darkness before passing out again.

I'm not sure how many days and nights had passed, but it couldn't have been too many if I lived through them.

I finally knocked the hatch loose and tumbled down the dirt slope. It took a while, but I climbed back up out of the pit. The ground was stained in several places, but the corpses were gone. Malcolm wasn't hanging from the trees anymore. All the shelters had been demolished and the wards scattered. The bleached cross was nothing but splinters.

There was no sign of Crawford or Syne. They could have been dead, but I'd thought that before. I'd eventually discover they were still alive, and would have to sneak past them a couple more times before I thought to return to Georgia instead of staying out there.

I'd see and hear the bone devils again a few times, but nothing like that last night in the woods.

I found some food in the debris of the camp. Drank my stale baptism water out of the skin-lined hole in the ground.

I wrapped myself in a bearskin and rested a bit more.

I ran across Avalon's head in the grass, staring blind up into the sky. Then, her milky eyes slid through their sockets and lighted on me. Her thrushy tongue slid out dry from between purple lips and licked them at me.

Stumbling away screaming, I brayed up at the sky. I shook all over and couldn't control my convulsions. I tasted blood in the back of my throat and kept looking for the wild donkey I was hearing before I realized I was the one making the noise. Kept making it until my voice broke on me, forcing me to silence for the next few days.

Sure, I might have imagined her severed head moving like that. A thousand things could have caused me to be seeing things at that point. But all the shit I already seen? That movement from her skull seemed the least unbelievable.

I cried all silent and husky, threw up, and cried some more. Drank a little more water and gathered some food. Her blood was dried to me in a warpaint it was going to take a few baths to get off me.

Then, I marched out of those woods with nothing but my scant supplies, a bear skin, and my boots. You should have seen me trying to explain myself to the next people I ran across about four or five days later, only being able to speak to them in throaty whispers.

What? Oh, sorry. I started to drift off there. How long have I been talking? My throat is dry. Can I get a drink and a rest before we continue on with all this?

36

IT WAS A good thing James Fanny had left early for work that morning. The protests in town had caused a real traffic jam in Scully, Alabama for the first time in as long as anyone could remember. What were they protesting anyway? There were a lot of signs about tyranny and freedom, but more than a couple about haircuts, too.

As far as James knew, none of the restrictions were being enforced in Scully. Not in the least. Maybe it was just the principle of the thing.

Violence broke out as he rolled past. A guy with wild hair jumped on the back of a bearded man in sunglasses, biting him on the shoulder. The poor guy dropped his sign about refusing to wear face diapers. The unmasked police ran in and fought to pull them apart as the violence spread through the crowd.

Fanny kept on driving.

The new girl who had done her first overnight was happy to leave her shift early. She reported nothing out of the ordinary with Stone's sleep as she was packing her bag.

James warned her to avoid the protest.

She said, "What's burning out here?"

They looked together. It did smell like smoke, even through their blue and white masks, and a billowing black cloud rose in the distance. Sirens wailed farther away, but still loud. It wasn't exactly coming from the direction of the protest, but over that way.

The landline phone on the front desk started to ring.

"Most excitement this town has seen in a while," she said, as she walked toward her car.

Fanny ran for the phone behind the desk. Dawes was here somewhere. He needed to lock the door back. He was supposed to answer the phone.

James answered with his name and the facility name.

Mandy Crawford from the Alabama State Prison System introduced herself and said she would be there in a couple hours for an evaluation of the prisoner.

James agreed to have Inmate Wicked dressed and ready for an interview.

"Crawford," James said, "any chance you're related to lawmen from years ago? I've heard tales of a few Crawfords."

She laughed and then coughed before she said, "Crawford is my husband's name, and his family is full of teachers as far back as we can track."

"It's a common name, I guess," James said. "I'll have him as ready as he can be. He's not always lucid and talkative though."

Stone was quiet through breakfast and only complained a little about having to wear day clothes. He complained of the smell of smoke and James apologized for that.

"You have visitors coming, Stone. Said they'd be here in a couple hours."

"I don't know anybody and my family is all dead."

"It's someone from the prison system."

"That Perkins asshole again?"

"No . . . well, I don't think so. She didn't say for sure whether she was coming alone or not. It's a lady named Mandy Crawford."

Stone looked at James and James smiled back. Stone shook his head. "It's a common name."

"It is. Do you want to watch some TV until they get here?"

"Nah. I think I've seen everything."

"You want to tell me more of your story instead?"

"It's hard to remember things that far back sometimes, Fanny. Not good memories, either. I don't think I have very many good memories, from what I recall."

"You want to tell me how you ended up getting arrested the last time? We've never gotten to that part of the tale after all this time."

"You sound like Perkins. It's not all that exciting. No ghosts or bony devils in that part of things."

"Stone, I think they may be closing this place down after this next interview today. You'll end up in an elder care wing of some other prison, I'm guessing. I'll get work somewhere, too. Hospitals are begging for workers right now, and paying better than here. But this may be the last chance for me to hear the end of your story."

Stone Wicked considered the orderly and then looked away. "You can never tell everything. There's always more story, and most of people's stories are boring as shit."

"It's yours to tell or not," James said. "I thank you for the parts you did share with me."

"You've been good to me. Better than you probably should have been," Stone said. "Maybe better than anyone in my life. So, you want the arrested part of the story?"

"If you'll tell it." James sat down on the couch next to Stone.

"You said time is short." Stone gave a chuckle. "And I've been told that before a few times. I'm tired and a little cloudy today, so I'm going to keep it brief this time."

James sat quietly.

Stone continued, "I came back to Georgia, like I said earlier, I think. Eventually, I went home when all my prospects at all points west dried up. I never got sick a day in my life after that last time in Avalon's cabin. My brother was mad at me for refusing the war that started some years later. I claimed to be unwell, which I sold to the authorities that mattered, but my brother didn't buy it. All my scars healed up, you see. So, we got in a bar fight and I hurt him pretty bad. Got him out of the war, too. I ended up in jail for it. The war started, I refused to join up for release, and ended up in the same prison camp with the Union officers down in south Georgia. Terrible conditions."

"What war was this?" James interrupted.

"The War of Northern Aggression."

James swallowed and his eyes lost focus. The Civil War? The fucking Civil War?

Stone continued, "I got out after it was over. That camp was as bad or worse than anything I'd experienced. My brother kept going around town telling everyone I was a traitor. The South fucking lost and I was the traitor? I considered leaving town, but then went to visit him in our old family home he occupied alone. He started up on me and I ended up choking the life out of him. It took a long time, but I was enraged and I stuck with it. My brother was dead."

Stone Wicked shifted on the couch, but stared down into his lap as he kept speaking. "I left with my brother's body still warm on the floor of our family home. I hadn't been welcome in there for many years. I guess I proved that out, didn't I? I hopped a train and headed west again, like old times. I changed trains in Birmingham. Um . . . No, that's not right. It was Elyton where I changed trains. It was just a cluster of small farming towns out there where two railroads crossed each other. No reason anyone there should have known me from Adam, but I got spotted. She followed me onto my next train and cornered me in the back car. Care to guess who?"

"Annabelle Syne?" James asked.

"That fucking Annie Syne, the one and only. Pure coincidence she was in the station as I was passing through. I tried to fight her, but she gave me a beating my late brother would've appreciated, and she subdued me. She had this whole speech worked out when she saw me on that train all these years after we lost each other in the wilderness. 'Heading back out looking for trouble, Stone? Mind if I tag along? There's people looking for you a long time, me included. Be a real shame to keep them waiting.' Shit like that. I had some stuff I said back to her, but I promised to keep this short.

"She took me off at the next stop and processed me for a laundry list of crimes out west. Sent word for Crawford to help her transport me. He was long retired by then. In the meantime, word of the killing in Georgia got out.

"There weren't many folks left that remembered anything I'd done out west, but the murder in Georgia was fresh. So, they took me back for that, as they still tried their best to arrange things out the other direction. I was convicted of murder, eventually, just the one in Georgia, and nothing else from my past materialized.

"The federals were in charge at that point and handling a lot of shit. I spent a long time in the town jail. Drunks came in and out, but I stayed.

"Had myself a black judge that sentenced me for the killing of my brother. The town was more upset by the color of the judge than the crime I committed. They had no sympathy for me, though. I was the trash that didn't even go to fight to help keep black judges from taking over, you see?

"Elliot Crawford started visiting me. Syne wanted nothing to do with me and thought it was weird Crawford did. At first, I think he was still trying to make sense of what we had seen and experienced out there, although we mostly talked about other things.

"She moved north before I was transferred to Blood Mountain finally. Made me miss that cramped cell back home. I didn't see him for a while, but he started coming up there to visit me on occasion, too. We both got older, but him faster than me. He started having trouble getting around, but I was healthy as a horse. His visits got further and further between as he became real old.

"Wasn't sure what had happened to him until Syne mailed me a letter saying he had passed a few months earlier. It was posted from Vermont, I think. She had handled the arrangements because he had no family left. Didn't give me any other details, not about herself or anything. Never heard from her again. I tried to look her up a few times, but I have no idea what happened to her."

Stone finally looked up, "And that was it."

"And you've been in prison ever since," James said.

"Every fucking day, for years on end, yes, sir."

"What was your sentence?"

Stone laughed and said, "Life."

"Usually means twenty years, tops, these days, Stone."

"You going to bust me out and put me on a train headed west?"

"Probably just fix your lunch is all."

Stone nodded. "Can you put on something with superheroes in it for me to watch? If I get bored, I'll go back to one of the *Star Treks* maybe."

37

AGENT JOHN PERKINS was with Mandy Crawford as she entered the facility.

"Pull your mask up over your nose, please, Mr. Perkins," James said.

The smell of smoke came through strong as the door closed. The fires were no longer billowing up and the ongoing sirens had paused for a while, but the carbon stink of it was still in the air.

She sniffed once and said, "He's right. The inmate is elderly. We need to protect his health."

Perkins coughed into his elbow, despite wearing the mask, but then pulled the adjustable band up over his nose. "I'd like to apologize for my demeanor last time I was here, Orderly Fanny. I'm here now in an advisory role to Assistant Director Crawford. We're going to conduct a final evaluation and interview with your sole inmate, then send a joint recommendation to the prison board about his future and the future of this satellite facility."

"Understood," James said.

Perkins coughed and leaned out to peer around James. "Is the guard in today?"

John Perkins's eyes were watering.

"Dawes is on duty, sir. Had a bit of a sniffle and is dealing with that in the back. We have the situation under control."

"Well, we're all on good terms and on the same side here," Mandy said. "Running this entire facility for one inmate is costly, especially in a time where the pandemic and the resulting economy have things so tight."

"I understand, ma'am."

"You have an exemplary work record, Mr. Fanny, and I'm sure we'll have something for you after the location is shuttered, if that does indeed happen."

"Thank you, ma'am."

"Is Inmate Wicked up and about?"

"He's on the couch. I got him to shut off the TV as you pulled up. I'll take you to him."

Perkins busied himself setting up the camera, like he had done earlier times. It looked like the same one they had taken from him last time and sent to the board with a complaint. All the good it had done.

Mandy sat down on the coffee table, off to the side from where the camera aimed on Stone. "Are you up for a little chat, inmate?"

Stone Wicked stared down between his knees and said nothing.

She turned her attention on James. "Is he having a bad day?"

"He talked a little this morning, but has been pretty quiet since then. It's hard to tell."

"This is mostly a formality anyway." Perkins started the recording and identified everyone present on his own, before naming the facility and the date. He leaned away from the camera and gave a croupy cough. His mask had slipped down past his nose again. "It's just allergies, I swear."

"Dawes said the same thing," James mumbled.

"Inmate Wicked," she started. "Can you tell us where and when you were sentenced?"

Nothing to say.

A horn honked in the distance and another answered it back, louder and longer.

Mandy sighed and then asked, "Can you tell us your prison of origin?"

Another pause.

Someone outside shouted something loudly, but unintelligible through the walls and distance. It sounded like they laughed jovially on the end of whatever they said. Small town shooting the breeze, it sounded like. Better communication out there than in here, it seemed.

"It's been like this every time," Perkins said, and wiped his exposed nose on his sleeve.

Mandy patted her knees. "Well, you have his health records

handy, Mr. Fanny? Anything that would preclude his transfer to a larger facility with elder care resources?"

James began, "Nothing that would—"

"Blood Mountain was my first prison, after they sent me up from the local jail finally," Stone said.

"Local jail where?" Perkins asked.

"Georgia. In my hometown."

"Where was that? Give me a name, please."

Mandy said, "Agent Perkins, please . . . "

Stone said, "Called Marthasville when I first lived there. They changed the name a few times and then had to rebuild after the fires. I was moved on to Blood Mountain by the time all that was finished."

"Then, Grinder State, before it changed names," Perkins said. "Then, on to a half dozen prisons in Alabama before you landed here and got forgotten, right?"

"Perkins?" she tried to interrupt again.

Stone met eyes with the agent and held his gaze strong and clear. James wondered how much of the story he might retell, given the chance. And then what would their reaction be to all that blood, magic, and bone devils?

"That's about the shape of it. Yes."

"What disease was it in Georgia?"

"How's that?" Stone asked.

"The disease that wiped out that prison and turned it into lost ruins up in the woods outside Ringgold," Perkins said. "What disease was it that you survived but everyone else perished under?"

"Cholera, I believe," Stone said.

"It was the flu, the first one," Perkins corrected.

Stone nodded. "It was in the spring, as I recall."

"It always is," Perkins said. He coughed again, but then continued. His eyes were glassy with tears and his nose ran visibly into the top of his mask resting just over his lip. He looked less clear than Stone did in that moment. "It got bloody, too, didn't it?"

"Always does," Stone said back, with an edge to his voice.

"What disease was it in South Carolina? What'd everyone come down with at the Grinder? Before the hurricane? Before the riot?" Perkins stepped around from behind the camera. He had to be blocking the view a little bit with his shoulder.

"Mrs. Crawford," James said.

She spoke up. "Agent Perkins, I need you to back up and settle down, please, sir."

"Tuberculosis, wasn't it?" Stone asked.

"It damn well was," Perkins agreed.

"Are you well, John?" James asked. "Are you having trouble controlling your—"

"Tell me about Talladega 1991, Stone Wicked," Perkins shouted over.

Mandy Crawford stood up, but didn't take a step toward Perkins.

"You want to know who won that year?" Stone asked. "I'm not much of a racing fan. Cars scare me."

"You were in the prison down in Talladega in 1991, before you ended up here," Perkins said. "There was a riot. One hundred and twenty Cuban refugees. You mentioned the Cubans a few times in our interviews. I looked back over the tapes."

"It got bloody," Stone said.

"Kind of an understatement when it comes to your path of destruction," Perkins said. "They lost their minds down there. Went feral almost. The Grinder was worse than that, the more I look into it. Beheadings. Mutilations. Stringing people up by barbed wire."

"Perkins, you need to stop," she said. "This is all on record, remember."

"What happened with the motherfucking Cubans, Stone?! Tell me!"

Mandy demanded, "Perkins, stand down right this instant. Step outside and wait for me there. That's an order."

He didn't move and she made no motion to physically intervene.

"Dawes? You back there, buddy?" James called out, without much hope.

Stone chuckled and Perkins took a step forward with his fists balled. James moved around behind the couch to get around to Perkins and Stone. He still had the couch between him and them for a while, and that might have been what saved his life, for a little while anyway.

Stone stared up with his head cocked at Perkins' red face. "The

Cubans turned cannibal, didn't they? They got real bloody. People kept coming in while the rest of us were on lockdown and asking them for demands. By the end, they couldn't even speak anymore, just stuffing their mouths with pieces they cut off each other and anyone else they could get to. Saw one of them eat his own dick."

"Jesus Christ," Mandy said. "End this, Perkins."

"And what diseases did they catch before they caught your curse, Stone?"

"No telling, really. They were passing everything around in there," Stone said. "Probably Aids, malaria, West Nile, Monkey Rash, and God knows what else."

"It was syphilis and hepatitis running wild right before the riot in '91," Perkins said.

"Sounds about right." Stone leaned back on the couch and crossed his arms over his skinny chest.

"Are you responsible for this Corona virus shit, Stone?" Perkins leaned down into the inmate's face with his mask hardly on at all. Stone didn't seem the least bit concerned. "Are you the one making the world so fucking crazy? The way you did in every prison you're crept along through since the beginning of time? Did we curse the whole world by keeping you alive too long?"

"Hadn't considered it, Perkins, but I think that might track."

Perkins reached for Stone. James shoved him away. Perkins shoved back.

"Both of you stop this right now. Right now!" Mandy cried.

"Dawes?! Get out here!" James yelled.

"Nothing's going to protect you from him. He *is* the curse. He's the plague." Perkins waved his arms like James was being unreasonable. He bumped the camera with a wild gesture. It rocked on its tripod, but didn't fall yet. "I swear to God, he goes on living forever and other people die from his curse. That's how this madness works."

Dawes finally emerged from the back, looking his usual sleepy self. He was casually thumbing through his keys as he approached. Clearly, he'd been woken from a deep sleep. He wasn't wearing a mask, but James was still happy just to see someone, anyone, approaching to help, even if it was particularly slowly.

"I don't think you're well," James said quietly. "I think you might have caught something. Try to calm down before it makes you lose your mind."

Perkins's blurry eyes grew wide. He looked back and forth between Stone and James. "Me?"

Mandy yelled, "You fucking motherfuckers, stop this right now or I'll tear your dicks off and force feed you all!"

Dawes looked up from his keys as if seeing them all for the first time. He launched himself forward and tackled Mandy Crawford through her side, hard enough to hear ribs crack. The coffee table collapsed under their landing weight. The camera tipped over and tumbled away in pieces.

"Not her," James said. "Him."

Dawes lifted Mandy's head up and slammed it back down a few times. He pulled out a chunk of her hair and part of the skin from her scalp with it.

She clawed up at his face and snapped her teeth. "I'm going to bite off your cock!"

Dawes growled back and jammed one of his keys into her eye. The eye tore and leaked. He twisted the key, grinding the eye meat into jelly.

James thought of Garacto, Grindfield, Honey or Sugar Brush, and every other strange tale Stone Wicked had told. It all appeared to be true. True, and happening again.

"Hey, stop that." Perkins reached down to help her by pulling Dawes off of her.

She sunk her teeth into his ankle. Dawes pulled the key out of her ruined eye before stabbing it into John Perkins's neck.

Stone tugged at James' sleeve. "Fanny, we need to get the hell away from here."

38

BLOOD SPREAD IN a growing pool across the clean tile out from under the couch. Mandy had torn through Perkins' face and throat. He was still screaming in muffled horror as she made good on her threat about his cock. He was still trying to fight back, but wasn't having much success.

As James Fanny walked Stone Wicked backward, away from the scene, Stone whispered, "A place in here with a lock on it? Somewhere we can lay low until help comes?"

"Not really," James said, "and Dawes has the keys."

"Is there another prison you can take me to real quick?"

"Shut up, Stone, and let me think."

Dawes launched himself up and over the couch. With the blood on his face, he couldn't possibly be seeing really clearly, and didn't quite clear the back. He flipped over in the air and landed in the pool of blood. He tried to get up twice, but kept slipping.

James stood there and hesitated.

"Fanny?"

Dawes hurled something from the floor. It was flying off to James' left, and he reached to move Stone out of the way. But Stone Wicked was suddenly on James' right. The bloody keys flew through empty air and landed on the floor in a long red streak.

James still didn't move. Dawes got his feet and advanced again.

"Fanny!? We need to get out of here."

James moved for the door and pulled Stone along. He burst outside and took Stone along to the car. He'd taken an inmate outside the facility without permission. The world felt completely wrong.

Dawes slammed into the inside of the glass and shattered it.

Stone broke away from James' grasp and suddenly stood at the car waiting.

James got his passenger door open and shoved Stone inside. As James rounded the back of the vehicle, Dawes crawled through broken glass toward him and someone else staggered into the parking lot from another direction. The man was naked, except for one shoe. He had wounds all over him, including cuts around his crotch.

"Help me. Please, help me!"

James got behind the wheel and backed out of his space. He was careful not to hit Dawes before shifting into drive and peeling out of the lot, leaving the naked man behind, too.

James didn't look back, but cut his eyes to the side, where he spotted a silver Audi in the lot. It paid to be high up in the prison system, it seemed. Well, until today, when she lost an eye and her mind.

They rolled to a stop at the first stop sign. James reached over, locking Stone's door and pulling on the seatbelt.

"You tying me up, marshal?" Stone asked.

"Just putting on your seatbelt. I don't know where we're going, just away from here."

"I know what a seatbelt is. I watch TV. I was just kidding."

James sat back up and looked in the rearview. No naked man. No Dawes. No Mandy Crawford. Certainly no Agent John Perkins anymore either.

The first of them slammed into the driver's side of James' car, rocking it on its shocks. The feral mob started to wrap around the front and back. They screamed and smeared blood on the windows. They clawed and attacked each other. This couldn't be happening.

"They're pinning us in, Fanny."

James hit the gas. The wheels spun in place at first, but then the car lurched forward. Bodies peeled off both sides and James prayed he hadn't run over anyone as he drove away.

"How far do we need to . . . " James stopped short. "Did you see that?"

"What, Fanny? What was it?"

The long claws swept by again. James sped up. The long digits that looked like nothing but bones smeared through the blood on the side windows and then scraped down the car. He swore he saw steam rising off those bones. And that purple thing slithering through the air couldn't have been a tongue. It just couldn't have been. He was just seeing things conjured up by his fear, he decided.

He forced himself to look in the mirror, but saw nothing behind them except the mob of mad people slowly falling behind. No bone devils.

"Was that them, Stone? Was that one of them? Did they follow you here?"

"I don't know, but wouldn't stop if I was—"

James slammed on the brakes and his car fishtailed out into the other lane before coming to a stop. The boy standing in the street wore a red baseball cap turned around backward. He had on denim shorts and a t-shirt that said "I'm Awesome Just Ask".

His eyes were sunken dark. His exposed skin was the color of aging newspaper, or an old photo being eaten by time and acid. He only stayed in focus a moment before vanishing up the road. He didn't walk, but the boy kept appearing and disappearing, in rapid succession, as he advanced on the car again. He raised his arms, his eyes blacked out into voids, and he showed sharp teeth, but vanished again, only to repeat the stutter up toward the nose of the car again.

Stone Wicked had been on his left when Dawes' threw the keys, but then had suddenly appeared on the right as they passed by in the air.

The spirit boy in front of them had a four-barreled rifle strapped over his shoulder.

An undeniable rich mineral water smell seeped moist through the car's vents.

"Is that him?" Fanny asked, without much breath behind his words. "Is that the boy you told about from the haunted ranch house?"

"It's been a while, but looks just like him."

"How many disappearing boys do you think are out there?"

"Not many."

"After all these years."

"We age slower."

"What?" James looked to Stone.

Stone still stared out the windshield at the boy. "They age slower."

"Can we get around him?"

"They don't do as well in the sun. We should be able to get away, if we do it before dark."

"Can he get into the car with us? Can he appear in here and then be protected from the sun enough to do some damage?"

"I hadn't considered that, Fanny. That's some scary shit."

The boy's shape morphed and distorted into a hideous shadow, leering further and further over the car with each attempt.

Stone said, "I wouldn't wait around to—"

The mob slammed into the back of the car and started climbing over the trunk. James pressed the accelerator and straightened the car as they picked up speed. He steered around the apparition of the boy as best he could.

Most of the people fell back, but a few held onto the trunk. They showed their bloody teeth and clawed at the back window.

James swerved from side to side until they rolled away and bounced on the street behind them. James showed his teeth, not wanting to be responsible for hurting anyone.

He glanced at Stone. They lived in different times, different worlds. Those worlds were coming together, it seemed. James double-checked to be sure his mask was still up.

"How far, Stone?"

Stone looked to James and then forward again. "How's that?"

"How far do we need to go to get away from all this?"

"From my experience, once the madness hits a town, you need to get as far away as possible. Things had been going fine for a long time. Why'd you have to keep bringing people in there with me?"

James wasn't sure how to answer that, so he just asked his next question. "What about those bone devils and the spirit boy? How far to get clear of them?"

"I thought I'd gone far enough already." Stone sounded exhausted. He slumped in his seat and closed his eyes. "Thought those days were behind me. Maybe our days are numbered, Fanny. Maybe they really are. Some monsters can only be survived, not defeated or outrun."

"That's not the answer I was hoping for, Stone. I need to think. I need to figure out what's next."

After a moment, Stone added, "While you're thinking, I'd keep driving, if I was you."

James turned up the air. The well water smell was gone, but he was never going to forget it. He kept checking the mirrors as they left Scully, Alabama behind. He turned south, toward Birmingham. To report what happened? To turn Stone Wicked back over? He didn't know yet.

The longer he drove, the more surreal everything seemed. He was in shock, he told himself. Stone Wicked's shape was not flickering around the edges, he told himself. When he pulled his eyes away from the road to view the old man straight on, he looked as solid as ever.

They marked him, Stone had said. And what did that mean, exactly? He was the only one to tell the tale, so what if he left out parts? What if the old man was less passive in the violence than his version of the story told? We age slower, he'd said. He counted himself among the devils.

Traitors and deserters.

If I could remember how to teleport . . .

Was there more to this story? Was there another version of this story not shaded by Stone Wicked's memory or agenda?

Never let your guard down around them. They can be more dangerous than they let on. Monsters. Devils.

"You want to tell me another story?" James asked, as he merged onto a larger highway, wondering if the blood on his windows was too obvious.

Stone Wicked snored in his seat without responding and James Fanny kept driving. There was always more story, but not always more time to tell it.

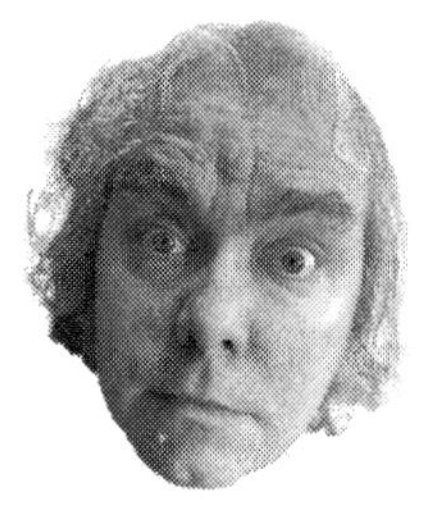

Jay Wilburn is a Splatterpunk Award nominated author with work in Best Horror of the Year vol. 5.

JayWilburn.com

Patreon.com/JayWilburn

Twitch.tv/JayWilburn

CURSE OF THE
RATMAN
BY JAY WILBURN

The cover kind of says it all.

A 50,000 word action scene of zombie fun and apocalyptic survival. Waldo Bloodfist must punch his way out of a zombie-infested city before it's too late

Made in the USA
Middletown, DE
03 November 2022

14053094R00142